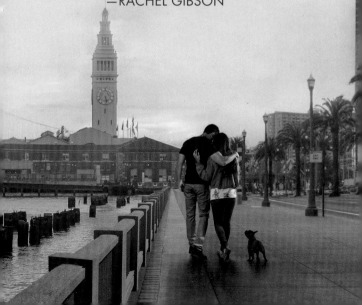

"What kind of a kiss?" he asked.

She was momentarily bewildered. "I don't know. It was a kiss. A normal kiss. A nice kiss." She cocked her head at him. "How many kinds of kisses are there?"

He just looked at her for a long moment before coming toward her. He backed her to the wall and pressed his big hands on either side of her head. "There are many kinds of kisses," he said.

Her breath had backed up in her throat, where her heart had lodged, pounding wildly. "S-s-such as?"

"Such as this one." And then he leaned in and covered her mouth with his.

Only when he'd thoroughly plundered and pillaged and left her boneless did he lift his head and look into her eyes.

"Wow," she whispered, fully aware she was still holding on to him like he was a lifeline, but the bones in her legs had liquefied. "I mean . . ." She shook her head. "Wow."

He nodded. "Yeah. So to be clear, that wasn't 'a normal kiss' or even 'a nice kiss.' It was a 'wow' kiss. Any questions?"

By Jill Shalvis

Heartbreaker Bay Novels

SWEET LITTLE LIES
THE TROUBLE WITH MISTLETOE
ACCIDENTALLY ON PURPOSE
CHASING CHRISTMAS EVE
ABOUT THAT KISS

Women's Fiction Novels

LOST AND FOUND SISTERS

Lucky Harbor Novels

ONE IN A MILLION • HE'S SO FINE
IT'S IN HIS KISS • ONCE IN A LIFETIME
ALWAYS ON MY MIND • IT HAD TO BE YOU
FOREVER AND A DAY • AT LAST
LUCKY IN LOVE • HEAD OVER HEELS
THE SWEETEST THING • SIMPLY IRRESISTIBLE

Animal Magnetism Novels

THEN CAME YOU • RUMOR HAS IT
RESCUE MY HEART • ANIMAL ATTRACTION
ANIMAL MAGNETISM

JILL SHALVIS

about that kiss

A
Heartbreaker Bay
Novel

AVONBOOKS

An Imprint of HarperCollinsPublishers

Excerpt from *Rainy Day Friends* copyright © 2018 by Jill Shalvis.

ABOUT THAT KISS. Copyright © 2018 by Jill Shalvis. All rights reserved. Printed in the United States of America. No part of this book may be used or reproduced in any manner whatsoever without written permission except in the case of brief quotations embodied in critical articles and reviews. For information, address HarperCollins Publishers, 195 Broadway, New York, NY 10007.

First Avon Books mass market printing: February 2018
First Avon Books special mass market printing: February 2018
First Avon Books hardcover printing: January 2018

Print Edition ISBN: 978-0-06-274177-6
Digital Edition ISBN: 978-0-06-274181-3

Cover design by Nadine Badalaty
Cover illustration by Aleta Rafton
Spine photograph © Jagodka/Shutterstock

Avon, Avon & logo, and Avon Books & logo are registered trademarks of HarperCollins Publishers in the United States of America and other countries.
HarperCollins is a registered trademark of HarperCollins Publishers in the United States of America and other countries.

FIRST EDITION

18 19 20 21 22   QGM   10 9 8 7 6 5 4 3 2 1

*To the best readers on the planet—
romance readers!
I'm grateful to each one of you
every single day.
Happy Reading! XOXO!*

about that kiss

Chapter 1

#LifeIsLikeABoxOfChocolates

Kylie Masters watched him walk into her shop like he owned it while simultaneously pretending not to notice him. A tricky balancing act that she'd gotten good at. Problem was, like it or not, her attention was caught and captured by the six-foot, leanly muscled, scowling guy now standing directly in front of her, hands shoved in his pockets, body language clearly set to Frustrated Male.

She sighed, gave up the ridiculous pretense of being engrossed by her phone, and looked up. She was supposed to smile and ask how she could help him. That's what they all did when it was their turn to work the front counter at Reclaimed Woods. They were to show potential clients their custom-made goods when what they really wanted was to be in the back workshop making their own individual projects.

Kylie's specialty was dining room sets, which meant she wore a thick apron and goggles to protect herself and was perpetually covered in sawdust.

And she did mean *covered* in sawdust. Wood flakes dusted her hair and stuck to her exposed arms, and if she'd been wearing any makeup today, they'd have been stuck to her face as well. In short, she was not looking how she wanted to be looking while facing this man again. Not even close. "Joe," she said in careful greeting.

He gave her a single head nod.

Okay, so he wasn't going to talk first. Fine. She'd be the grown-up today. "What can I do for you?" she asked, fairly certain he wasn't here to shop for furniture. He wasn't exactly the domesticated type.

Joe ran a hand through his hair so that the military short, dark, silky strands stood straight up. He wore a black T-shirt stretched over broad shoulders, loose over tight abs, untucked over cargos that emphasized his mile-long legs. He was built like the soldier he'd been not too long ago, as if keeping fit was his job—which, given what he did for a living, it absolutely was. He shoved his mirrored sunglasses to the top of his head, revealing ice blue eyes that could be hard as stone when working, but she knew that they could also soften when he was amused, aroused, or having fun. He was none of those three things at the moment.

"I need a birthday present for Molly," he said.

Molly was his sister, and from what Kylie knew of the Malone family, they were close. Everyone knew this and adored the both of them. Kylie herself adored Molly.

She did *not* adore Joe.

"Okay," she said. "What do you want to get for her?"

"She made me a list." Joe pulled the list written in Molly's neat scrawl from one of his many cargo pants pockets.

Bday wishlist:
—Puppies. (Yes, plural!)
—Shoes. I *lurve* shoes. Must be as hot as
    Elle's.
—$$$
—Concert tickets to Beyoncé.
—A release from the crushing inevitability of
    death.
—The gorgeous wooden inlay mirror made by
    Kylie.

"It's not her birthday for a while," Joe said as Kylie read the list. "But she told me the mirror's hanging behind the counter, and I didn't want it to be sold before I could buy it." His sharp blue eyes searched the wall behind her. "That one," he said, pointing to an intricately wood-lined mirror that Kylie had indeed made. "She says she fell in love with it. Not all that surprising since your work's amazing."

Kylie did her best to keep this from making her glow with pleasure. She and Joe had known each other casually for the year that they'd both been working in this building. Until two nights ago, they'd never done anything but annoy each other. So that he thought of her as amazing was news to her. "I didn't know you were even aware of my work."

Instead of answering, his eyes narrowed at the price tag hanging off the mirror, and he let out a low whistle.

"I don't get to set the prices here," she said, irritating herself with her defensive tone. She had no idea why she let him drive her so crazy with little to no effort on his part, but she did her best to not examine the reasons for this.

Ever.

Joe had been Special Ops and still had most of his skills, skills he used on his job at an investigation and securities firm upstairs, where he was, for the lack of a better term, a professional finder and fixer. He was a calm and impenetrable badass on the job, and a calm, impenetrable smartass off it. On the worst of days, he made her feel like a see-saw. On the best of days, he made her feel things she liked to shove deep, *deep* down, because going there with him would be like jumping out of a plane—thrilling, exciting . . . and then certain dismemberment and death.

While she was thinking about this and other things she shouldn't be thinking, Joe was eyeballing the opened box of chocolates on the counter, which a client had brought in earlier. A little card said HELP YOURSELF! and his gaze locked in on the last Bordeaux—her favorite. She'd been saving it as a reward if she made it all day without wanting to strangle anyone.

Mission failed. "It'll go right to your hips," she warned.

He met her eyes, his own amused. "You worried about my body, Kylie?"

She used the excuse to look him over. Not exactly a hardship. He was lean, solid muscle. Rumors were that he'd done some MMA fighting right after his service and she believed it. He was perfect and they both knew it. "I didn't want to mention it," she said, "but I think you're starting to get a spare tire."

"Is that right?" He cocked his head, eyes amused. "A spare tire, huh? Anything else?"

"Welllllll . . . maybe a little junk in the trunk."

He out-and-out grinned at that, the cocky bastard. "Then maybe we should *share* the chocolate," he said and offered the Bordeaux to her, bringing it up to her lips.

Against her better judgment, she took a bite, resisting the urge to also sink her teeth into his fingers.

With a soft laugh that told her he'd read her mind, he popped the other half into his own mouth and then licked some melted chocolate off his thumb with a suctioning sound that went straight to her nipples, which was *super* annoying. It was February and blistery outside but suddenly she was warm. Very warm.

"So," he said when he'd swallowed. "The mirror. I'll take it." Reaching into yet another mystery pocket, he pulled out a credit card. "Wrap it up."

"You can't have it."

At this, he studied her with a hint of surprise, like maybe he'd never been told no before in his life.

And hell, looking like he did, he probably hadn't been.

"Okay," he said. "I get it. It's because I never called, right?"

She pushed his hand—and the credit card in it—away. But not before she felt the heat and the easy strength of him, both of which only further annoyed her. "Wrong," she said. "Not everything's about you, Joe."

"True. This is clearly about *us*," he said. "And that kiss."

Oh hell no. He didn't just bring it up like that, like it was some throwaway event. She pointed to the door. "Get out."

He just smiled. And didn't get out.

Dammit. She'd grounded herself from thinking about that kiss. That one drunken, very stupid kiss that haunted her dreams and way too many waking moments as well. But it all flooded back to her now, releasing a bunch of stupid endorphins and everything. She inhaled a deep breath, locked her knees *and* her heart, and mentally tossed away the key. "What kiss?"

He gave her a *get real* look.

"Oh, *that* kiss." She shrugged nonchalantly as she reached for her water bottle. "I barely remember it."

"Funny," he said in a voice of pure sin. "Cuz it rocked my world."

She choked on her water, coughing and sputtering. "The mirror's still not for sale," she finally managed to wheeze out, wiping her mouth.

I rocked his world?

His warm, amused gaze met hers, going smoky

and dangerously charismatic. "I could change your mind."

"On the mirror or the kiss?" she asked before she could stop herself.

"Either. Both."

She had no doubt. "The mirror's already sold," she said. "The new owner's coming for it today."

The buyer just happened to be Spence Baldwin, who owned the building in which they stood. The Pacific Pier Building, to be exact, one of the oldest in the Cow Hollow District of San Francisco. Since the building housed an eclectic mix of businesses on the first and second floors, and residential apartments on the third and fourth floors, all built around a cobblestone courtyard with a fountain that had been there back in the days when there'd still been actual cows in Cow Hollow, the entire place went a lot like the song—everyone knew everyone's name.

In any case, Spence had bought the mirror for his girlfriend, Colbie, not that Kylie was going to tell Joe that. For one thing, Spence and Joe were good friends and Spence might let Joe have the mirror.

And though she didn't know why, Kylie didn't want Joe to have it. Okay, so she did know why. Things came easy to Joe. Good looking, exciting job . . . hell, *life* came easy to him.

"I'll commission a new one," Joe said, still looking unconcerned. "You can make another just like it, right?"

Yes, and normally a commissioned piece would be a thrill. Kylie wasn't all that established yet and could certainly use the work. But instead of being excited, she felt . . . unsettled. Because if she agreed to the job, there'd be ongoing contact. Conversations.

And here was the thing—she didn't trust him. No, that wasn't right. She didn't trust *herself* with him. *I rocked his world?* Because he'd sent hers spinning and the truth was, it'd take no effort at all to once again end up glued to him at the lips. "I'm sorry, but maybe you can get Molly . . ." she eyed the list again " . . . puppies."

And speaking of puppies, just then from the back room came a high-pitched bark. Vinnie was up from his nap. Next came the pitter-patter of paws scrambling. At the doorway between the shop and the showroom, he skidded to a stop and lifted a paw, poking at the empty air in front of his face.

Not too long ago, her undersized rescue pup had run face-first into a glass door. So now he went through this pantomime routine at every doorway he came to. And she did mean every doorway. Poor Vinnie had PTSD, and she was his emotional support human.

When Vinnie was thoroughly satisfied that there was no hidden glass to run into, he was off and galloping again, a dark brown blur skidding around the corner of the counter like a cat on linoleum. He was half French bulldog and half Muppet, and no one had ever told him that he was under a foot tall and twelve pounds soaking wet. He actually thought he was the big man on campus, and he smiled the whole way as he ran straight for Kylie, tongue lolling out the side of his mouth, drool dribbling in his wake.

Heart melting, Kylie started to bend to reach for him, but he flew right by her.

Joe had squatted low, hands held out for the dog, who never so much as glanced over at Kylie as he took a flying leap into Joe's waiting arms. Arms that she knew were warm and strong and gave great hugs, dammit.

Man and pup straightened, rubbing faces together for a moment while Kylie did her best not to melt. Like most French bulldogs', Vinnie's expression often read glum. She called it his RBF—resting bitch face. But he was actually the opposite of glum, and the mischievous, comical, amiable light in his eyes revealed that.

"Hey, little man," Joe murmured, flashing that killer smile of his at her pup, who was valiantly attempting to lick his face off. Joe laughed and the sound caused an answering tug from deep inside Kylie, which was maddening.

She had no idea what was up with her hormones lately, but luckily they weren't in charge. Her brain was. And her brain wasn't interested in Joe, excellent kisser or not. See, she had a long history with his kind—fast, wild, fun, and . . . *dangerous*. Not her own personal history, but her mother's, and she refused to be the apple who fell too close to the tree.

"I'll pay extra," Joe said, still loving up on Vinnie to the dog's utter delight. "To commission a new mirror."

"It doesn't work like that," she said. "I've got jobs in front of you, jobs I have to finish on a schedule. A mirror I haven't yet even started isn't for sale."

"Everything's for sale," Joe said.

And how well she knew it. Shaking her head, she reached beneath the front counter, pulled a miniature tennis ball from her bag, and waved it in front of Vinnie, who began to try to swim through the air to get to the ball.

"Cheater," Joe chastened mildly, but obligingly set Vinnie down. The dog immediately snorted in excitement and raced to Kylie, quickly going through his entire repertoire of tricks without pause, sitting, offering a paw to shake, lying down, rolling over . . .

"Cute," Joe said. "Does he fetch?"

"Of course." But truthfully, fetch wasn't Vinnie's strong suit. Grunting, farting, or snoring—*these* were his strong suits. He also often went off the rails with no warning, zooming around a room in a frantic sprint until he started panting and then passed out. But he did not fetch, not that she'd admit it. "Vinnie, fetch," she said hopefully and tossed the ball a few feet away.

The dog gave a bark of sheer joy and gamely took off, his short bowlegs churning up the distance. But as always, stopping was a problem and he overshot the ball. Overcorrecting to make the sharp turn, he careened right into a wall. He made a strong recovery though and went back for the ball.

Not that he returned it to Kylie. Nope. With the mini–tennis ball barely fitting in his mouth, Vinnie padded quickly into the back, presumably bringing his new treasure to his crate.

"Yeah, he's great at fetch," Joe said with a straight face.

"We're still working on it," she said just as a man came out from the back, joining them at the counter.

Gib was her boss, her friend, and her very long-time crush—though he knew only about the first two since dating her boss had never seemed like a smart idea—not that he'd ever asked her out or anything. He owned Reclaimed Woods and Kylie owed a lot to him. He'd hired her on here when she'd decided to follow in her grandpa's footsteps and become a woodworker. Gib gave her a chance to make a name for herself. He was a good guy and everything she'd ever wanted in a man—kind, patient, sweet.

In other words, Joe's polar opposite.

"Problem?" Gib asked.

"Just trying to make a purchase," Joe said, nodding to the mirror.

Gib looked at Kylie. "Told you it was remarkable."

It was pretty rare for Gib to hand out a compliment, and she felt her chest warm with surprise and pleasure. "Thanks."

He nodded and squeezed her hand in his, momentarily rendering her incapacitated because . . . he was touching her. He *never* touched her. "But the mirror's not available," he said to Joe.

"Yeah," Joe said, although his gaze didn't leave Kylie's. "I'm getting that."

Suddenly there was an odd and unfamiliar beat of

tension in the air, one Kylie wasn't equipped to translate. Because her parents were teens when she was born, she'd been primarily raised by her grandpa. She'd learned unusual skills for a little girl, like how to operate a planer and joiner without losing any fingers, and how to place bets at the horse races. She'd also grown up into a quiet introvert, an old soul. She didn't open up easily and as a result, not once in her entire life had two guys been interested in her at the same time. In fact, for long stretches of time, there'd been *zero* guys interested.

So to have that bone-melting kiss with Joe still messing with her head and now Gib suddenly showing interest after . . . well, *years,* she felt like a panicked teenager. A sweaty, panicked teenager. She jabbed a finger toward the back. "I've, um . . . gotta get to work," she said and bailed like she was twelve years old instead of twenty-eight.

Chapter 2

#IfYouBuildItHeWillCome

Out of sight of both Joe and Gib, Kylie leaned back against the workshop door and put her hands to her hot face. *Good going. Way to be cool.*

"What's wrong?" asked Morgan, a new hire and a part-time apprentice to Gib. After a few missteps with the law, Morgan had recently turned her life around, and though she had no woodworking experience, she seemed eager enough to learn.

"Nothing," Kylie muttered. "I didn't say anything."

"No, but you moaned a little."

Kylie sighed and poured herself a huge mug of coffee from a sideboard against one wall where they kept caffeine and, if they were very, very lucky, sometimes snacks. "You want to know what's wrong? Men. Men are what's wrong with life."

Morgan's laugh said she agreed as she went back

to hand-sanding some teak for a project of Gib's. Other than that, the shop was quiet. There were two other woodworkers who were employed here as well, but neither was in today, leaving the big, cavernous workshop feeling peaceful and calm.

Typically, Kylie spent long stretches of hours at a time in here. For her, it represented home and comfort in more ways than one. But even standing at her workbench in front of several ongoing projects and her tools, with Vinnie asleep clutching his ball at her feet, she was short on comfort today. Shaking it off, she started up her joiner and went to work on the mahogany slab she was making into a tabletop.

Gib stepped through the doorway, looking big and brawny from all the physical labor of his work. He had a handsome face that made women sigh and Kylie had never been immune, not even when they'd been young. He gestured for her to turn off the machine. "What was that about?" he asked.

"What was what about?"

"That vibe out there," he said with a jerk of his chin to the front room. "Something going on between you and Joe?"

"No. No, of course not," she said. Flustered and needing something to do with her hands, she poured herself yet another mug of coffee while Gib studied her.

Having known him since she was in middle school, she could interpret his every expression. He was male, which meant he had only a few. Happy-mode, hungry-mode, sports-mode, work-mode, and pissed-off-mode. That was it, his entire repertoire. She knew he had a lust mode as well, although she'd never seen it aimed at her. But at the moment, his expression was new and completely unreadable to her.

"I'm barbecuing after work," he finally said. "You should come."

She stared at him in shock. "You want me to come over to your house for dinner?"

"Why not?"

Yeah, why not? She'd waited so long for him to ask her out, she didn't quite know what to do with herself. She glanced at Morgan, who sent her a surreptitious thumbs-up.

"So?" Gib asked. "You'll be there?"

"Sure," she said, trying for his same casual tone. "Sounds nice, thanks."

He nodded and moved off to his workstation, where he was making a shelving unit that looked like an actual oak tree. His creations were gorgeous and becoming more and more sought after. He was living his dream, just as Kylie's grandpa had taught him when Gib had apprenticed under him.

Trying to do the same thing, she turned away and busied herself with her tabletop. She was making it for one of Gib's clients, since he'd been kind enough to refer the customer to her. Hours later, she resurfaced and realized it was six o'clock and she was the last one in the shop. She vaguely recalled Gib and Morgan leaving an hour earlier and waving them off.

Alone, she went through the end-of-the-day routine, locking up, tucking Vinnie and his toys back into his carrier to lug everything up front. Her last stop on the way out the door was the shelf beneath the front counter to grab her purse, which had somehow tipped over and spilled onto the floor. Crouching low, she scooped everything back into the bag, freezing when she realized something was missing.

Her penguin. It was a three-inch-high wood carving that had been beautifully and lovingly handmade by her grandpa years ago, and was in fact the only thing she had of him. She kept it with her at all times because, silly as it felt to admit, it was her good luck charm. As long as she had the penguin, the last tie to her grandpa, everything would be okay.

But it was gone. Even just thinking it had her breath hitching as she searched the entire shop, top to bottom. Nothing. With an odd sense of panic clogging her throat, she called Gib. He hadn't seen it. She called Morgan. She called Greg and Ramon, the other two artists who worked at the shop. No one had seen her penguin. She called Gib again. "It's nowhere."

"Maybe you just set it down somewhere and forgot," he said in a rational tone.

"No. I know where I left it," she insisted. "I had it in my purse, but now it's gone."

"It'll show up tomorrow," he said. "Maybe with that slide rule of mine you lost last week."

Frustration choked her. "You're not taking me seriously."

"I am," he insisted. "I'm just in the middle of getting things ready for the barbecue, making my world-famous kabobs. For you. So get your cute ass over here."

Okay, now *this* should have made her day. He thought her ass was cute????? But she'd have to obsess over that later. Much later. "Gib, I think someone stole the penguin."

"I'll help you look in the morning, okay? We'll find it. Now move it."

"But—"

But nothing, as he'd disconnected. Kylie looked down at Vinnie. "He's not taking me seriously."

Vinnie, as comfortable in the shop as he was at home—or anywhere, really—just yawned.

Sighing, she carried him out the shop and through the courtyard. Here, she felt herself relax a little bit. She loved this building. The cobblestones were worn beneath her feet, as was the glorious old architecture of the structure around her: the corbeled brick and exposed iron trusses, the big windows.

It was a wet evening. Not raining exactly, but the moisture hung in the air. Night was falling, so the strings of lights wrapped around the wrought-iron benches lining the fountain were shining and sparkling with raindrops.

Kylie walked past The Canvas Shop and then the coffee shop, which was closed. Most of the other places were too, including the newest one—Pinot's Palette, a wine and painting shop.

But the pub was open and she decided to make

a quick stop. Most nights any of her friends from the building might be found here. Tonight it was the building manager, Elle, Joe's sister, Molly, and Haley, who worked as an optometrist on the second floor.

Sean, bartender and also co-owner of the pub, tan from a recent trip to Cabo with his new girlfriend, Lotti, slid Vinnie a doggy biscuit from the jar he kept beneath the counter.

Vinnie practically swallowed it whole.

"Your usual?" Sean asked Kylie.

"Not tonight. I'm not staying. But . . . maybe just a quick coffee?"

Elle and Molly were dressed in sharp business attire. Elle because she ran the world, Molly because she ran the front office of Hunt Investigations, where Joe worked. Haley was in a doctor's lab coat—she often forgot to take it off before leaving her office—and adorable specs.

Kylie, the fashion outcast, was in jeans, a Golden State Warriors sweatshirt, and some residual wood shavings. The fact that she had more clothes to sleep in than to go out in said a lot about her.

Haley was talking about her recent date, which had apparently gone all sorts of bad. The woman she'd gone out with had spread a rumor that they'd slept together in order to get back at an old girlfriend. Haley sighed. "Women suck."

"Yeah, well, it's not all that great on the other side of the fence either," Molly said.

"Gib finally asked me out," Kylie blurted.

Everyone gasped dramatically, which made her laugh. She'd been waxing poetic about him the entire year she'd been working for him. "He's barbecuing for me at his place tonight."

Another dramatic, collective gasp, and she knew they were happy for her. And she was happy too.

Wasn't she?

Of course she was. She'd wanted this for a long time. So then why couldn't she stop thinking about Joe and that damn kiss? How he'd slid one arm low on her hips, his other hand sinking into her hair to slowly fist it, holding her in place as he'd kissed her slow and deep, easily the hottest, most erotic kiss of her entire life . . .

Because she self-sabotaged, that's why. She'd inherited that particular trait from her mom, who was a professional self-sabotager. Her drug of choice was men. The *wrong* men. And Kylie was absolutely not going to follow in her footsteps.

A woman strode through the pub and up to the bar. She had jet black hair with a few purple streaks, most of it piled on top of her head and held there with a pencil. She wore a pretty flowy top that said *Keep Calm and Kiss My Ass,* skin-tight jeans, and some seriously kickass ankle boots that had both Elle and Molly nearly drooling.

Her name was Sadie and she worked as a tattoo artist at The Canvas. She nodded at Sean. "I need an order of buffalo wings, crispy fries, and whatever you have for dessert," she said. "And you know what? Double all of that." She slid a look over at Kylie and the girls. "When you gotta take a minute to compose yourself at work because violence is frowned upon."

"Amen to that," Molly said. "Nice outfit, by the way."

Kylie sighed. "I need to make fashion my hobby."

"My only hobby is trying to close the elevator door before someone else gets on," Sadie said.

Elle high-fived her. "Hey, so if someone said you'd slept with them when you hadn't, what would you do? Haley here has a situation."

"First of all, don't bother to deny anything. It won't work," Sadie said. "Instead, use it. Tell everyone how bad he—or she—was, and make up weird fetishes too, like . . . they called out their mom's name in the throes or something. Destroy 'em, I say."

"Damn, that's good," Haley said.

"Not my first rodeo," Sadie said.

Kylie gulped down her coffee and stood up with Vinnie. "Okay, well, we're off to Joe's."

Everyone blinked in shock at her and she quickly rewound and replayed her words in her own head and— Oh shit. *"Gib's,"* she said quickly. "I meant we're off to *Gib's.*"

Elle pointed at her. "She said Joe's."

Haley nodded. "She totally did."

"Wait. Like, Joe my brother?" Molly asked.

"I don't know any other Joe, do you?" Elle asked.

"And it's not like he isn't *really* hot," Haley said. "What?" she asked when they all just stared at her. "I'm gay. I'm not dead."

Molly grimaced and put her fingers in her ears. "Guys, please. He's my *brother.*"

Kylie desperately waved down Sean. "I'm going to need another shot of caffeine."

Molly tapped her on the shoulder. "And I'm going to need you to tell me what's going on with you and Joe."

"To go," Kylie said to Sean.

He eyed her undoubtedly crazed expression. "How much have you already had today?"

"Oh, not much." She took a grateful sip as he poured her more. Her hands were shaking. She could hear colors. But that wasn't the point right now. She looked at Molly. "The answer to your question is nothing. Nothing's going on with me and Joe, although I'm pretty sure we don't like each other very much—no offense intended."

Molly shrugged. "He's an acquired taste, so no offense taken."

"Not only don't we like each other," Kylie said, "we irritate each other. Just by breathing. Like, all the time."

"Huh," Molly said and looked at Elle. "You hearing what I'm hearing?"

"Yep. It's a classic case of protesting too much."

"No," Kylie said. "Really."

"Definite denial," Elle said.

"See, *that's* why you don't ever deny," Sadie said calmly.

"I'm denying because it's not true!" Kylie said. "The Joe thing is nothing."

"And now there's a Joe *'thing,'*" Haley said, using air quotes. *"Fascinating."*

"Okay, we're out," Kylie said, lifting Vinnie's carrier. "We're going to the barbecue now."

Vinnie perked up at this. Vinnie loved food.

"Which is at . . . whose house again?" Haley asked innocently.

"Joe's." *Shit.* Kylie slapped a hand over her mouth. "What the hell *is* that?" she asked around her fingers.

Her so-called friends grinned.

"Gah. I'm going to *Gib's*," she corrected herself, horrified, enunciating his name carefully. "*G-I-B*, Gib's." Then, before she could make anything worse, she left.

She dropped Vinnie off at home with a hug and his dinner. Then, thirty minutes later, she stood on Gib's front porch. He'd inherited a tiny Victorian on the edge of Pacific Heights. It was a cute, little old lady place, and everyone who came here made fun of Gib for keeping it.

He couldn't care less. Property in San Francisco was priced out of the atmosphere and so he made this house work for him. He'd added some modern touches, such as an eighty-inch LED TV and an extra fridge, and called it good.

Kylie knocked but he didn't answer. Probably because his music was on loud and there were people inside. As in *lots* of them.

This wasn't a date. It was a party.

Feeling stupid, she turned to go just as Gib finally opened the front door. "Hey!" he said, smiling at the sight of her. "You came! Listen," he said more quietly, taking a quick peek over his shoulder. "A few friends showed up unexpectedly and brought—"

From behind him, two arms wrapped around his

waist and then the smiling face of Rena, his beautiful, perfect ex-girlfriend, appeared over his shoulder. "Hey, Kylie," she said sweetly. She squeezed Gib affectionately, resting her chin against him. "How you doing?"

"Good," Kylie said automatically, eyes still locked in on Gib, who winced and mouthed, *I'm sorry.*

But Kylie was the sorry one, sorry that she felt like a complete idiot. "I can't stay. Something's come up and I've gotta—"

Gib tugged her inside, shook off Rena, and put a glass of wine in Kylie's hand. "Stay. Drink. Be merry." He lowered his voice. "Seriously, I'm so sorry. I didn't expect her. Stay? Please?"

Mostly Kylie preferred to eat her carbs but tonight she downed the glass and, bolstered by liquid courage, even danced with Gib. Twice. And she stepped on his toes only one of those times.

When it became clear Rena wasn't going to leave before she did, she finally headed home just before midnight, because like Cinderella, she had to work in the morning.

And because she was also a little frustrated and very tired, she didn't notice the manila envelope that had been shoved through the mail flap on her front door. It wasn't until she'd greeted a sleepy, adorable Vinnie and then gone straight to the kitchen for the ice cream in her freezer that she looked back as she leaned against the counter to inhale her dessert.

On the floor, just inside her front door, lay the

envelope. Odd, as she'd gotten all her mail the first time she'd been home, but she set down the ice cream and picked it up. Inside was an instant Polaroid and it stopped her heart.

It was a close-up of her missing penguin in mortal danger, staged to look like it was falling off the Golden Gate Bridge into the bay.

What. The. Hell.

Someone *had* stolen her statue. And worse, was now taunting her with it. Why? She couldn't think of one good reason and knew she needed to confide in someone. But who? Not Gib. You didn't go running to your crush to play the damsel-in-distress in the twenty-first century. Or at least, she didn't. She could try the police but she could already see how that would go. *"Hello, someone stole my beloved but worthless penguin carving and is pretending to knock it off the bridge."*

They'd laugh her out of town.

She could also do absolutely nothing, but whoever had done this knew her, or at least knew where she lived. Suitably creeped out, she double-checked all the locks on her windows and doors. Then she tucked Vinnie into his crate, turned out the light, and climbed into bed.

And lay there, jumping at every creak.

Two minutes later, she got out of bed, retrieved Vinnie, and climbed back beneath the covers. Excited to be where he wasn't usually allowed, he snuggled her, curling up on her pillow with her. A gust of wind brushed a branch against her window and she stilled. "Did you hear that?"

Vinnie, apparently secure in his safety, closed his eyes.

But not Kylie. She didn't sleep a wink, and by morning she knew she not only couldn't go on like this but also needed answers. And to get them she was going to need help.

The thing was, she really hated needing help of any kind. She'd been raised to count on herself and only herself. So it went against the grain, but fear was a big motivating factor here. She needed someone good at this stuff.

Archer, the head of Hunt Investigations, was the first person to come to mind. She could go to him. He'd help for sure. But the problem was that he knew she was strapped for cash so he wouldn't charge her, and she'd feel guilty taking him away from his own work.

She racked her brain for any other way, but the only answer that came to her was . . . Joe. She could make him the mirror in exchange for his help.

Dammit.

Chapter 3

#FastenYourSeatbeltsItsGoingToBeABumpyRide

Joe Malone wasn't a big fan of mornings and never had been. Growing up, his alarm clock had been his dad banging a pan on the stovetop. Later, in the military, it'd been some higher ranked asshole screaming into his ear.

Today it was 100 percent pure responsibility that had him rolling out of bed. He worked on a team of independent contractors who took on criminal, corporate, and insurance investigations along with elite security contracts, surveillance, fraud, and corporate background checks. There were also the occasional forensic investigations, big bond bounty hunting, government contract work, and more. The guy in charge, Archer Hunt, was a tough taskmaster, but it was the best job Joe had ever had. He was second in command and the resident IT genius. Not that he'd started out in IT.

Nope, he'd begun his illustrious career in . . . breaking and entering.

Shrugging the old memories off, he pulled on running gear and managed to get to the previously arranged meeting spot without killing anyone for looking at him cross-eyed. A real feat for how early it was.

Spence was waiting for him and wordlessly handed him a coffee. He was kind enough to wait for the caffeine to kick in before saying, "You're late."

"Alarm didn't go off," Joe said.

"Because you don't use an alarm."

True enough. Joe had an internal clock, one of the things he could thank the army for beating into him.

"You alright?" Spence asked. "I mean, you're always a bitch in the mornings but you look *particularly* bitchy today."

"Bite me."

Spence was richer than God and brilliant enough that he'd once been recruited to work for a government think tank. Joe was *not* richer than God, and though he'd also once worked for the government—in special forces, to be exact—it hadn't been his brain that had been coveted, but his ability to be as lethal as needed.

To say he and Spence were unlikely friends was an understatement. It'd started at the weekly poker game that went on in the Pacific Pier Building's basement. Spence owned the building, so he played poker with an easy abandon. Joe played poker the same way he lived his life—recklessly. It'd bonded them.

Spence, not really a morning person either and

certainly not a coddler, accepted Joe's "bite me" for "I'm fine," and they tossed the coffee cups in a trash and took off running. Today they hit the Lyon Street stairs, which—talk about being a bitch—were a straight-up torture rack of 332 steep steps, made all the more daunting by the early morning fog hiding the top third of them from view. This made it feel like an endless, unobtainable goal, not that they let this stop them. If anything, they each pushed harder, trying to outrun each other.

When they finally got to the top they didn't stop, instead entering the Presidio, a park where one could run along forested trails for miles. Almost immediately the city vanished behind woods of thick eucalyptus and, still goading each other, they went all out.

Spence was in excellent shape, but Joe trained for a living. Five miles later Joe inched ahead of Spence and beat him back to their building, gasping for breath, dripping sweat.

"You're insane," Spence managed, bent at the waist, hands on his knees. "You outrun your demons, I hope?"

"Can't run fast enough for that," Joe said.

Spence straightened with a frown. "See, some- thing *is* wrong. Your dad? Molly?"

"No, they're both fine and so am I." Joe shook his head. He didn't know what was up with him, other than a general restlessness. His dad was . . . well, his dad.

"The job?" Spence asked.

Joe shook his head. His job was fulfilling and solid, and served the additional purpose of giving him his daily adrenaline rush as needed. "I'm fine," he repeated.

"Yeah, so you keep saying." Spence paused and then shook his head. "I'm around. You know that, right? We're staying in San Francisco for the next few months."

Not that long ago, Spence had fallen hard and fast for Colbie Albright, a YA fantasy author based out of New York. They'd been splitting their time between San Francisco and New York, but both preferred San Francisco and resided on the private fifth floor penthouse suite of the Pacific Pier Building where Joe worked.

Colbie had been great for Spence, making him seem more human than he'd ever been, and clearly far happier. Joe was glad for him, even if he didn't completely understand the life Spence was making in the name of love. It wasn't that he didn't understand the need or yearning to share his life but that he didn't feel like he had anything to offer. As a hardened soldier turned security expert, he knew how to protect, but what else could he give to a woman? Teach her how to hold a gun? How to incapacitate a man in 1.5 seconds? Hardly things a normal person would want or need to know.

And he could give even less emotionally. After all he'd seen and done, he wasn't even actually sure if he could open up or allow himself to be vulnerable enough to sustain a serious relationship. And what woman would want a guy who couldn't? But not sure if Spence would understand, he simply nodded. "Thanks," he said, and he meant it.

They fist-bumped and went their separate ways. Joe headed home, showered, and then got to work at two minutes past seven a.m.

"You're two minutes late," his sister, Molly, informed him from behind the front desk, where she ran the show at Hunt Investigations. She stood up and moved to her credenza to grab her iPad.

Her limp was more pronounced today than usual, which meant she was in pain, and an age-old guilt sliced through him. Not that he said a word. She got mad whenever he brought it up, but even worse than that, the last time he'd done so, she'd cried.

He *hated* when she cried. So they played a game he was very familiar with. A game called Ignore All The Feels.

"I'm aware that I'm late, thanks," he said. He was the older sibling by three years, but twenty-seven-year-old Molly seemed to believe she was in charge of him. Which was not how it really went.

They'd grown up hard and fast. In their neighborhood, they'd had no choice. Their dad suffered with prolonged PTSD from serving in the Gulf War. As a result, Joe had been in charge from a young age. Being poor as dirt hadn't helped any. He'd gotten in with the wrong crowd early, doing things he shouldn't have in order to keep a roof over their heads and food in their bellies.

"Archer's pissed," Molly warned quietly.

Archer had a thing. Being on time meant you were already late. Being two minutes late was unforgivable. Joe lifted a bakery box. "I brought bribes."

"Ooh, gimme," she said, using both hands to do the *come here* gesture.

Joe held out the box but didn't relinquish it when she tried to take it. "Pick one."

Again she tried to take the box, huffing out a breath when he held tight. "Whatever happened to trust?" she asked, relenting and taking only one doughnut.

"It's not about trust. It's about if I let my guard down, you'll chew my fingers off to get to all the other doughnuts."

"And?" she asked.

He shook his head. "Annnnnnd . . . you made me swear on Mom's grave that I wouldn't give you more than one doughnut per day."

"That was last week."

"Yeah. So?"

"So," she said. "I was PMS-ing last week and feeling fat. I *need* another doughnut, Joe."

He had looked death right in the eye more times than he could count but Molly's tone was more terrifying than anything he'd ever faced. "You said you'd kill me dead in my own bed if I caved to you," he reminded her.

"That could still happen."

He stared her down, but she was a Malone through and through and she wasn't playing. Between a rock and a hard place, he relented and let her take a second doughnut. Because who was he kidding? He'd never been able to tell her no.

"Thanks. And good luck," she said, mouth full, giving him a chin nod toward Archer's office. "He's waiting for you."

Great. Yet another battle to survive. Some days his life felt like a real-life video game. He headed down the hall to Archer's office, where Archer and his significant other, Elle, were on the couch, arguing.

"I need the remote to show you my PowerPoint presentation," Elle was saying.

Archer shook his head. "Told you I don't have it."

"You just don't want to suffer through my PowerPoint," Elle said.

Archer apparently pleaded the Fifth.

"You're sitting on it, aren't you?" she demanded.

Archer almost smiled. "Funny how all trust goes away when the remote's involved."

Elle sighed. "You're impossible."

"And irresistible," Archer said. "Don't forget irresistible."

"Hmm," Elle said.

Archer was grinning at her as Joe stepped inside the office to make his presence known because if he gave them another minute, chances were that they'd decide to settle this by getting naked. Yeah, they were polar opposites and drove each other nuts, but they were also passionately in love.

Which was great for them. Personally, he'd rather face battle. War he knew how to handle. War had rules. You fought. You won, no matter the cost.

Love didn't have rules. And as far as he could tell, you couldn't actually win at love.

He endured a blistering look from Archer that would've caused most anyone else to lose the contents of their bladder. But Joe didn't scare easily. Still, he stayed a good distance back from the couch and tossed the box of doughnuts their way.

Archer caught it in midair and nodded.

Bribe accepted.

"Where's everyone else?" Joe asked, referring to the rest of the team of guys who worked at Hunt Investigations.

"I postponed the morning meeting," Archer said, biting into a chocolate glaze. "Which you would've known if you'd been here on the hour."

He was literally four minutes past the hour but he didn't try to defend himself. Archer hated excuses.

"Heading to work now," Elle said and walked to the door. "Oh, and do you know why it's called *man hours?*" she asked, turning back. "Because a woman does the job in twenty minutes." With that, she left.

With the box of doughnuts.

Damn. That'd teach Joe not to grab a doughnut when he had the chance.

"So what's going on with Kylie?" Archer asked.

Joe prided himself on always being prepared, but this caught him off guard. "Nothing," he said. "Why?"

"Nothing?"

Well, shit. Archer didn't do small talk. Which meant he knew something.

"Let me help you out here," Archer said easily. "There's rumor of some sort of kiss between you two. Does that sound familiar?"

Jesus. That kiss had been in the alley off the courtyard in the pitch dark. They'd been alone, he was sure of it. "How the hell do you always know everything?"

Archer shrugged. "One of life's little mysteries. Do we need to discuss the risks of hurting one of Elle's friends?"

"Hell no," Joe said, looking over his shoulder to make sure Elle had really left. "Nothing personal, boss man, but your woman is crazy."

Archer smirked. "Man, if a woman hasn't shown you her crazy, she's just not that into you."

While Joe processed that, Archer went on. "I put you in charge of the Rodriguez case," he said. "You've got Lucas riding shotgun. You've got an opening to get into the family compound at ten for some surveillance—the notes are in the file. Don't miss your window."

Joe nodded. Lucas, a good friend as well as a co-worker, was always a good choice. The guy was a sharp partner with even sharper skills, and as badass as they came. Joe would use the couple of hours before their meeting to catch up on the file, which was a probate case. Hunt Investigations had been hired to gather evidence to prove assets were being hidden from key family members. It was a large, dysfunctional family and there was a web of civil cases going on because everyone was suing everyone. It most likely wouldn't involve a threat to life or limb—always a

nice bonus. Leaving Archer's office, he headed down
the hall toward his own, texting Lucas as he went.

Joe: I'm e-mailing you the notes on our new case.

Lucas: Already got them. You were late.

Joe: Two minutes!

Lucas: You still owe.

Whoever was late owed doughnuts. Shit. Joe
texted Tina, who owned the coffee shop downstairs
in the courtyard, and put in another order because
Lucas liked to be paid in either time in the ring or
doughnuts. Joe had done some MMA and even he
couldn't beat Lucas in the ring. Plus he liked his face
as-is. So doughnuts it was. He'd barely sunk into his
office chair before someone stormed in.

Kylie.

She wore a sunshine yellow peacoat dusted with
Vinnie's dark dog hair, and faded jeans with one
knee torn out that snugged to her sweet bod and were
tucked into work boots. She was work-ready and a
juxtaposition and a challenge all in one, and God
help him, he did love a challenge. Especially one in
such a pretty package. And the thing about her was
this. She was a brilliant woodworker with an artist's
temperament, which meant she wasn't afraid to say
what she was thinking as she thought it.

She'd first come on his radar when she'd started
working at Reclaimed Woods last year. He'd been

insanely interested, even going so far as to occasionally stop by the store just to catch glimpses of her working those big tools—a ridiculous turn-on, he could admit.

But though he'd swear he'd seen an answering flare of interest in her eyes, she always squelched it so quickly he couldn't tell if it'd been just wishful thinking on his part. So he'd not gone there.

Not until three nights ago at a party at O'Riley's, the pub in the building courtyard. The party had been for Spence and Colbie, and it'd involved drunken karaoke and pool, and—to Joe's ongoing disbelief—that one insanely hot kiss.

They'd stepped outside the pub for fresh air at the same time. One minute they'd both been standing staring at the fountain and the next they were in the alley. She'd turned toward him and laid one longing look at his mouth and the next thing he knew, they were attempting to swallow each other's tonsils.

In the time since, he'd given up fighting the undeniable truth, which was that he'd wanted her for a long time now. Exactly when the power driving his urge had shifted from being okay with just the fantasy to actually needing her and being so attracted to her, he had no idea. It'd happened before he'd even realized it was possible.

But ever since Kissgate, she'd gone back to pretending he was a bug on her windshield, which, he had to admit, rankled. "Morning," he said easily. "Let me guess. You're here for another kiss." He smiled. "They always come back for more."

At this, she stopped short halfway between the door and his desk and narrowed her eyes, and he had the single thought that she was sexy as hell when she was pissed. And then his next thought—he was grateful that her job as a woodworker didn't require her to be armed, since she was looking as if she'd like to kill something. Or someone, anyway, most likely him. He had that effect on women. "Speechless," he said. "I like it."

She was hands on hips now. "I'm here in a business capacity."

"Disappointing," he said.

She let out a wry laugh. "Come on. We both know that I'm not even close to your type."

She was smart. Tough. Sexy. All without knowing it. She was *exactly* his type. "Why do you think that?" he asked.

"Because I'm not half-dressed with oversized store-bought breasts."

He grinned. She was teasing him, and for some sick reason he loved it. "You're also not all that nice," he said. "And I really like nice."

"Uh-huh. I bet 'nice' is right up there on your list next to, let me guess . . . a good personality?"

He laughed. "So young and yet so cynical." He *tsk*ed, enjoying the hell out of himself. "You're assuming the worst of me."

"I have a long habit of assuming the worst." She slapped an envelope on his desk. "I need to hire you to find something."

Since she appeared to be quite serious, he picked

up the envelope. Nothing on the outside except her name. Inside was a Polaroid picture of what looked like a wooden penguin poised to fall off the Golden Gate Bridge into the water beneath.

"I need you to find that carving," she said.

He met her gaze as he slid the picture back into the envelope. "Funny."

"I'm not kidding."

He took a second look at her. Her light brown eyes were solemn and serious, with shadows both in and beneath them. Her mouth—the one he could still feel under his—was grim. She was right. She wasn't kidding. He pulled out the photo again. "Okay, tell me what I'm looking at."

"A three-inch wood carving of a penguin."

He made a show of looking around the room, beneath his desk, behind his chair.

"What are you doing?" she asked.

"Searching for the cameras. You're punking me."

"No, I'm not! Someone stole this from me yesterday."

"So call the police," he said.

"Are you kidding? They'll laugh at me." She sighed when she clearly read in his expression that he wanted to laugh too. "I want that wood carving back, Joe."

"Yeah? Like I wanted to buy that mirror for Molly yesterday?"

She blew out a sigh as if maybe she'd expected this reaction and plopped into the chair in front of his desk. "About that," she said. "Do this for me, find my carving, and I'll build you a new mirror for Molly."

"So . . . we're making a deal?"

"Yes."

Interesting. He met her gaze, the color of the whis-key he'd been drinking the other night just before their infamous kiss. And he thought *sure, why the hell not.* Given that his jobs usually involved death and mayhem along with dealing with the bottom-feeders and scum of the population, this might be some welcome comedy relief. He could help out the cute, crazy chick, and as a bonus he'd be able to get his sister the birthday present she wanted. "Okay."

"Okay?" she asked, still very serious. "Okay as in we have a deal?"

Joe might be a little slow on the uptake, but clearly there was more here than she was saying. Way more. For one thing, he realized that the shadows in her eyes weren't just annoyance at having to deal with him. She was unnerved. She was hiding it well, but she was scared, and hell if he didn't react to that. "When did you last see it?" he asked.

"If I knew, I wouldn't be here."

He sighed. "When did you *notice* it was missing?"

She thought about it. "Last night right before I closed up the shop," she remembered. "I last saw it yesterday morning, so it could have vanished at any point during the day. The problem is I keep my purse up front under the counter, but sometimes, if I'm in charge of the retail store, I'm in the back until a customer comes in, which I might not always notice right away."

"So your purse is often unsupervised."

"Yes."

He didn't bother to point out that she was lucky something like this hadn't happened sooner. She knew. It was all over her face. As was the fact that she hated having to come to him for help. "Why would someone steal this thing and then taunt you with it?" he asked.

"I don't know and it doesn't matter," she said. "I just want it back."

"It *does* matter."

"Why?"

"Because," he said, "I feel like I'm missing all the good parts of this story. Is this going to be like the game Clue? Colonel Mustard in the library with the revolver?"

She stood up. "This isn't a game, Joe. And if you're not going to help me, I'll find someone else who will." With that, she headed to the door.

Which was when Joe realized he'd finally met someone more stubborn than himself. And according to his friends and family, that wasn't even possible.

Chapter 4

#ICouldaBeenAContender

Joe caught Kylie at the door of his office, barely. Wrapping his fingers around her wrist, he tugged her around to face him. "I didn't say I wasn't going to help you, Kylie."

As her name fell from his lips, her gaze went to his mouth. Just for a single heartbeat, but it told him something he hadn't realized he needed to know.

She most *definitely* remembered everything about their kiss.

"So you *will* help me?" she asked.

A missing penguin? Seriously? But the absurdity of the task was eclipsed by the way her pulse raced beneath his fingers, by how her gaze slid briefly back up to his mouth before returning slowly, almost reluctantly, it seemed, to his eyes. He'd had a taste of her and yeah, it'd been . . . off the charts. But he wasn't a man who went back for seconds. Ever. So he was as surprised as she was when his mouth opened and he said, "Yes. I'm going to help you."

"In exchange for the mirror," she said, clearly not trusting him and wanting to clarify and lay out the terms. "Nothing more."

He smiled. "Where's the fun in that?"

Her eyes narrowed. "Say it, Joe."

He let out a low laugh. "Fine. My help for the mirror. You know, you might just be the most stubborn woman I've ever met, and that's saying something."

"Do me a favor and don't compare me to the women you date," she said. "Or whatever you do with them. We all know the only reason you even remember their names is that you take them to the coffee shop in the morning and then read what gets written on their cup."

Okay, there'd most definitely been a time in his life when that had been true, but he was slowing down in his old age. Having just turned thirty, he was discovering that he wasn't nearly as entertained by hooking up as he used to be. Not that he planned on admitting that. "If I'm going to do this," he said, "I need details. All of them, Kylie."

"Sure," she said so quickly that he knew she was full of shit.

But it took someone else just as full of shit to recognize it. "Then come back and sit down," he said. "Fill in some blanks."

She headed past him, shoulder-checking him as she did, which made him want to laugh.

Even up against the wall, she came out fighting.

She moved past his visitor chairs to his window, looking down at the courtyard below. "The penguin is a wood carving that has no value to anyone but me," she said. "It was my grandpa's." She paused. "It's all I have of him."

"Your grandpa . . . Michael Masters, right?"

"Yes."

"He was an artist," he said. "A woodworker like you. Is his stuff valuable?"

"It wasn't," she said to the glass. "At least not until he died. Almost ten years ago now."

There was something in her carefully emotionally blank voice that gave her away. His second inkling that nothing about this was a joke to her. "How many of these carvings exist?"

"All I know about for sure is this one," she said. "My grandpa made it for me as a toy. He said penguins stick with their families for life. Like him and me." She paused. "I think I remember him mentioning once that there might be another, but I never saw it."

"Who knew this one existed?" Joe asked.

"No one," she said. "The penguin was a toy to amuse me when I was little. As far as I know, he never made any for sale."

But clearly someone else *had* known it existed. He watched as she turned from the window and looked at him, and he saw a depth of hidden pain and vulnerability that nearly took his breath. Shit. He was really going to do this. He was actually going on the hunt for a toy, a chunk of wood. He *never* made decisions from a place of emotion. At least not anymore, not since that long-ago time when what he'd had to find was his sister. Then he'd run on pure emotion and it'd nearly gotten her killed. "Tell me more about your grandpa."

She turned away from him again and took a moment to speak. "He died after a fire in his shop."

"Were you close?" he asked.

"Yes." There was another long pause. "I lived with him at the time."

Hell. He gave her a moment to get herself together and took a deep breath himself. So much for the emotional distance. "Were you hurt?" he asked quietly.

"I wasn't there that night."

Joe wasn't completely heartless, and his chest got tight at the guilt in her voice. "Damn, Kylie. I'm sorry."

"It was a long time ago."

Yeah, but as he knew, time didn't heal shit. Just as he knew—at least in his experience—that crime didn't discriminate. Bad shit happened to good people. "What about your parents?"

"What about them?" she asked.

"Why were you living with your grandpa and not them?"

She shrugged. "They weren't really parent material." She met his questioning gaze. "They were kids when the stick turned blue. They weren't a couple or anything. My dad didn't stay around, and my mom wasn't . . . equipped to deal back then."

"Do you see them now?" he asked, curious about her. He knew that she was quiet, thoughtful, creative. He'd always wondered what made her tick. Now that he knew she'd been raised by her grandfather, things made more sense, like the way she seemed like such an old soul, or could walk into a room and turn heads but never even realized it.

"My dad works on the oil rigs in the Gulf," she said. "He blows through San Francisco every few years. My mom's living *la vida loca* in the Mission District with her current boyfriend, but we do best with a little distance between calls and visits."

Joe and his mom had been incredibly close before she'd died when he'd been ten. And though he never knew how to describe his relationship with his father, they were in each other's lives, forever bound by the ties of blood and family. Same with Molly. The three of them had many faults, but not caring wasn't one of them. They were in a love/hate and undoubtedly dysfunctional relationship, but he had no doubt they'd stand at his back in any situation, no questions asked.

Well, okay, there'd be questions. And yelling, *lots* of yelling, but they'd still be at his back.

It seemed the only person Kylie had ever had at her back was gone, and though he knew she wouldn't want him to feel bad for her, he did. It sucked. It also made her life and her success in the artistic world all the more amazing for the fact that she was accomplishing it on her own. "Tell me more about the fire," he said, not daring to risk her wrath by offering sympathy. "His entire shop burned? And what about any inventory in it?"

"Everything was destroyed," she said.

"Which would've made any work of his that had already sold instantly more valuable," he said. "Right?"

She turned to face him, her brow furrowed. "Yes. I guess I hadn't thought of it that way."

"That's why you're paying me the big bucks." He smiled, hoping she knew he was teasing. "Okay, we'll start with some paperwork."

She looked startled. And annoyed. "You mean like forms?"

"No, a list," he said. "How many people knew the both of you? Anyone have anything against either of you, a grudge, a vendetta? Anything?"

She stared at him like he was crazy. "No one had anything against my grandpa. He was the sweetest, kindest, most generous man on the planet."

Uh-huh. Call him jaded, but *everyone* had secrets. And everyone had a bad side.

She took in his expression and shook her head. "No one was mad at him." She paused. "Or me."

He went brows up.

"Hey," she said. "I'm a delight."

He laughed and she rolled her eyes. "Okay, fine, I'm a pain in the ass, whatever. Just find my penguin."

The way she said that, "my penguin," like it'd been her most treasured possession, dried up his good humor. He knew what it was like to love family so deeply it hurt and he also knew what it was like to lose them. His dad was still kicking, but Joe had lost him just the same. "So you're saying no one was pissed off at him or you."

"That's what I'm saying."

"Then let's try another angle," he said. "Greed instead of revenge."

"Okay," she said slowly. Doubtfully. And Joe got it. Most people didn't give a lot of thought to motives behind a crime. Most people's minds didn't go there.

He wasn't most people.

"It's someone who knew the both of you," he said. "Or someone who might have heard something from someone who knew the both of you, or they wouldn't have had any idea that this wood thing even existed."

"Penguin wood carving," she corrected him. "It's a penguin wood carving, not a 'wood thing.'"

"Right," he said. "Penguin wood carving."

"My grandpa was simple," she said. "And quiet. He didn't go out, didn't have friends he hung out with. He liked to stay home and be with me."

Joe was really glad that she'd had him when it seemed as if she'd not been able to count on her parents, but he could only imagine how lonely and sheltered she'd been. "How about employees?"

"He didn't have any."

"No one? Not an office helper or apprentice? No one at all?" he asked, finding that hard to believe.

"I handled his phones and the books," she said, "although he did have apprentices here and there. I didn't think about them."

He nodded, not liking the vision he was getting of how her younger years had gone. She'd lived lean and isolated. "Can you list all the apprentices?"

"I think so. But—"

He pulled out his desk chair, gestured for her to sit, and pushed a pad of paper and a pen in front of her.

"Okay." She bent over the pad in concentration, her long, wavy, light brown hair falling into her face. With a sound of annoyance, she coiled it up on top of her head with an elastic ribbon she'd had on her wrist. She went back to the list and wrote in silence for a few minutes before handing him the pad.

"Here are the apprentices during the time I was with him," she said. "There are nine. I've given you their names and where they were from. One was older than my grandpa and isn't a viable suspect. Another has passed away. Two are living out of the country. And out of the ones that are left, I honestly can't see a single one of them doing this. They all loved my grandpa as much as I did."

This was a biased point of view and as was habit on this job, he ignored all bias and emotion. "Is there anything else I need to know?" he asked.

She pulled her lower lip into her mouth and gnawed on it with her teeth. After a pause, she shook her head.

He resisted a sigh. She was a shitty liar. "Going to actually need the words, Kylie," he said, holding her gaze, knowing it was next to impossible to hold a lie while looking someone in the eyes and speaking at the same time. At least for someone like Kylie. Him, he could look into the eyes of a saint and give a good run for his money.

But Kylie didn't hold the eye contact. She looked away as she spoke. "There's nothing else you need to know."

Right. He didn't believe her, of course, but he knew better than to push a woman who'd dug her toes in the sand. Instead, he scanned her list and stilled. "Your boss is on here."

"Gib? Yeah," she said. "But I marked him *not* a possibility."

"You've marked them *all not* a possibility," he said dryly. "But let's start with Gib. Why isn't he a suspect in your eyes?"

"Because we grew up together," she said. "My grandpa taught him everything he knows. He considered Gib one of his own, even gave him a place to stay when he needed it."

"So Gib would know exactly how important the thing—er, *penguin wood carving* was to you, right?" he asked. "Not to mention what it must be worth."

"It's not Gib," she said stubbornly. "He's been good to me, very good to me."

He didn't like where this was going. "How good is very good?"

"What do you mean?" she asked suspiciously.

Joe's instincts were razor sharp and they'd gotten that way because he was a master at studying people. He'd been in Reclaimed Woods several times. He'd seen little to no sexual tension from Gib aimed at Kylie, but he still had to ask. For the case, he told himself, and absolutely not for personal knowledge. "You and Gib a thing, Kylie?"

"What does this line of questioning pertain to?" she asked.

Him being jealous, which was asinine. "Motive," he said. Look at him showing off his lying skills . . .

"No," she said. "In the past, Gib and I have never been a thing."

She spoke with 100 percent honesty. But there'd been a hesitation there that told him he was definitely still missing a piece of this puzzle. "And how about the present or the future?"

She crossed her arms. "I don't see how this is relative."

Shit. She had a thing for Gib. He studied her for a minute. "I'm going to ask you that one again. You and Gib going to—"

"None of your business," she said with surprising finality. "Drop it, please."

That would certainly be the smart thing to do. "Fine. But he stays on the list."

"Whatever. Now what?" she asked.

"You go to work, and so do I. I've got a surveillance job to get to." To save time, he began to load up, sliding his comms case into one of his cargo pockets for later. He laced up his boots and unlocked his weapons safe to start strapping on weapons. Glock on his right hip. Knife clipped to the inside of a pocket. Cell phone in front pocket. Sig strapped to a leg. Giants cap on backward, flak vest strapped across his chest and back, and a fucking partridge in a pear tree.

He looked up and realized that Kylie's eyes had darkened as she stared at him. He was male enough to smirk but smart enough to keep it on the inside. "I'll get back to you once I make my way through this list. I'll start tonight after work."

"What? No," she said. "I want to be involved. We're partners in this."

"I work alone, Kylie."

He was surprised when she stared him down. "Not this time," she said.

"Listen—"

"Do you want that mirror for Molly or not?" she asked.

He felt the muscle in his jaw tick. She had balls, he'd give her that. Her courage was shockingly attractive too. "You know I do," he said.

"Then I'll see you later. *Partner*."

Shit. He was so screwed.

Chapter 5

#FranklyMyDearIDontGiveADamn

After the meeting with Joe, Kylie went to work, but for once her heart wasn't into her dream job. Her thoughts were on her missing penguin. And also on how Joe had looked strapping on his weapons, because holy cow. For years she'd harbored her not-so-secret crush on Gib because he was handsome, steady, and—let's face it—safe.

But Joe. *Nothing* about Joe said *safe,* and yet the inexplicable yearning she had for him said a good part of her didn't care. She hadn't taken many risks in her life, if any. That needed to change, and if that change included more time with Joe's incredibly sexy mouth on hers, she was thinking that wouldn't be a bad thing. His mouth. His body . . . And with that thought, she stupidly overmilled the tabletop she'd been working on for weeks. Trying to correct the mistake, she ended up with a huge splinter jammed in her right palm. "Dammit!"

She flipped off the machine and stared at her palm and then the wood, now rendered unusable.

Not good. Hand throbbing, she called her supply source to get more wood and received bad news. More mahogany lumber would put her overbudget. By hundreds of dollars. Worse, it would take two weeks to arrive.

The whole thing was a costly rookie mistake that would probably also cost her the client.

Both over herself and the day so far, she spent an hour trying to dig the splinter out with her left hand, which only made things worse. Finally, bloody and frustrated, she ran upstairs to Haley's office.

"Help," she said and held out her hand, palm up.

"Oh my God, what the hell did you do?" Haley asked. "Stab yourself with a pocketknife—repeatedly?"

"I was just trying to get out the splinter," Kylie said.

"With what, your pocketknife?"

"Hey, I get a lot of splinters," she said in self-defense. "And we have a saying in the shop. Mark 'em and take 'em out on our own time—*after* work. So I was in a hurry."

"You're all a bunch of barbarians," Haley said and brought her into a patient room. She poured some sort of antiseptic over Kylie's hand and then directed a mobile bright light over her entire palm and went to work with a set of tweezers.

"Ow!" Kylie said.

Haley snorted but didn't stop working. "You're okay stabbing yourself repeatedly with your pocket-knife, but you're flinching over my tweezers?"

Kylie sighed. "It's different when someone else is the one poking around—*Ouch!*"

"Done." Haley held up her tweezers, revealing a splinter a good inch long.

"Wow."

"Yeah, and you're welcome," Haley said. "You owe me a bag of Tina's muffins."

"Thought you were on some sort of ridiculously strict diet. Something about a bikini and summer season ahead . . ."

Haley sighed. "I just don't know how I went from being sixteen years old and eating pasta for every meal and wearing a size zero to being twenty-six, drinking kale, and debating wearing a T-shirt to the pool."

"Well, I think you look great," Kylie said honestly.

Haley hugged her. "Thanks. And I'm over myself. I really do want—no, make that *need*—muffins."

After Kylie was bandaged and had paid the bill in the form of the promised muffins, she was headed back to Reclaimed Woods via the courtyard when she was waylaid by a call from her mom. They talked every few weeks, with just long enough between calls to grow the fondness.

"Hey, baby, thanks for the birthday gift certificate to Victoria's Secret and Charlotte Russe!" her mom said happily. "New fancy undies and club dresses, here I come! However did you know?"

Kylie had to laugh. "Because it's all you ever want every year."

"Well, it was very sweet. Thank you. How's work? You with your cutie-pie boss yet?"

"Mom." Kylie pinched the bridge of her nose. "No."

"Good. I mean, he's a decent guy, but he's not *The Guy*. I know you don't want to hear this from me, but you need someone who pulls you out of your shell."

Kylie grimaced. "I'm not in a shell."

"You're so far in your shell, you can't even see out of the shell."

Kylie rolled her eyes. This was a common refrain between them. Her mom felt Kylie didn't have enough fun in her life, and Kylie thought her mom could do with a little more life and a little less fun. "I've gotta get back to work."

"See? All work. Come out with me sometime. We'll have a drink, loosen you up a little bit, and find you someone to light you up."

"Mom, a man isn't going to solve all my problems."

"Well, of course not, silly. But he'll sure help you forget about them. Just think about it. Call me once in a while."

Kylie sighed, shoved her phone away, and went back to work. Problem was, now she was short the wood she needed for her table, her hand hurt like a bitch, and she couldn't stop thinking about the fact that though Joe had agreed to partner with her on this, he apparently planned to work his way down her list.

Without her.

She knew that was just his usual lone wolf mentality, but it felt a little bit like he'd told her that she wasn't wanted. She'd hired him and he'd taken over, and it was yet another rejection.

Man, she was really on a roll.

But she wasn't going to be set aside that easily. She'd been texting with Molly. Nothing happened at Hunt Investigations that Molly didn't know about, and according to her, the guys were all up to their eyeballs in work at the moment. Topping things off, they'd gone out on an unexpected big bond bounty hunt that needed to be handled today due to a court deadline.

Which meant that Joe wouldn't even think about starting on her list until he was back. The hours crawled by until late afternoon when Molly texted a heads-up that the team was coming back into the office.

"Is there anything else I need to know?" Joe had asked.

Yeah, but not that she planned on telling him about. Or anyone. She turned off the planer she'd been using and quickly cleaned up. Vinnie tried to help by picking up wood scraps and spreading them everywhere under her feet so that she kept tripping. Trying to distract him, she tossed him one of his own toys. "Fetch," she said.

He gave a bark of pure joy, went after the toy, and . . . took it back to his bed. She sighed and continued to close up. She'd just finished and grabbed Vinnie to go when Gib poked his head in and smiled.

"Hey," he said. "Everything okay?"

"Sure," she said. "Even though right about now would be a really great time for someone to tell me that I'm Princess of Genovia."

"Who?"

"Never mind. What's up?"

"I thought maybe we'd do dinner," he said.

She froze. Was he asking her out? She actually wasn't sure. "The kind of dinner where we've both been working late and you're hungry so I go get us takeout?" she asked, which they'd done a million times and definitely wasn't a date.

"No," he said. "The kind of dinner where I take you to a restaurant." He smiled and ran a hand over the sexy scruff on his jaw. "I think it's about time, don't you?"

She waited for the burst of excitement to hit, but . . . it didn't. She wasn't exactly sure when or where or how, but the painful crush she'd had on him forever now didn't seem quite as painful. Suddenly, wanting Gib felt like the safe option.

And for whatever reason, safe was no longer what she craved. "I'm sorry," she said, "but I can't tonight. I've got plans."

"With Joe?"

"Yes, but it's not what you think." Instead of using the carrier, she tucked Vinnie into the large pouch of her hoodie sweatshirt—his favorite place to be—and rose to go, but Gib grabbed her hand.

"I really am sorry about the party last night," he said. "I honestly didn't know Rena would be there."

"It's okay. It doesn't matter."

"No, I think it does." He reeled her in closer and bent a little to look into her eyes. "I've made some mistakes with you, Ky. I'm trying to fix them."

"What kind of mistakes?" she asked curiously.

"For starters, the kind of mistake that had me letting you leave last night."

She stared up at him, into the eyes of the man who'd been the only one she'd wanted for as long as she could remember—aside from Justin Timberlake. "Why?"

He looked confused at the question. "Why?"

"Yeah, why were you hoping I'd stay when we haven't really seen much of each other outside work?"

"Because I realized something." Holding her gaze, he pulled her in to him. "That I wanted to do this." Then he leaned in, lowered his head, and brushed his mouth over hers. His lips were warm and very nice, and though she froze at the contact, her brain didn't.

Gib was kissing her!

She was still stunned when he pulled back and smiled at her. "Think about it," he said.

And then he walked away, leaving her staring after him. Hell had frozen over. The fat lady had sung.

Because Gib had just made a very real pass at her.

She should be doing cartwheels. Why wasn't she doing cartwheels? She locked up and left, more confused than ever. She'd planned to sit on a bench at the fountain in the courtyard where she could see to the second floor and the entrance of Hunt

Investigations. She'd thought to lie in wait for Joe to leave his office, and then waylay him. But five minutes into her wait, Molly sent a text.

He's delayed thirty minutes by a meeting with Archer.

Great. Head still spinning, Kylie headed into the pub for a drink. She stepped up to the bar next to Sadie.

Sadie smiled distractedly, but didn't say anything.

"You okay?" Kylie asked.

"Good question," Sean said from the other side of the bar. "I just asked her the same thing."

"And?" Kylie asked.

Sean slid Sadie a look. "She told me not to mistake her silence for weakness, that no one plans a murder out loud."

Kylie laughed.

Sadie didn't.

"Okay, so . . . whose murder are we planning?" Kylie asked her when Sean moved off.

"Still up for debate," Sadie said, reaching over to pet Vinnie's head. He'd stuck it out of Kylie's sweatshirt pocket. "I'm having a late lunch and thinking it over."

"What is that you're having?"

"Fruit salad."

"That's funny," Kylie said, "cuz it looks like a sangria."

"Huh. Weird." Sadie sipped her "fruit salad."

Kylie laughed. "Okay, so you had a bad day too." She sighed. "Adulting never looked so hard from the other side."

"It's not our fault," Sadie said. "Monopoly gave us all these false expectations. Like, why can't I buy property? Where's my get-out-of-jail-free card? Or my two hundred bucks for passing Go?" She fed Vinnie a pretzel. Vinnie loved pretzels. Actually, Vinnie loved all food. Well, except for pickles, which Kylie had discovered by accident when he'd eaten her lunch the other day, every single bite except for the pickles that he'd so thoughtfully left on the floor for her to step on.

A guy walked into the pub, his phone to his ear. He was long, lean, wearing a really great suit, and looking like a million bucks. Kylie knew his name. Caleb. He was Spence's business partner who also sometimes dealt with Hunt Investigations. He always seemed very serious, but beyond that all she knew about him was that he was *very* nice to look at.

"Relax, Susan," he said into his cell phone as he came up to the bar. "I won't be late. I'm in my car right now, on my way."

"No, he's not, Susan!" Sadie yelled toward his phone. "He's in a bar!"

Caleb sent her a long look.

"Sorry, Suits," she said unapologetically as she casually sipped her lunch. "No one lies to Susan in front of me."

Caleb narrowed his eyes. Sadie smiled without showing teeth. In response, he pointed at her and then moved away from them.

"'Suits'?" Kylie asked Sadie.

Sadie shrugged. "He wears more money on his broad shoulders than I make all year. It's annoying."

"There's a story here," Kylie guessed. "I think I want to hear it."

"He's just too uptight."

"You two a thing?"

"He's too uptight," Sadie repeated. "Plus, I actually like being single. I get to be selfish with my time and personal space. I can leave the top off the toothpaste and sleep like a starfish."

All true.

When Molly finally texted her that Joe was preparing to leave, Kylie exited the pub. She made her way to the parking lot where Joe kept his truck. She was leaning against it when he strolled up five minutes later. He was in work gear, which never failed to trip her pulse. Dark cargos, a long-sleeved T-shirt that fit him like it'd been made for him, and God knew how many weapons she couldn't see. He had a duffle bag hanging off one broad shoulder and his phone to his ear.

He wore dark aviator sunglasses, but she knew he was looking at her as he finished up his call before slipping his cell into one of his million pockets. "What happened to your hand?" he asked.

She looked down at the gauze wrapped around her palm. "Splinter."

"You get it out?"

"Haley did."

"You clean it good?"

"Again, Haley."

He nodded and studied her. "So . . ."

"So . . ." She bit her lower lip.

He raised a brow. "So what are you doing here, Kylie?"

"Catching a ride." She wished she had a pair of sunglasses that made her look even half as badass cool as he did.

And though he hadn't smiled in greeting at her, he did so at Vinnie, reaching out to ruffle the top of the dog's head affectionately. "And where are you catching a ride to?" he asked.

"Wherever you're going. I presume to someone on the list, right?"

He didn't sigh. Joe didn't give away his emotions that easily. But she sensed his irritation as he gave Vinnie one last pat and beeped his truck unlocked. Kylie jumped into the passenger seat before he could turn her away.

Joe slid behind the wheel, expression a little tight. He wasn't happy. The irony didn't escape her. After a very long dry spell, she'd kissed two men in the past week. One who wanted to be with her and one who didn't.

And here she sat with the man who didn't. Clearly she needed help. And as she clicked the seatbelt, she told herself she was *doubly* grateful Joe hadn't called her after the infamous kiss, because seriously? She'd gotten a little drunk at a bar and kissed some guy? *This* guy? The wrong-for-her guy? Who was she, her own damn mother?

Kissing the *wrong* man was her mom's MO, as was making poor decisions when it came to the male species. Or life, really. Kylie didn't want to be that person or make those mistakes. And Joe, sexy and hot as he was, represented exactly that—the mistakes she'd seen all during her growing-up years, the kind of men her mom had always brought home, the guy who burned hot and fast and then disappointed and disappeared.

But for all her determination to not be her mom, to live life more seriously and be content just watching the fun happen around her, she had an embarrassing truth. For that five minutes she'd been in Joe's arms, she'd been transported. Transfixed.

And aroused beyond belief.

None of which she'd felt in Gib's arms earlier. Shaking that off, she asked, "So where are we going?"

"The Embarcadero," Joe said. "Rowena Butterfield was your grandpa's last apprentice."

"Ro," Kylie said with a smile. Rowena was a throwback to a flower power child of the sixties. She was in her forties, but seemed timeless, and she was a real talent as well. Her grandpa had loved her and so had Kylie. "She's great. She didn't have anything to do with this, Joe."

"She was fired from her last job for questionable behavior and she's now selling her wares at a little stand near Pier 39."

"No," Kylie said. "No way."

"Yes way."

She slid him a look. "Define 'questionable behavior.'"

"She stole a hundred-year-old bottle of wine from

a winery and, when confronted, hit the winery employee over the head with the bottle."

Okay, so that was definitely questionable behavior, but she shook her head. "That can't be right."

Joe didn't comment. He drove them through the city to the Embarcadero, where he parked. She started to get out of the truck along with him but he pointed at her.

"No," he said.

She arched a brow. "I'm sorry. What?"

"You're staying here. The rug rat too. I'm starving, so if I pick up some food, what do you want?"

The guy was a contradiction from head to toe. Badass and ready to save the world one minute, deceptively playful the next. He was constantly hungry and on the perpetual search for food. She had no idea where he put the million-plus calories he consumed in a day. "I'm not staying in the truck," she said.

He pushed his sunglasses to the top of his head and gave her what was surely a patented *you're driving me crazy* look. "Yes, you are."

She crossed her arms. "The only way that's going to happen is if you handcuff me," she said. "You going to handcuff me, Joe?"

There was a very slight softening around his mouth and his eyes heated. "Only if you ask me real nice."

Her every single erogenous zone quivered, and she had more of them than she remembered having. "You do realize this is the twenty-first century and men don't get to tell women *no* anymore, right?" she asked.

"Kylie, this woman can ID you."

"Well, yes," she admitted.

"So you stay here. You too," he said to Vinnie, who licked Joe's finger.

"Wait." She was so not okay with this, even if a little part of her wanted to lick Joe's finger too, amongst other body parts. "I—"

"She knows you, Kylie. Presumably she likes you. She's never going to admit to stealing your carving if you're standing right there while I question her."

Okay, so *maybe* he had a point.

Joe studied her for a moment and then, apparently satisfied that she was going to stay, he nodded. "I'll be back."

She waited three minutes and then got out of the truck, but not before "borrowing" a big black hoodie from his backseat and what was clearly a spare pair of sunglasses in his console. She pulled the sweatshirt on over hers, hood up, slid on the sunglasses, and glanced at herself in the mirror. She was so keeping the sunglasses.

"There," she said to Vinnie. "Incognito. What do you think?"

Vinnie cocked his head to one side and then the other, his ears quivering with excitement. He sensed an adventure. He loved adventures. She put him on a leash and headed to Pier 39, eyes peeled for Joe.

There was an area in front of the pier where individual vendors sold their wares. The place was crowded with people, mostly tourists, giving her plenty of cover.

She and Vinnie stopped at the first vendor, who was selling pet costumes. Perfect! She scooped up Vinnie and showed him a lion costume, complete with mane. "What do you think?"

Vinnie licked it.

Good enough. She paid for the costume and put it on Vinnie. "Now you're undercover like me," she told him. She could see the line of vendors going up the Embarcadero. Several ahead of her was Rowena, who appeared to be selling all sizes of handcrafted, ornately carved wooden boxes.

She didn't see Joe. Huh. She was still standing there in indecision when someone set a hand at the nape of her neck and squeezed lightly.

Chapter 6

Kylie nearly leapt right out of her own skin. And then a familiar low male voice said in her ear, "I knew you wouldn't be able to stay."

"Joe," she gasped, sagging a little. "You startled me. I didn't see you."

"No shit. But we all saw you," he said, his hand warm on the back of her neck. "You and your vicious pet lion."

Kylie looked down at Vinnie, who'd fallen asleep at her feet, mouth open, snoring at maximum volume. She scooped him up. He snorted and snuggled in, setting his head on her shoulder, going right back to sleep.

And back to snoring.

"Ruthless guard dog on the job," Joe said, steering her away from the vendors and toward where he'd parked. "Are you wearing my sweatshirt?"

"Yes, and your spare sunglasses too," she said. "It's my disguise."

His mouth quirked. She was pretty sure he was laughing at her on the inside.

"What did you learn?" she asked.

"Not here."

When they got back to his truck, he took a call on Bluetooth.

"Four a.m. tomorrow," Archer's voice said. "Be locked and loaded."

"Ten-four." Joe disconnected with a flick of his thumb on a button on his steering wheel.

Kylie stared at him.

Joe kept his gaze on the road.

"What was that?" she asked.

"Tomorrow's job."

"Four a.m., locked and loaded?" she repeated. "What kind of a job is that?"

"The kind I can't talk about."

She sighed and tried to let it go, but curiosity killed the cat and all that. "Is this job dangerous?"

He spared her a quick glance, eyes amused.

Right. *All* his jobs had the potential to be dangerous. Very much so. It hadn't been too long ago that Archer had been shot on the job. And Joe himself had taken a bat to the back of his head in a terrifying incident as well. She was thinking about that, the differences in their lifestyles, when his phone rang again.

It was Molly on speaker that time. "I need backup on Dad," she said.

Oddly enough, this had him looking far more tense than needing to be "locked and loaded" tomorrow morning at four a.m. He pulled the truck over and took the phone off Bluetooth. "What's wrong?" he asked. He listened and then pinched the bridge of his nose. "Yeah. Got it. I'll take care of it."

Then he disconnected and speed-thumbed a long text. He sent, waited a minute, got a response that he read, and returned with another, a short one this time, before he started driving again.

All without a word.

Kylie couldn't hold her tongue. "Is everything okay?"

"Yeah."

"This would be a lot more satisfying conversation if you used more than one word at a time," she said.

She thought maybe she detected the slightest exhalation from him at that. His version of a sigh. "My dad's got some problems I need to take care of," he finally said.

Her heart squeezed with worry. "Do you need any help?"

He slid her a look.

"Hey," she said. "I'm good at helping."

This got her a ghost of a smile. "Thanks, but this one's all on me." He stopped at a light. "My dad's got a lot of medical bills," he said. "I try to pay them all, but sometimes he hides the mail."

"Why does he do that?"

"God knows," he said on a mirthless laugh. "But apparently a collection agency called earlier and he threatened them quite inventively. They called the cops."

She didn't know what to say to this. "Did he get arrested?"

"No. I've got friends on the force. It's taken care of."

He was quiet for the rest of the drive. Must have used up all his words. Kylie spent the time thinking about what kind of guy takes care of his dad and sister with everything he had.

A good guy, she decided, and sighed. Dammit.

Joe pulled up in front of her apartment building, and she looked over at him in surprise. "How did you know where I live?"

"I know a lot of things about you," he said, coming around to open the door for her and Vinnie.

"Like?"

"Like the fact that someone else *also* knows where you live, someone who shouldn't." He pulled her out of the truck and walked her to her front door. "Keys?" he asked.

"Hold on." She was searching her bag, but couldn't find them. Then she remembered the rush she'd been in that morning. Vinnie had gakked all over her rug, throwing up the pinecone he'd eaten at the park the night before. She'd stepped in it with her bare feet, which had pretty much set the tone for her entire day. "I think I must've forgotten them this morning," she said. "I was running late and almost missed the bus. *Crap.*"

Joe didn't say anything, just pulled something from one of his pockets, and not five seconds later her door clicked open, faster than she could've used her key in the first place.

"Wait—" she exclaimed. "Did you just break into my apartment?"

"That would be illegal," he said and discreetly slipped the small tool back into his pocket. He nudged her inside and bent to pick up an envelope on the floor, taking in the handwritten KYLIE on the front.

Same as before with no stamp or postmark.

"Another one," she breathed. She set Vinnie down and took the envelope from his fingers. She was staring at it like it was a rattlesnake ready to strike when she realized that Joe was quickly and efficiently walking through her apartment and looking hot as hell while he did it.

When he came back to her, he nodded at the envelope. "We're all clear. Open it."

"It might be nothing."

"All the more reason to open it."

Right. But she didn't want to because she knew—as Joe clearly did—it *wasn't* nothing.

Vinnie trotted off toward the kitchen, stopping just short of the doorway to lift his paw and poke at the air. When he was satisfied that he wasn't going to encounter a glass door, he happily made his way to his water bowl.

"What was that?" Joe asked.

"He has trust issues."

Joe let out a low laugh. "Well, at least we know where he gets them from."

"Hey," she said. But also, it was true. With a deep inhalation, she opened the envelope.

This time there were two Polaroids. The first one was of her beloved little penguin—sitting in a jail cell this time. "Is that . . . Alcatraz?" she asked in shock.

Joe took it in, mouth dialed to Not Happy. "Yeah."

Kylie pulled out the second Polaroid and stilled in confusion. There were two items in this pic, one of a small entry table, ornately handmade. The other was a bench to match. She stared at them both before Joe turned the photo over in her hand. On the back was a scrawled note:

Authenticate the table and bench as Michael Masters's work for the auction listed below and you'll get your carving back. To do this, make an appointment at the auction house where the items are being held. You'll ID yourself, authenticate, and sign off on the items. They'll contact me when you've done so.

"I don't understand," Kylie said. "This table looks like my grandpa's work, but I know all of his pieces that are out there. This never hit the market. But it couldn't have been something he had in his unsold inventory either, since everything burned."

"And the bench?"

She took a pic of the pic with her phone's camera and then used her finger and thumb to enlarge the back, getting a close-up look before shaking her head. "I really don't think this is his at all. It's nowhere as good as the table."

"You can tell from just a photo?"

"I can. But I don't know if anyone else could. It's not his, Joe."

"Actually," he said slowly, "I think that's probably the point."

"What do you mean?"

"I'm guessing as Michael Masters's granddaughter, someone who's in the field as well, you're probably one of the only people who could authenticate his work. And if you do, this person makes bank."

"But how does he have something of my grandpa's at all?"

"That's what we have to find out," he said. "But I can guess the reason for the bench. If you authenticate it along with the table, he makes potentially a lot of money on something he either made himself or had made. This could be just the beginning of a very profitable scam."

She stared at him in horror and anger. "This isn't Rowena. She'd never do this."

"Agreed. I already ruled her out."

"How?"

"Back at the pier, she cleansed my aura and told me that money is the root of all evil and that if I believe, the universe would fill my cup with love."

That broke through her temper and she had to smile. "Aw. Is the universe going to fill your cup?"

"Jury's still out," he said. "But I asked for her autograph." He pulled a piece of paper from another of his million pockets and held it up next to the back of the photo. "Her handwriting doesn't match this or what's on the envelopes."

Kylie pulled out her phone and Googled the auction details. "The auction he's talking about is in two weeks' time," she said. "Which means . . ."

He met her gaze. "We've got less than that to find this asshat so you don't have to do something you don't want to do."

"But that won't get me my penguin back."

"I'm going to get the penguin back for you," he said with such confidence that she wanted to believe.

"Maybe I should call the auction house and find out who the seller is or try to see the items," she said.

"We can try," he said. "But I'm betting you'll get stonewalled on the seller details. Auction houses protect their sellers and buyers with everything they have. If one of them wants anonymity, never the two shall meet."

"But I don't get it," she said. "Surely there's an easier way to make money."

"Not if this guy is just getting started," Joe said. "With your grandpa gone, his work is only going to continue to go up in value. So I'd bet whoever this is, they're out there making or commissioning other pieces. The bench is probably just the beginning. Once you authenticate it, everything else he makes could be authenticated as your grandpa's stuff as well—without you." He turned and headed toward her front door. "Lock up tight behind me."

"Wait—where are you going?"

He looked back at her. "There're *nine* other apprentices out there."

"No, not nine. I told you, one's old, one's passed away, two are out of the country, and Gib isn't a viable suspect. With Rowena out, that leaves only three."

He shook his head. "I haven't cleared any of the others yet, including Gib."

"It's not Gib!"

Their gazes met, his as stubborn as hers probably was. "Look," she said. "You're going to have to trust me on this. He's not a thief."

Joe studied her. "I asked you once before, but now I'm going to ask you again. Is there something going on between you two?"

She tossed up her hands. "Why do you both keep asking me that about each other?"

His eyes narrowed. "I thought nothing was going on."

"And before today, I could've passed a lie detector test on that," she said.

"What happened today?"

She paused. Not because she had anything to be ashamed of, but because she wasn't quite sure what had happened.

"Kylie."

She sighed. "It's nothing."

"Try again," Joe said and gave her the very male universal *go on* gesture.

She rolled her eyes. "Fine. He . . . finally made a move on me."

Joe didn't budge. Not a blink, not a muscle twitch,

nothing, but she could've popped corn off the electric tension coming off him.

"Describe 'made a move,'" he finally said.

She crossed her arms. "And again, how is this relevant to my case?"

He just gave her that careful stare again and she thought *wow, those eyes of his should be registered as a lethal weapon,* because she found herself opening her mouth and spilling her guts. "He kissed me."

"He kissed you."

"Yeah," she said. "Do you know that you often repeat what I say?"

"What kind of a kiss?" he asked.

She was momentarily bewildered. "I don't know. It was a kiss. A normal kiss. A nice kiss." She cocked her head at him. "How many kinds of kisses are there?"

He just looked at her for a long moment before coming toward her. He backed her to the wall and pressed his big hands on either side of her head. "There are many kinds of kisses," he said.

Her breath had backed up in her throat, where her heart had lodged, pounding wildly. "S-s-such as?"

"Such as this one." And then he leaned in and covered her mouth with his.

Chapter 7

#TheresNoPlaceLikeHome

At the touch of Joe's mouth, Kylie's brain stopped being capable of rational thought. His tongue gave a knee-weakening stroke against hers and she let out a shockingly needy moan as she clutched at him, fisting her hands in the material of his shirt at his chest.

Only when he'd thoroughly plundered and pillaged and left her boneless did he lift his head and look into her eyes.

"Wow," she whispered, fully aware she was still holding on to him like he was a lifeline, but the bones in her legs had liquefied. "I mean . . ." She shook her head. "Wow."

He nodded. "Yeah. So to be clear, that wasn't 'a normal kiss' or even 'a nice kiss.' It was a 'wow' kiss. Any questions?"

"Just one," she said softly. "Can I have another?"

Joe didn't have to be asked twice. His mouth immediately descended again, his fingers sliding into her hair to change the angle of the kiss to suit him. It was a controlled, alpha thing to do, but she had only one thought—nothing about the usually carefully, purposely leashed Joe was in control at the moment.

And she liked it.

She had no idea how long they went at it because she was in absolute heaven. Who knew that the man could use his preferred *silent mode* to communicate in a way that she finally approved of?

Only when she was completely breathless and about to strip him down to his birthday suit did she manage to pull back.

"Any more questions?" he asked, also a little bit breathless, which was more than slightly gratifying.

Dumbly, she shook her head.

His eyes softened and he gently he stroked his thumb over her bottom lip. "And FYI? Gib's an idiot."

She'd forgotten all about Gib, and she bit her lower lip as she stared up at the man who'd made her forget everything but his very talented mouth. And sexy body. And knowing hands . . . "I think I need you to go now," she murmured.

Again he just looked at her before turning slowly away from her and heading to her front door. His movements were different from his usual decisive, calculated ones and she wondered if he was even halfway as discombobulated as she was. "You're going home, right?" she asked. "To bed, since you have to be at work so early?"

He paused and then kept walking.

"Dammit, Joe. After all that, you're really going to leave me here and check out another apprentice without me."

When he turned to her this time, he was back in control. "You've got a time frame now," he reminded her. "Less than two weeks."

"But you have to be up early. You have to be at work at four a.m."

His mouth curved in a small smile. "Don't worry. I'm a big boy."

Of that she had no doubt. "I'm coming with. I can help."

"Look," he said. "No offense, but I'll be faster alone. I'll call you—"

"No way. Just give me a minute." She started to dash into her bedroom to get a few things she thought she might need, but pivoted first and snatched his keys from his fingers.

"That's not going to stop me," he said mildly.

"No, but here's something that might. If you don't take me, I'm not going to work on Molly's mirror."

He rubbed the back of his neck and tipped his head down, staring at his shoes. Whether to keep from strangling her or just to count to ten, she had no idea. She raced into her room, shoved some stuff from her closet into her bag, and then was back in a flash. "Love you," she told Vinnie. "Be a good boy. Don't wait up. I'll be home late."

Two minutes later they were in Joe's truck. His breathing was relaxed and deep. His eyes were vigilant. He was back to his regular cool and calm.

She was not. "Where are we going?"

"The Castro."

He parked just off Market Street. When he got out of the truck, so did she, pausing at the rainbow-colored crosswalk to look at him. "You're not going to tell me to stay in the car?" she asked.

"Why, when you're going with me anyway?"

Good point. And look at him with the learning curve. They headed up a steep walkway to a narrow six-story building. Inside the lobby, Joe pushed the elevator button. The elevator didn't come.

Fine with Kylie. She *hated* elevators. Correction— she was *terrified* of elevators. Well, not of elevators, necessarily, but of any small, enclosed space. She was a terrible claustrophobic. "We should just walk up," she suggested, trying to hide her panic.

"It's six flights," he said and looked at her boots.

They were work boots. Heavy, steel-toed. Great in the shop, not great for going up six flights. "I don't mind," she said quickly. "I need the extra steps today anyway."

Of course just then the elevator doors opened and Joe held the door for her, gesturing for her to go first.

Great. "This is a *really* bad idea," she muttered but stepped onto the elevator, albeit with the same enthusiasm she would've walked to the guillotine.

The doors slid closed with an audible click, like the last nail on her coffin might sound.

And then, just like that, they were enclosed in the tiny space together. Joe was looking amused, his blue eyes on her, warm but curious. "You okay?" he asked.

"Sure. Yes. Yep," she said, popping the *p* sound.

"Maybe one more and I'll believe you."

She opened her mouth—to say what exactly, they'd never know, because suddenly the elevator lurched and went on the move. At a snail's pace. "Seriously? I could've climbed the stairs backward faster than this."

But then, as if the elevator had heard her, it jerked and . . . *screeched to a halt.*

"Oh shit," she gasped before she could stop herself. One time she'd been sitting on a bench in her building's courtyard in front of the fountain when a spider had dropped out of a potted tree and landed next to her. She'd literally shot up into the air using only the muscles of her butt cheeks and had come down into the lap of the perfect stranger sitting next to her.

What happened in the elevator was pretty much the same. One second she was standing on her own two feet. The next she'd leapt at Joe.

His hard arms closed around her and he put his jaw to hers. "If you wanted another kiss, all you had to do was say so."

"I'm begging you not to talk," she moaned and dropped her forehead to his chest. "Just get me out of here."

He paused and she felt him looking down at her. "You're claustrophobic."

"Maybe. Just a little tiny bit." But she was also a big girl, so she pried herself away from him and turned to stare at the doors, willing them to open.

She half expected Joe to make a joke or laugh at her. Instead she felt his bigger, much warmer hand slide into hers. Not proud, her dignity long gone, she held on like he was her personal life buoy.

"One sec," he said calmly and opened the control panel to take a look.

She lifted her head. "Do you know how to fix elevators?" she asked hopefully.

"I could probably figure it out."

He could probably figure it out . . . "Oh my God." She squeezed her eyes shut and heard him laugh.

"It's going to be okay, Kylie. Just hang on."

She was pretty sure he didn't mean that literally but she did just that, fisting her hands in his shirt and holding on. "This is all your fault," she said tightly. "I really want to hit you right now."

"Take a few deep breaths," he said.

"*Then* can I hit you?"

He snorted and kept doing something in the electric panel.

"Doesn't *anything* bother you?" she asked a little bitterly.

"Plenty." He looked at her as if gauging the level of her panic. Apparently deciding it was extremely high, he said, "I go with the five-by-five rule. If it's not going to matter in five years, I don't spend more than five minutes upset by it."

She tilted her head to his, startled to realize that since he'd bowed his, their mouths were nearly lined up.

All you have to do is not kiss him, she told herself. But she licked her suddenly dry lips, a gesture that had his eyes darkening and a very rough, very male sound coming from deep in his throat. He leaned in even closer, but just before their mouths touched, the elevator jerked and began its upward motion again.

Kylie let out a shaky breath and stepped back from Joe. "I told you this was a bad idea!"

"Yeah, that was close," he said. "You almost kissed me again."

"I meant getting on the elevator!" She glared at him. "And *you* kissed *me* that last time!"

"You were going on about a kiss being *nice*. But there was nothing nice about that kiss you planted on me in the alley. It was raw and sexy and dirty in the best possible way. You needed to be reminded of that."

She covered her face. "Oh my God."

"God had nothing to do with it," he said smugly. "Kylie, you kissing me like that was hot as hell and . . ."

She dropped her hands and stared at him. "And . . . ?"

He held her gaze prisoner. "The thought of you not remembering it the same way made me crazy."

Oh, she remembered it the exact same way. The memories of it were imprinted on her brain much as the Polaroids she'd been receiving. First having drinks with her friends, and then at some point realizing that most of them were paired up and in love, and she'd felt . . . alone. Needing air, she'd stepped outside into the courtyard.

Joe had been there looking dark and dangerously

alluring. She'd tossed some change into the fountain like a tourist and he'd laughed with her, making her feel . . . well, less alone.

Then she'd done something wild, at least for her. She'd taken him by the hand and pulled him into the alley. And the rest was history. "I'm not going to do that again," she said. "Kiss you."

"Okay, how about I kiss you again then?"

He was infuriating. And way too sexy. The elevator doors opened and she stormed off the elevator. Joe followed, still smiling, the ass. He knocked on an apartment door.

"I forgot to ask," she whispered. "Which one of the apprentices is this?"

Joe didn't have time to answer before the apartment door opened, revealing a man who looked older than time itself. He was ninety if he was a day, hunched over a cane.

"Mr. Gonzales," Joe said respectfully.

"Eh?" Mr. Gonzales asked. "Speak up, boy!"

Kylie recognized him from years ago when he'd worked at her grandpa's shop after a late-in-life career change from carpenter to furniture maker. She waved at him. "Hi, Mr. Gonzales. Remember me? You were my grandpa's first apprentice. I was just a kid, maybe five years old?"

"I remember you." He blinked at her through his spectacles. "You were a runny-nosed, whiny little thing who rode her bike through the shop and knocked my work over."

And he'd been a grumpy, curmudgeonly old man even back then, but she kept that to herself.

"Never saw you after your grandfather died." His voice softened. "It was awful what happened, to the both of you."

She felt Joe look at her, but she kept her face averted from his, heart feeling tight.

"We're wondering if you're still doing any woodworking," Joe said.

Mr. Gonzales laughed so hard he would've toppled over if Joe hadn't steadied him. "Haven't left this apartment in several years. The only woodworking I do is picking my teeth with a toothpick. Can't even take a shit in peace anymore." He gestured to a bag attached to him at the hip.

Joe winced and nodded. "Thank you for your time, sir."

"Yeah, yeah, whatever. If you show up again, bring me some of that greasy fried food from the deli on the corner."

"Done," Joe said.

Mr. Gonzales slammed the door on their noses.

Joe looked at her. "What did he mean, sorry for what happened to the both of you? You said you weren't hurt in the fire."

Kylie didn't want to go there with him. Not now, not ever. Just thinking about the horrific warehouse fire gave her nightmares, even all these years later. "I wasn't." She started walking. "I'm sure he just meant he was sorry for my loss. I told you that there was an elderly apprentice and he didn't need to be investigated."

Joe was unapologetic. "I like to cover all the bases myself."

She shook her head. "And clearly, you'd already looked into him. You *knew* he was two hundred million years old when you said I could come up with you."

"To be fair, I never said you could come up," he reminded her. "I said I wouldn't stop you."

"Whatever!" she exclaimed, tossing up her hands. So he'd only *pretended* to trust that she could take care of herself. She should have known. Shaking her head at the both of them, she headed straight to the stairwell. No way in hell was she taking the elevator back down.

"You afraid of getting stuck or afraid you're going to jump me again?" Joe asked.

She ignored him. Which was, admittedly, getting harder and harder to do.

Chapter 8

#WhereWereGoingWeDontNeedRoads

By six o'clock the next day, Joe was exhausted after fourteen hours on the job. Still, and against his better judgment, he met Kylie at the courtyard as she'd insisted by text.

She had her huge bag over her shoulder and Vinnie in her arms, who snorted in excitement at the sight of him. Kind of how Joe felt like doing at the sight of Kylie. Instead, he ruffled the top of Vinn's head. "Hey, little man. Whatcha up to?"

"He's been very busy," Kylie said. "He ate one of my socks. And in other not-so-surprising news, he's constipated."

As if on cue, Vinnie farted audibly.

"Nice one," Joe told him on a laugh. "Bet you feel better now."

"Sorry." Kylie grimaced and fanned the air with

her hand. "I don't dare leave him at home alone. What's our plan?"

Joe ignored the "our." "I've a lead on two more of the apprentices. Jayden and Jamal Williams."

"Yes, they're brothers," she said. "They're the ones I told you left the country. They went to England a few years ago."

"They're back and in business together, right here in San Francisco. I'm going to go check out their warehouse."

She looked surprised, but nodded. "Then let's go."

He put a hand on her arm to stop her. "There's no 'let's,'" he said. "I'll go. You and Vinnie can wait in the comfort of your place and—"

"I'm not good at waiting, Joe. I probably should've warned you about that."

He didn't bother sighing. Or trying to hinder her as she turned to walk through the alleyway, stopping to talk to Old Man Eddie, the homeless man sitting on an upside-down crate near the Dumpster.

An original hippie, Eddie looked like Doc from *Back to the Future*. He wore a tie-dyed shirt and board shorts that he'd probably had since the sixties. He'd lived in the alley forever, and in spite of many people's loving efforts to get him into a place of his own, he'd held firm.

He said he was meant for the great outdoors.

Playing a game on the phone that Spence, his grandson, had forced on him last year, Eddie looked up and winked at Kylie. "Hey, darlin'."

"How are you? You warm enough out here? The nights have been pretty cool."

"Well, I sure wouldn't complain about having the dough to buy a new sweatshirt," he said wistfully.

Kylie patted Old Man Eddie on the hand, a sweet smile on her face as she reached into her bag. Joe started to open his mouth to stop the cutest pushover he'd ever seen from giving away her own hard-earned cash because one, he knew Spence made sure Eddie had everything he could ever need, and two, Eddie's usual MO was to con money out of the cute ladies he charmed—and he could charm a snake—and then use the money for the weed he liked to bake into his homemade brownies.

But Kylie surprised both men by saying, "I gave you a twenty last week, which we both know you used to buy pot, so this time I have something better than cash . . ." She pulled a black hoodie from her backpack. It had a peace sign in the colors of the rainbow on the front. "Got it in your size too."

Sweet, but *not* a pushover, Joe revised with a shake of his head, impressed in spite of himself.

Eddie put on the sweatshirt and stood to give Kylie a kiss on the cheek. "Thanks, dudette. Come by later in the week. I'll have my mistletoe packs on deep discount since the season is over."

Mistletoe, Joe's ass. Undoubtedly, it'd be weed.

Kylie started walking before turning back to Joe to give him a *what's keeping you?* look.

Yep. Sweet, not a pushover, and . . . also a tyrant.

Once in his truck, she pulled a wig from her apparently bottomless bag and set it on her head so that suddenly she had long, dark brunette waves. "Okay," she said, tucking in some stragglers. "Ready to do this."

Joe stared at her as she applied a dark gloss to her lips, which, combined with the wig, had him spinning. "Kylie—"

"Ready," she said.

Yes, but the question was, ready for what? Shaking his head to clear it, he navigated the roads without speaking again, which he knew drove her nuts. Good. She could join his club because she drove him nuts too. Especially as she used the ride to add horn-rimmed glasses to her ensemble so that now from the neck up she looked like a naughty librarian while from the neck down she was the girl next door. It was like Christmas for his eyes so he forced himself to stop looking at her as he drove into Hunter's Point, a district by the water and the ballpark in the southeast corner of San Francisco.

"Interesting neighborhood," she murmured.

He parked, going still when she leaned in to him to look up and down the street. He nodded, speechless, because her breast was pressing into his biceps and killing his concentration as he attempted to keep an eye on their surroundings at the same time.

Usually he multitasked with no problem in his work zone. But Kylie had shot his zone straight to hell. She looked so different in that wig it was startling. Different and damn sexy. Not that she wasn't always sexy. She *was,* incredibly so. But it was messing with his head a little—or a lot—to see her looking like herself and yet not.

"So?" she asked. "What's next?"

Right. What was next—beyond wanting to haul her into his lap so that she could straddle him and grind them both to an earth-shattering finish? He cleared his throat. "Jayden and Jamal work here in Hunter's Point. I want to get a look at their inventory and see if we find anything resembling the workmanship of that table or bench you're supposed to authenticate."

She pushed some of the brunette strands off her face and he told himself to be careful. If the woman had enough skills to hide her identity, she could just as easily hide other things—like his dead body.

Although the truth was that though he did have to be careful around Kylie, it wasn't his life he was worried about but his damn heart, an organ he'd thought long dead. She was an irresistible dichotomy of sweet charm and heart-stopping sexy, and she threw him off guard with every look, be it a smile or a glare. In fact, he kinda liked when she gave him dirty looks, which meant he was seriously losing his shit. And he never lost his shit.

Never.

Yeah. He was royally screwed and the thing was, even knowing that, he didn't want to walk away because he enjoyed her so much. How crazy was that?

"I'm going to go try to get a look inside," he said. "Trust me, I know this area. It's not good, so you should—"

She held up a finger. "Let me stop you right there.

If you're about to let out your inner caveman and say 'stay in the truck,' I'm going to sic Vinnie on you."

Joe took in the sight of Vinnie snoring and snorting in his sleep from his perch in her lap. "Yeah, you're right. That five-pound rat is terrifying."

"I'll have you know that he's *twelve* pounds. And fine, I'll find some other form of payback."

"Payback away," he murmured, enjoying the blush that lit up her cheeks. It suitably distracted him from the reason he had a ball of dread low in his gut—that they were, literally, parked in his past, in his old neighborhood, and it was every bit as rough and ugly as he remembered.

Although undoubtedly it was mostly his own memories making it so. Still, Hunter's Point had always been San Francisco's radioactive basement. It was dirty and dangerous, and he'd have really liked for Kylie to have stayed as far away as possible.

"I've never been here," she said quietly, as if sensing his mood change. "Have you?"

"Yeah."

He felt her turn to face him and he met her gaze. "Grew up here," he said.

He could feel the weight of her concern. But he didn't want or need it. Instead he concentrated on the night and any trouble that was most certainly lurking in it. The decommissioned naval shipyard up the street was quiet. Still. *Too* still.

There'd been efforts to clean up the area, including redevelopment projects two decades back. In some areas, such as the former navy shipyard water-front property, they'd been fairly successful. In other areas, not so much. Drug and gang activity was high, as was the murder rate.

"Not exactly warm and cozy," Kylie said.

She had no idea. They were parked across and down the street from the warehouse. On the north-east corner in front of them, he'd once been confronted by a few of his friends who'd turned into gangbanger wannabes. In order for them to get into the gang they wanted, they'd been challenged to steal a car—except none of them had known how to hot-wire a car, so they'd tried to get Joe to do it.

When he'd refused, they'd stolen something of his to hold over him and force his hand.

Molly.

They'd held his sister for nearly three full days before he was able to get to her. He'd retaliated by nearly killing the guys who'd kidnapped her. A judge had then forced Joe to decide between jail and the military for his restitution.

He'd chosen the military, and though he'd hated it at the time, with dubious maturity he'd come to see it as the best thing that could've happened to him. It'd been a way out of here, a lifeline he hadn't realized he'd needed. Granted, the army hadn't been easy. In fact, they'd practically beaten discipline and temper management into him.

But there was no doubt he'd grown up. He was different now, slower to rile for one thing, and yet not so different that he couldn't remember what it'd felt like to be trapped here in Hunter's Point, thinking there was no way out.

Kylie slipped her hand in his, bringing him back to the present. Which thankfully was very different than his past. Although he was still armed and dangerous, so maybe not all that different after all.

"Do you have a specific plan of action here?" she asked quietly. "For getting a look inside the warehouse?"

He did. He always did, and had ever since that long-ago day when he'd pulled Molly out of the rat hole they'd held her in. There was a plan A, and a plan B, C, and Z too.

First, he wanted to stake the place out from right here for a little bit, get a feel for the layout and make sure they were really alone. No way was he getting Kylie into something that he wasn't prepared for. He knew she'd think he was being overprotective, and hell, given the fact that they were seeking a three-inch piece of carved wood—excuse him, a penguin—maybe he was.

But his instincts had saved his life more than a few times and they were screaming now. It felt like the threat to Kylie was escalating and he wasn't going to ignore that, no matter what she thought. This whole thing had gone from a way to amuse himself to something far more serious.

And yeah, maybe his life experiences had jaded him, made him cynical. After all, he spent a lot of time knee-deep in the scum of the earth, seeing the worst humanity had to offer—everything from abusive and cheating spouses, to criminal and civil crimes, to far worse. But he could live with being cynical and jaded. He couldn't live with something happening to Kylie because he didn't take this seriously enough.

"The brothers close up their shop by five or six every night," he said. "There're windows in their warehouse. I should be able to keep to the shadows and get a good look inside without any trouble."

"How?" she asked.

"I grew up here. I know every nook and cranny like the back of my hand."

"That's good," she murmured, clearly trying to hide the horror in her voice as she looked around at the decayed buildings and dirty streets that symbolized his very ugly past. "Maybe . . . maybe it wasn't so rough back then, when you were a kid?" she asked with sweet hope.

He gazed out the windshield, trying to see the neighborhood from her point of view. "This is cleaned up. It was far rougher back then."

She squeezed his hand. *Comforting* him, he realized, and felt something in his chest tighten.

"Where did you live?" she asked softly.

"Right down that street." He gestured with a jerk of his chin rather than take his hand from hers. "This used to be a navy base. In and around all the gangbangers' hideouts and graffiti are old Victorian homes that once upon a time were captains' or generals' homes."

She nodded. "I love the architecture of the time,"

she said. "All the ornate woodworking on the bevels and crown moldings, and the attention to detail. Would've liked to see it back then in its height of glory."

Trust her to imagine the forgotten beauty in a place like this.

"You should be proud," she said. "You came from here and made something of yourself."

His chest tightened again. Emotion, he realized, which he couldn't afford. Not now, not ever. But still, in spite of himself, he turned his hand over and entwined their fingers.

She gave him a small smile with those dark lips he wanted wrapped around his—

"So what do we do now?" she asked.

Definitely not act out the X-rated porno playing in my mind. "Watch a little bit longer and get a feel for things."

She nodded her agreement, but not ten minutes in she began to squirm.

He slid a questioning look her way, making her grimace. "It turns out that stakeouts are kind of boring," she said.

"I like boring. It means nothing has gone fubar."

Yet.

"I'm just wondering about you," she said. "You've got a lot of secrets."

"So do you."

"Me?" she asked. "I'm an open book."

He had to laugh. "If that's true, then why don't you tell me what this scavenger hunt is really about? Why does that carving mean so much to you?"

She looked out the window and didn't speak for a while. "I'm guessing you don't usually get a lot of quiet time like this on the job," she finally said.

"No." He didn't call her out on the change of subject. She wanted her secrets? Fine. That would keep his own safe as well.

"Your job can be pretty dangerous," she said.

"Only if I get stupid."

She looked at him. "I can't imagine you doing anything stupid on the job. You're sharp and focused, and the very best at what you do."

He was pretty sure the words weren't supposed to turn him on. "And you know this how?" he asked.

"Archer speaks highly of you. So does Spence. A lot of people talk about you, actually. Like Molly."

"Molly's my sister. She's not going to talk shit."

"Oh, she talks shit," Kylie said on a laugh. "Just not about your work skills."

He narrowed his eyes at her. "And what shit might that be?"

She smiled and bit her lower lip, looking away.

Oh hell no. Leaning in, he cupped her jaw and turned her face back to his. As he studied her, he realized she was blushing again. "Okay," he said. "I definitely want to hear this story."

"It's nothing."

"Try me," he said.

"It was last week. Girls' night out. We were going to the pub, but we had to go for a walk first because half of us needed money from the ATM down the street. We were laughing because Haley didn't want her receipt. She said that sometimes you have to hit no on getting a receipt because you don't need that kind of negativity in your life."

Joe laughed. "Let me guess. At which both Elle and Molly had heart failure."

"Yes." Kylie smiled in memory. "Anyway, once we got back to the pub and had a few drinks, Haley said that if she didn't bat for the other team, she'd want to ride you like a bronco all night long and that though she's never really been sure if she believes in monogamy or not, she'd want to keep you."

Not much surprised Joe, but he felt his brows vanish into the hair falling over his forehead.

"Yeah," Kylie said. "And then Molly said that Haley would have to get in line for the bronco riding part because you usually had women on the line. But as for the keeping you part, many have tried, yet none have succeeded."

Joe snorted.

"So it's true," she said.

"She's talking about my feral early years," he said. "But I'm an old man now. I've slowed down some."

"You think thirty is old?" she asked.

"Not for normal people, but I put a lot of living in my first thirty years, so yeah, sometimes I feel ancient."

He'd meant it as a joke but her gaze was serious, her tone quiet. "I knew you grew up rough even before you brought me here," she said.

"How? And if you say another girls' night, I might have to muzzle my sister."

She laughed softly. "Not a girls' night, no. But a couple of months ago, a few of us went with Molly to your mom's grave site and left some flowers." She broke the eye contact and looked down at her hands. "Molly told us how she died when you were young and how your dad suffers from PTSD so badly that there were long stretches of time when he couldn't work. She said that you took care of the both of them."

Joe shook his head. "Molly did plenty of taking care of me too," he said and paused. "I wasn't easy."

"Well, that's a shock."

He met her gaze across the dark interior of the car. Clearly she was trying to lighten the mood for him. Her mouth was curved but her eyes were still serious. "Your life might have been ugly and hard, Joe," she said, "but from the outside looking in, you had all the important things."

"Such as?"

"Acceptance," she said. "Love."

There were few people who could wade through the bullshit that life had to offer and find the small, necessary kernels of truth. Kylie had been through her own sort of hell, far different than his but hell nevertheless, and yet she was still the optimist to his cynic.

The light to his dark, he realized with not a little shock.

He reached for her hand, entwining their fingers to bring them up to his mouth. He brushed a kiss over her knuckles, then got out of the car and had to clench his jaw in order to not let out a litany of warnings as Kylie got out as well.

"I can take care of myself," she reminded him quietly.

Yeah, and that's exactly what Molly said all those years ago, right before the nightmare that had followed. He looked into Kylie's fierce, adventure-seeking face and swore to himself. Maybe she *could* take care of herself, but he still wasn't going to take that chance. "Stick close."

"Of course," she said with a bright smile in spite of the fact that he'd practically growled the two words at her. "I'll do whatever you say."

And with that, she pierced his fierce concentration, making him laugh. "If only that was really true," he said and had the pleasure of seeing her blush again.

Chapter 9

#LoveTheSmellOfNapalmInTheMorning

Kylie put on a good face for Joe, but she was no fool. The neighborhood around them was clearly a rough one, the streets dark and dank and not exactly welcoming.

So stick close? *No problem.*

There was a storm coming and the wind kicked up dust and debris, further masking their surroundings. It was like being in her own personal horror flick. She reached out and put a hand on Joe, fisting her fingers in the back of his shirt. "Close enough?" she murmured.

He stilled at the touch and she felt him turn to look down at her in surprise. Whatever he saw, he laughed at. Quietly, but his amusement was genuine and deep as he bowed his head, shoulders shaking.

"What?"

"Your . . ." He swiveled a finger at her head and she put a hand on it.

Her wig was crooked. "Dammit."

"Give up on the wig, Kylie," he said, still grinning. "It's not a disguise."

"It's not?"

"No. I'd know you anywhere."

She tried really hard not to think about why that gave her a tingle. Leaving the wig in place, she demanded, "Are we doing this or not?"

His eyes darkened.

Oh boy. "You know what I mean!" She started walking toward one end of the warehouse only to be caught up by the back of her shirt.

"This way, Slick," he said, redirecting her to the other end of the warehouse.

"Right," she said, but then hesitated at all the shadows.

"Just wait in the car with Vinnie," he said. "I'll lock it and—"

"No. I'm fine with you." And wasn't that just the shocking truth. She was *more* than fine with him. With him, she felt like Wonder Woman.

When they got close, she eyed the gate surrounding the building. "Locked," she whispered, looking it over. "And no simple lock either. This one's keyless."

"With a side bolt," he agreed and pulled a tool from his pocket to tackle the bolt first.

"Nice," she whispered as he opened it. "I wouldn't mind learning a skill like that. Maybe you'll teach me sometime."

"Sure." He cocked an ear to the lock, spinning the dial before cursing to himself.

"Problem?" she asked.

"More like problem-*esque*." He ran a finger over her wig.

"What are you doing?" she whispered.

"I'm having a hard time concentrating. You look so different and yet the same."

Because his voice combined with his touch was turning her on, she waved her finger in front of her face. "I'm really hot in this thing."

"You're right on that."

She huffed out a laugh. "Seriously?"

"Seriously," he murmured, voice an octave lower now and sexy as hell, as was the heated look in his eyes.

And she realized that there was something incredibly liberating about wearing a costume or disguise and pretending to be someone else. It allowed her to be more . . . free than she'd be otherwise. And even the knowledge that she was acting like her mom wasn't enough to stop her. "You really think I'm hot in this wig?"

"Actually, I think you're hot in anything," he said as he went at the lock. "Your work aprons, the kick-ass steel-toed boots, the ripped jeans, the dark hair, your own hair . . . it's *all* hot to me."

She shook her head. "Men are weird."

He stopped working and stepped in to her, nudging their bodies together, lining them up. "You telling me you don't think it's kinda hot to pretend to be someone else?"

She bit her lower lip and he laughed. "You do," he said in naughty accusation and made her laugh too.

But then he suddenly froze before turning around, using an arm to keep her behind him as a guy strode down the dark street their way. Though at first they'd appeared to be alone, Kylie could see more than a few shadows behind him. The shadows stayed back as the guy came forward, his hands out of his pockets and loose at his sides.

"Don't shoot, jefe," he said to Joe.

If she hadn't known Joe, she'd say he appeared to be perfectly relaxed. But she *did* know him and knew he wasn't relaxed at all, but . . . ready. He didn't speak.

"Been a long time," the stranger said, coming to a stop in front of them while his shadows remained back.

Joe still didn't move or say a word.

The guy smiled without showing his teeth. "Been so long that maybe you forgot how to greet an old friend."

Kylie's knees got a little wobbly and her palms began to sweat.

"I've forgotten nothing," Joe said.

"Good." The man paused, slid a gaze over Kylie, then concentrated on Joe again. "So you know I owe you more than I can ever repay. You're safe here."

Joe smiled then, also without showing his teeth. "And I should believe you, why?"

"Because you're not the only one who can make changes."

The two men, both lean and tough and built in a way that said a fight might be terrifyingly equal, stared at each other and then suddenly they were doing some complicated male handshake.

Kylie sucked in some badly needed air as the guy stepped back and nodded. "You're safe here," he repeated and then vanished into the dark, his shadows on his heels.

Joe took Kylie's hand. He'd gotten the locks open. "This way," he said, taking her around to the back of the warehouse, where they could peek in the dark windows.

Kylie was still processing the conversation she'd just heard. Joe had done something to help that guy. Something so big that he'd risk himself to help keep her and Joe safe. Whatever Joe had done had stuck, and she wondered what it might have been.

But he wasn't much for talking, which of course made him very different from anyone else she'd ever met. Especially her own mother, who liked to make sure everyone knew her positive attributes at all times.

But not Joe. He was trying to do something good. His job wasn't just a paycheck to him. It was so much more. "Why does that guy owe you?"

"Five minutes," he said.

"What?"

"You've been trying not to ask me that question for five whole minutes. I'm impressed."

She rolled her eyes and waited.

He said nothing.

"So . . . ?" she pressed.

"It was a lifetime ago." He flashed a penlight through the dark warehouse windows. "Are you seeing what I'm seeing?"

The clearly handmade, high-end furniture was beautiful, but not in the same style as her grandpa's, not even close. Nothing here even remotely resembled the table in the pic she'd received, the one she had thirteen days left to authenticate or lose her grandpa's penguin forever. "I don't think it's them," she whispered.

"I don't either," he said. "But not because of the warehouse. They also have places in Los Angeles, New York, and London."

"They must be doing well then."

"Yeah," he said. "And they've carefully cultivated a reputation, one they're proud of. They do their own work, they pride themselves on that work being 100 percent green, and they give back a percentage of every dollar they make."

"They wouldn't risk all that to toy with me."

"I can't see it," Joe agreed.

He drove her home and walked her up to her door, and then several things happened at once. For the second time that night, he grabbed her and shoved her behind him just as her front door opened. And then suddenly he also had a gun in his hand, pointed right in the face of the man who'd opened her front door.

Gib.

Chapter 10

#YouTalkingToMe?

Joe couldn't think of one good reason for Gib to be coming out of Kylie's place when she wasn't even home. So he held the gun steady, letting it ask the question for him.

But clearly Kylie had other ideas. "Gib," she gasped, stepping out from behind Joe. *"What the hell are you doing?"*

Joe didn't budge, not his stance or gun, and when Gib didn't speak, she turned on him next. "And what the hell are *you* doing?" she asked, pointing to his gun. "Put that away."

What am I doing? Was she serious? She had some asshole playing with her, toying with her emotions, and she didn't understand why he'd pull a gun on a guy coming out of her locked apartment? "I'm wondering why your boss is coming out of your place like he owns it," he said calmly.

"Oh my God." Kylie shifted from standing at his side to standing in front of him with the gun pointed right in her face as she blocked Gib from him.

Shit.

He immediately lowered the gun but didn't put it away.

Kylie rolled her eyes.

And maybe in another time and place he might have marveled at her bravery—or stupidity. In his world, he was typically actually respected, even feared, for his shooting abilities. And yet she stood there toe-to-toe with him, protecting his target, eyes flashing with temper.

When *he* was the one who should be pissed. So it was a damn good thing the good old U S of A had taught him how to handle himself and put his emotions and temper aside.

Real good.

He hadn't yet gotten around to mentioning to Kylie that he'd put Gib through Archer's invasive search programs. He knew the guy's secrets. Such as he'd gotten married at age eighteen and divorced less than a year later. Three years ago he'd gotten a DUI. And he'd just spent way too much money on a new Lexus. And . . . he was also pretty much exactly who he seemed, an okay enough guy if not a little self-centered, who worked in his own style and not Michael Masters's style and who'd put away a good amount of money—which he'd earned, not stolen.

He wasn't Kylie's thief.

Did it piss Joe off that Gib overcharged for his work while underpaying Kylie? Hell yes. Ditto for the way he was suddenly playing with Kylie's feelings. Gib being the bad guy would've really worked for Joe, selfishly, but his gut told him it wasn't him. He knew he'd have to tell that to Kylie sooner or later, but later was working for him at the moment.

Kylie stood there staring at him like *he* was the asshole before turning to face Gib. "What are you doing here?"

"I went back to the shop and saw that you forgot your paycheck," he said, not taking his gaze off Joe, which earned him a single, solitary point in the respect category.

But only one.

"I knew you'd want it," Gib said. "I left it for you on your kitchen table."

Kylie nodded. "Okay, thanks. I'll see you tomorrow."

Gib didn't leave. In fact, he crossed his arms and set his feet, still holding Joe's gaze. "Thought maybe we could catch up on one of our shows. *Iron Chef*?"

"Cute," Joe said.

"It's one of her faves," Gib said.

Right. And Joe didn't know her faves because they didn't watch TV together. They didn't do anything together because . . . well, because he was an idiot who'd let Kylie think he didn't want anything serious, that he *couldn't* be serious. He turned to go, but Kylie put a hand on his arm.

"Joe."

He stepped back so that her hand fell away. "It's late," he said. "I've got to go."

"Joe."

Resisting a sigh, he met her gaze.

She stepped in to him and said quietly for his ears only, "Look, I'm sorry. He has a key because, as you know, I tend to lose or forget mine and—"

"You don't owe me an explanation, Kylie."

She stared up at him. "Fine," she said.

"Fine." He held her gaze, saw the bad temper in it, and thought *fuck it*. He didn't need this. Hell, he didn't even *understand* this. So he turned and walked away.

Behind him, her front door slammed shut. With both her and Gib on the other side.

"Fine," he repeated to the night. Yeah. He was a fucking fine asshole, is what he was.

Kylie turned from her front door, leaned back against it with her arms crossed and stared at Gib. "What was that?"

"I told you, you forgot your check—"

"The truth, Gib."

He held eye contact before he blew out a breath and looked away. "I hate the way you're suddenly so into him, okay?"

"Not okay."

He sighed and stared down at his shoes, rubbing the back of his neck. "Things aren't the same between us anymore. It's all wrong." He lifted his head. "And it's scaring me."

"What's wrong is that you've confused me," she said. "You knew I had a crush on you since the fifth grade and yet you never let on that you had any feelings toward me in that way. Not until Joe showed up in the shop. Then suddenly you're asking me out and trying to get closer."

"Maybe seeing Joe look at you like you're lunch opened my eyes to what I've felt all along," he admitted. "But what does that matter?" His eyes warmed as he took a step toward her. "There could definitely be something between us. I know it."

She stared at him, trying to reconcile her feelings. It wasn't easy, but there was a big difference between a childhood crush and an adult love. "Just tell me this," she said quietly. "If you felt something for me all this time, why did you wait so long?"

He shook his head, his expression earnest. "I couldn't go there with you. Not when your grandpa . . ." He shook his head, looking pained. "He gave me everything, Ky. No matter how I felt for you, it never seemed right."

"He's been gone a long time."

He opened his mouth and she held up her hand. "No, wait. I don't want to do this right now. I'm tired. Please, just go."

"You want me to leave?" he asked in disbelief.

"Yes, I do." She opened the front door. "Because at the end of the day, I still want to be your friend and employee. And I'm afraid if you keep talking, that would all be in jeopardy because I might kill you."

He shook his head. "So we're seriously not even going to try?"

"I think you missed your shot."

He looked startled, like that had been the last thing he'd expected her to say, which somehow made her feel even stronger about her decision. "We aren't each other's the One, Gib."

His eyes held sincere affection and equally sincere regret. And also carefully banked lust. All this time she'd yearned to see just that and here it was, and the only thing she felt was . . . unmoved.

"If I could change things," he said, "if I could go back and kick my younger self in the ass and tell him not to save the best for last, I would." And then he was gone.

And she was digging into her freezer, soothing her what-ifs and uncertain heart with cookie dough ice cream.

The next afternoon, Joe sat at work, distracted as hell as the team meeting went on without him. He tried to mentally check in before Archer kicked his ass. But it'd already been a rough day. They'd gone after a high bond that had been about to be forfeited if the bondee, Milo Santini, didn't show up for his court date. Milo had a record, was known to be armed at all times, and wasn't a nice guy. So it was no surprise when his takedown had gone bad.

He'd been holed up in a basement of a building in the financial district when they caught up with him, and an innocent cleaning crew had nearly burned to death when Milo, cornered and spitting mad, had set fire to a huge laundry bin for a diversion.

As a result of the ensuing takedown, Milo had gotten a little roughed up, which had led to a police inquiry. Everyone at Hunt Investigations had been cleared of misconduct, but Archer was pissed off and had spent the past hour chewing them out and going over protocol.

Thing was, protocol *had* been followed.

Well, mostly.

Sometimes in the heat of the moment—such as when an asswipe perp had made a break for it, starting a dangerous fire that threatened innocent bystanders—things happened.

Things like the bad guys getting punched in the face.

It hadn't been Joe. It'd actually been Lucas, who'd lost a brother to an arson fire. Not that any of the guys would spill on Lucas. They'd each take a bullet first. This job wasn't easy, and they were a team by both necessity and choice, even if they each did it for their own personal reasons. In Joe's case, he liked that they were fighting the fight for good, and in doing so, maybe he was also cleaning up his karma, even a little bit.

He thought maybe that was Lucas's reason too, though Lucas carried around a lot more anger than he did. Anger he channeled into doing the job really, *really* well.

"Let's review," Archer said with a deceptively mild tone, taking a hard look around the table at his guys, Joe, Lucas, Trev, Reyes, and Max—along with Max's Doberman, Carl—all carefully trained by Archer himself. "What steps would you take in the event of a fire?" His gaze landed on Lucas.

Shit, Joe thought. He knew. Not that he was surprised. Archer knew *everything*.

Lucas shrugged at the question. "Fucking big ones?"

Wrong answer. Archer was *still* going on and on when Molly came in and dumped a couple of big brown bags on the conference table.

Carl sat straight up and licked his big chops.

So did the guys.

"Grub," Molly said, shooting Joe a careful once-over.

She was making sure he hadn't gotten hurt in any way. She was still freaked out about the bat he'd taken to the back of his head a few months back. But hey, he'd recovered. And it irritated him that she tried to be the protector when that was *his* role. He'd taken care of her his whole life—well, except for that one time he'd failed so spectacularly. His gaze traveled to her right leg as she limped her way around the table.

Her leg and back were bothering her today, and that just about killed him because if it hadn't been for him, she'd never have gotten hurt.

No one dared touch the bags of food while Archer was still going off, but he'd wound down at the sight of Molly, softening enough to smile and thank her for the food. "Okay," he said, pushing the bags down the table so everyone could reach. "I promised the cop shop I'd say all that. Now let's move on."

Fucking finally. Joe listened with only half an ear as, while they all inhaled the food, Archer went over their upcoming caseload.

When Carl whined in protest, Max tossed him a dog bone. With a longing look at Max's food, Carl sighed but took the bone.

Joe ate everything he could reach. In his opinion, the best thing for adrenaline letdown was sex. In lieu of that, food would do. It was quiet in the conference room now except for the chowing down and the occasional grunt, and Joe let his mind drift to a woman. Not Ciera, the pub's newest and sexiest server who'd slipped him her number not too long ago. Nor Danielle, who he'd met a few months back at the gym and had rocked his world three nights running before he'd had to leave town for a job and then hadn't called again.

Nope. He was thinking about the one woman who could drive him crazy without trying.

Kylie.

He hated the way he'd left things the night before with her.

And Gib.

Kylie and Gib . . .

Shit. Logically, he knew she and Gib weren't a thing because one, she'd told him so and two, he knew Kylie. For a year now he'd watched her. She hadn't gone out much. She needed to really feel something for a guy.

And yet she'd kissed *Joe* with her entire heart and soul.

So why had he lost it? *Because you're an asshole. Because you know you're taking something from her you can't return.*

He knew she still hadn't told him the entire story about why that carving meant so much to her. He was missing more than a few pieces of that puzzle. It was frustrating that she didn't trust him, but on the other hand, just as well. He didn't do trust either and he was real good at keeping people at arm's length.

But even as he thought it, he knew he was full of shit when it came to her, proven by the fact that she wouldn't get out of his head. Her and those big see-all eyes. The way she'd looked when she'd told him about her grandpa still haunted him because though she hadn't said it, she felt alone now that he was gone.

And then there was how she felt in his arms.

Like she belonged there.

He'd tried kissing her again to get her out of his system but that had been an epic mission-fail. Every time he laid eyes on her, she was the most desirable woman in the room. *Any* room. It was those jeans and boots and tough 'tude, softened by her smile and the way she looked at the world. And when she worked those big power tools . . . holy shit. *Huge* turn-on.

Maybe one last time would be the winner. *Yeah.* Warming up to the idea, he closed his eyes and pictured it, how he'd back her to a wall and—

"He's *completely* gone," Lucas said, sounding amused. "I think he's dreaming. Probably about that hot chick at O'Riley's who slipped her number in his pocket last week."

Joe's eyes flew open to see Lucas waving a hand in front of his face. He shoved it away. "I'm not dreaming."

Lucas gave him a rare smile. "I don't know, man. You were smiling and everything."

Joe rolled his eyes so hard they nearly came out of his head.

Archer raised a brow. "Something you want to share with the class?"

Most definitely not. But the vultures had the scent of roadkill and were circling now.

"Maybe it's that new hottie at the coffee shop," Reyes said. "She always times her morning coffee run with his."

"I bet it's Kylie," Trev said.

Even though he knew better than to react, Joe froze.

Max let out a short laugh. "Nah. Kylie hates him. Thinks he's a jackass. I know this because every time I go visit Rory when she's at work at South Bark Pet Shop, she and the girls are talking. Carl's my cover," he said, grinning at his dog. "They throw themselves at him and don't pay me any attention."

"Kylie thinks I'm a jackass?" Joe asked before he could stop himself and knew when Max grinned that he'd been caught. Shit.

"If we're done discussing our love lives . . ." Archer said with deceptive casualness.

"You say that because you have one," Reyes said. "Some of us aren't in a relationship and we take all the scraps we can get."

"I don't know. You might be better off," Max said. "I mean, I love Rory, but sometimes being in a relationship is about getting a large fry when you really just wanted a small—but you know your girlfriend's gonna eat 'em all even though she said she didn't want any."

Archer snorted but wisely didn't say anything because they all knew Elle was maybe even more badass than him. "Back to work," he said and just like that, fun time ended.

Joe was grateful for the intervention, but he knew it wasn't over. These hyenas were going to drive him crazy wanting details. He could ignore them but what he couldn't ignore was . . . *Kylie thinks I'm a jackass?*

That evening, Joe pulled up to his dad's place. He'd promised to show up early, but the job had kept him longer than he'd planned and then he'd gotten caught in construction traffic.

Grabbing the two grocery bags off the passenger seat of his truck, he headed up the walk to the modest duplex on an equally modest but relatively safe street filled with identically styled homes in the Inner Sunset District.

Joe had bought the place five years ago. Since Alan Malone was too proud and stubborn and mean to allow live-in home care, he was only visited twice a week by a nurse who checked up on him. When and if he opened the door to her, that is.

This meant that Joe had to live on the other side of the duplex, mostly because Molly refused to. He'd tried to give her the place rent-free but she lived in Outer Sunset, "just far enough away," she always said, "so you two can't try to run my life."

They split up the shifts, each checking in on their dad often. Tonight Joe was up. The lights were on, but the front door was locked. This was not a surprise. The retired veteran always kept his windows and doors locked and bolted.

Joe had a key, but letting oneself in without warning was bad for one's health. He knocked on the door, four hard raps and then a pause, and then one more. This was their code because his dad needed one.

There was no answer so he called his dad's cell.

"You're late," came a surly voice and then a click. He'd disconnected.

"Son of a bitch," Joe muttered. He tried texting.

Joe: Traffic.

Dad: Tough shit.

Joe: I brought food.

No response.

Joe knocked again, same pattern as before. "Open up, Dad."

Nothing.

Joe sighed. "Dad. Open up or I'll just break in."

To this he got a definitive answer. The unmistakable sound of a shotgun ratcheting.

Chapter 11

#GoAheadMakeMyDay

There were probably some people who could hear their dad ratchet his shotgun and stand firm, secure in the knowledge that their own father wasn't going to shoot them.

Joe was under no such illusions. If his dad felt like shooting, he would most definitely shoot. Joe had long ago taken away all of the bullets in the house, but there was no betting against the old man. He was as wily as they came.

And skilled.

"Seriously?" Joe called out to him. "I'm only a few minutes late."

There was no response and it was like being fifteen and stupid all over again. There'd been many, many nights when he'd had to sleep on the porch without so much as a blanket to keep warm because his dad had locked him out of the house for being late.

Late being anytime after dark.

His dad didn't do the dark and hadn't since he'd come home from the Gulf War a different man from the one he'd been before he'd left. Because he couldn't keep a job for any length of time, Joe had stepped up to help provide from a young age, although not all his methods had fit into the niceties of society. But letting his dad and sister go hungry hadn't been an option.

Thankfully those days were long behind him now and Archer paid him more than well enough to cover what they needed. He set the bags of groceries he'd brought with him on the stoop, pulled out a small tool, and . . . took his life in his hands by breaking in. When he got the locks opened, he nudged the door. "Don't shoot me."

"Why not?" came the gruff reply.

"Because then you won't get dinner." But Joe wasn't stupid, so he stepped to the side of the door and out of direct sight range until his dad responded.

"Fine, but it'd better be good."

Joe grabbed the bags of food and headed in, still cautious. One never knew with his dad. He relocked the door and then, to soothe the man he knew damn well was watching his every move, he checked the locks four times, paused, and then checked one more time. OCD was a bitch. He turned and found his dad indeed watching him in his wheelchair in the doorway between the living room and kitchen, a shotgun across his legs, wearing only his underwear.

"Where are your pants?"

"I don't like pants."

"Well no one does," Joe said, passing him to head into the kitchen. "But we still have to wear them."

His dad wheeled along after him, looking pale and surly at the same time.

"You doing your stretching exercises like you're supposed to?" Joe asked. "To reduce your pain?"

"Fucking doctors. They don't know shit."

"It wasn't the doctor who taught you those stretches. It was your PT. You like her, remember?"

"No, I don't."

"You told me she smells nice," Joe said.

"And she does."

Joe drew a deep breath, feeling his already thin patience waning. He loved his dad, loved him a whole hell of a lot, but that didn't mean he didn't want to strangle him sometimes. He put water on to boil for spaghetti and began to brown some sweet Italian sausage for the sauce. "I don't understand what the problem is."

"She's not your mom."

Joe stilled and then turned from the stove. "Dad, no one is. But . . . Mom's gone."

"Fucking cancer. Fucking doctors."

She'd been gone for twenty years now but there was no arguing with the man.

"Where's Molly?" his dad asked. "Thought she was coming tonight."

"She'll be by tomorrow. Said to tell you she'll bring you pizza if you want."

"Yeah, I want. She's nicer than you. She brings me cigars, too."

Joe stopped stirring the meat and stared at his dad. "She's not supposed to be doing that."

His dad patted his wheelchair side pocket smugly.

Joe shook his head but didn't get dragged into a fight. He knew damn well there were no matches or lighters anywhere in the house. He and Molly had PTSD-proofed the house years ago and they kept a clean ship. So his dad could hold on to those cigars all he wanted if they made him feel better. And seeing him defiant and pleased with himself was far better than the depression and anxiety he usually displayed. "You need to get out more."

His dad shrugged.

"What about Janice?" Joe asked. "The nice lady who lives down the street who makes you brownies. She offered to take you to the movies."

"She's old."

"She's forty-five," Joe said dryly. "Seven years younger than you, by the way."

His dad looked up in surprise. And guilt.

Well, shit. "Dad, what did you do?"

Silence.

"Tell me you weren't . . . yourself with her," Joe said.

"That's all I know how to be."

"What did you say exactly?"

His dad shifted in his chair, his only concession to feeling bad about whatever he'd done. "She wanted me to join some Bunko club. And learn to line dance with her."

"And?"

His dad stared at him like he'd grown a second head. "Bunko is a stupid chick game and hello, I'm in a chair. I can't dance."

"Men play Bunko," Joe said and hoped that was true. He actually wasn't sure what Bunko was. "And you're in a chair that has wheels. Good ones." He'd seen to it himself. "But I'm begging you—put on pants first. And then, if a woman likes you enough to want to share her life with you, don't be stupid about it. You share her life."

"How about I'll take that advice when you do the same?"

"No problem," Joe said. "But no one's asked me to play Bunko or line dance."

"You know what I mean. You're just as much a loner as I am."

"Yeah, well." Joe blew out a breath. "Maybe it's time a couple of old dogs learn some new tricks."

"Like I said, you first."

Joe's mind went immediately to Kylie, and he had to admit, he hoped she didn't play Bunko or line dance.

They ate in contemplative silence, and afterward Joe quickly cleaned up and got his dad through his nighttime routine. Shower, pills, bed.

"What's the bum rush for?" his dad asked, pulling up his blankets.

"No rush," Joe said, putting a glass of water on the nightstand.

"Can't bullshit a bullshitter, son. The other night we watched a whole season of *Pretty Little Liars*.

Tonight, though, your ass is on fire to get out of here, which I suppose means I don't have to feel bad that I watched the first episode of the next season with Molly."

"Wow," Joe said. "Your TV etiquette sucks. And I'm leaving because I have work." It was true. Sort of. He was meeting Kylie at seven at her place to check out another apprentice. Eric Hansen, who by lucky coincidence was having a showing at a nearby gallery tonight. It'd be a perfect way to get in close. He'd called Kylie earlier to let her know, and predictably, she'd insisted on going.

And that was the thing about Kylie. She wasn't looking for a hero. Guys like Joe were used to women looking for them to solve all their problems, but Kylie wasn't like that. She was out there doing the work, trying to solve it herself. And hell if that didn't draw him in.

As did their explosive chemistry.

It made no sense. She was a huge contrast to the rest of his life. She created beauty with her hands and assumed the best about people. He'd been torn between annoyance over that and something that was just about the opposite of annoyance . . .

"It's a girl, right?" his dad said. "Christ, tell me it's a girl. Ted's son left his wife for some guy that wears eyeliner and nail polish. Don't know what the fuck this world is coming to."

Ted had been in his dad's unit. He was in a long-term care facility and had been since they'd both gotten back stateside, but they kept in touch via texts. "There's nothing wrong with Kelly coming out as gay," Joe said.

"Well, Ted asked for it, giving his boy a sissy name like Kelly."

Joe checked the lock on the window just for something to do rather than react to his dad's words. The doctor had told Joe on numerous occasions that his dad was angry at everyone equally, which meant he was an equal-opportunity bigot. Not that this made it any easier to take. "Things are different now, Dad. Gender and orientation are fluid."

"So you wouldn't care if I started wearing makeup? Or got a boyfriend?"

"Not in the least," Joe said. "Mostly because I'm assuming you'd have to get way nicer to catch a man in the first place."

His dad surprised him by laughing. He was still laughing when he turned over in bed and gave Joe his back.

Joe left and drove through the city to Kylie's building. He knocked on her door and felt her looking at him through the peephole. He expected her to still be pissed at how he'd left her after Gib had shown up, so he was surprised when she spoke first.

"You over yourself?" she asked through the door.

He lifted a shoulder. "Pretty much."

"Good." She opened the door and that was that. No passive-aggressive retorts, no pouting, no nothing.

He'd never met a woman like her.

Ever.

He took in her appearance and went brows up.

She was wearing a blond wig tonight, huge dark sunglasses, and a trench coat.

"Tell me you're butt-ass naked beneath that trench coat," he said. "It'd really turn my day around."

She crossed her arms. "I'm in costume!"

"I can see that," he said. "Slutty nurse? Oh please, God, be the slutty nurse."

"Are you serious right now? I'm dressed in disguise so I can go to Eric Hansen's show and not be recognized."

Joe couldn't help it. He burst out laughing. And he couldn't stop either.

She narrowed her eyes at him and he tried to get it together. "Ah, shit," he said, swiping his eyes. "I needed this after the fubar day I've had."

"I'm not trying to amuse you," she said in her pissy voice. "I'm going into the gallery as a secret shopper."

"Kylie," he said, doing his best not to laugh again. He wasn't sure she wouldn't slug him. "I'm going in as a normal person."

"But you're not normal."

"Okay, smartass," he said. "I just want to look around and, if I can, talk to Eric."

"Fine. Then what's my part?"

"Part?" he asked.

"My motivation. Actors need motivation."

He looked her over from head to toe and had to shake his head to clear the heat. "Your motivation is going to be keeping me from getting into that coat to see what you're wearing beneath."

Her mouth went a little slack, as if maybe she was imagining the ways he might coax her out of that coat. Yeah, he thought. *Go there, Kylie. Think about it. Picture it.* It just might put them in the same boat.

But as fast as it'd come, her dazed expression cleared. She tightened the coat around her. "Is your mind always in the gutter?"

"Always," he said, and steered her to his truck. "You might want to remember that."

Thirty minutes later, they had a new problem. They were stymied by the fact that the showing was a ticketed event, sold out, and no amount of cajoling at the front entrance could get them inside. Joe was prepared to sneak them in through the back, but one look at the fancy-ass party being thrown inside told him they weren't dressed to sneak in. Plus he hated champagne and fancy froufrou food.

They'd just have to wait until the thing was over. To waste some time, he went through a drive-thru for Kylie, whose stomach he could hear rumbling in protest of the lack of food, and then he parked in back, where he eyed Eric's vehicle.

"What are we doing back here?" Kylie asked, inhaling her French fries.

"Stakeout."

She nodded. "How long do we wait?"

"Long as it takes," he said distractedly because she was sucking the salt off her thumb.

Then she sucked on the straw to her soda and he nearly had a brain aneurysm.

"What's the longest you've had to wait?" she asked.

He met her gaze with some difficulty. The woman had the most gorgeous mouth he'd ever seen.

"Well?" she demanded, cracking through the lust and making him smile. She was impatient as hell. *What is the longest I've had to wait?* Well, let's see . . . he'd waited an entire year before getting his mouth on hers, but he was pretty sure that was *way* too revealing, not to mention *not* what she'd meant. "It won't be much longer."

"What if we miss him back here?"

"We won't. That's his car," he said, pointing to the Tesla Roadster on the corner. "He's not going anywhere without us knowing about it."

She slid him a look. "And as a bonus, by waiting back here you don't have to put on a suit."

He went brows up.

"Molly told me you hate to wear suits. That your idea of dressing up is tucking in your T-shirt." She smiled. "Molly's pretty funny."

"Molly has a big mouth," he said.

"Molly's amazing."

True story. Molly *was* amazing. Didn't mean he wanted his baby sister giving away his secrets. "What else did she say about me?" he asked.

"That heroes don't wear capes, they wear dog tags and camo, and that you and your dad are her heroes."

Ah, hell. "I'm no one's hero, Kylie."

Their gazes met and then hers dropped to his mouth. Great minds, he thought as she shifted closer in that sexy blond wig and the trench coat that was still fucking with his mind. He had his arm along the back of her seat and let his fingers stroke the soft skin at the nape of her neck.

She shivered and her eyes darkened, and that was all the invite he needed. He lowered his head to hers and—

She jumped back like she'd been stung by a bee. "Oh!" she said. "I almost forgot." She dove into her huge purse and came up with two penknives.

"I'm already armed," he said.

"What?" She blinked. "No, I'm going to teach you how to carve." She paused. "Wait. You're armed?"

"Yes."

"Are you always armed?"

"On the job, yeah."

She looked him over, her gaze slowing in certain spots that had him getting a little heated. "Where?"

"Kylie—"

She shook her head a little. "Never mind. Don't tell me. Carve. We're going to carve."

"Why?"

"So you can understand why I want my grandpa's penguin back." She then proceeded to pull two small blocks of wood from her bag.

"How much shit does that bag hold?" he asked in marvel.

"A lot, and that's the point of it." She also came up with a bag of chocolate kisses, grinning in triumph. "Dessert!"

He wasn't much of a dessert guy but she looked so pleased with herself. The chocolate went down sweet and so did the way she so carefully showed him how to hold the wood and how to carve. He opened his mouth to tell her he didn't have the patience for art but she bent over him, her brow furrowed in cute, bossy teacher mode. The long blond wig strands swept across his forearms and he forgot what he was going to say. He followed her instructions and they carved.

It was nearly impossible to make anything except notches in the wood but he did his best. After a few minutes, Kylie lifted her face to his, their mouths only an inch apart, hers smiling. "Wow," she said. "You're really bad at this."

No doubt. And something else he was—hard and getting harder by the moment. It was unbelievable to him just how uncontrolled he was around her. He had no excuse for it, but he was damned tired of fighting it. So he hauled her into his lap so that she straddled him, cupped her sweet ass in his hands, and kissed her until it was *him* letting out a groan for more, *him* sweating because he wanted her more than he could remember ever wanting anything, *him* actually losing his ability to keep vigilant and aware of his surroundings.

He stopped only when she put a hand on his chest and pulled back.

"Don't you need to keep a lookout?" she asked, as if she hadn't just completely rocked his world into next week.

They could have been surrounded by gangbangers and he wouldn't have even noticed. He had it bad, and worse, he didn't care. He still had a hand gripping a cheek, the other fisted in her hair to hold her head. "Yeah." Jesus. He shook the lust off with shocking difficulty, even as a small part of him recognized this wasn't just sheer animal magnetism. But that problem would have to get in line.

"So . . ." She smiled. "Back to carving?"

"Sure." He was glad his voice sounded so normal because he didn't feel normal. He felt like howling at the moon. But though she was flushed from the kiss, she looked equally happy to teach him to carve.

Talk about humbling. So when she climbed off him and back into her seat, he pretended to give a shit about using a knife for something other than threatening someone and told himself to just enjoy having her hands on his.

Even though what he really wanted was to have his hands back on *her*.

Chapter 12

#HeresLookingAtYouKid

Kylie didn't carve very often anymore. When her grandpa had been alive, they'd carved together at night after work and chores were done. It'd been a way they could connect, and for Kylie, who hadn't had a lot of connections in her life, it'd been everything.

After her grandpa's death, carving had lost some of its appeal. But tonight, getting her hands on the knife, the movements came back as easily as getting on a bike after a long absence, and it gave her . . . peace.

Being in such close contact with Joe gave her other things too. Like a soul-deep yearning and a hunger she'd denied for far too long now. She watched him work the knife over the wood, cutting deep instead of shallow, and she had to admit, it was kind of fun to find that he wasn't good at everything. She put her hands over his again, trying to show not tell that he needed to caress and finesse. Wrapping her fingers around his, she guided them as he worked the knife up and down.

His eyes landed on hers. "If you keep that up," he said, "we're not going to have any problem with the wood."

He said the word *wood* in a low, suggestive tone, and her hands stilled as she felt her cheeks flush pink. He held her gaze for a long moment, smiled, and then . . . went back to concentrating on the carving.

She adjusted the angle of his wrists, but mostly it was just to keep her hands on him. He was warm to the touch and she could feel the sinewy muscles in his forearms flexing with each stroke of his knife. She squirmed in her seat, and again he met her gaze. At whatever he found in her expression, a full-blown smile lit up his face, transforming him into a regular guy for a minute. "It's been a long time," he said.

"Since . . . ?"

"Since I've had fun on a stakeout."

She laughed. "I thought you were going to say since you've had a woman in your car who you weren't trying to sleep with."

"Who says I'm not trying to sleep with you?" he asked.

Note to self: Don't tease him. He's better at it than you.

"Come here, Kylie."

His voice was deep and steady and she didn't

hesitate. She scooted close and hard arms pulled her in. Lowering his head, he kissed her. He tasted like chocolate, smelled like aspen wood, and felt like heaven. It was the best kiss she'd ever had and she didn't want it to end, but out of the corner of her eye she saw Eric come out the back door of the gallery. "Joe."

"Yeah?" His mouth was making its hungry way along her jaw to her ear, where he took her lobe in between his teeth and gave a slight tug, causing an answering tug between her legs.

"D-don't we need to talk to Eric?"

He licked the spot he'd just bitten. "Uh-huh."

She put her hand on his chest and pulled back enough to meet his gaze. "So are we going to do that now?"

He jerked upright and looked out the window to see what she had, that Eric had just come out the back door of the gallery. *"Shit."* He was out of the truck so fast her head was spinning. But that might have been the kiss.

Or . . . the knowledge that she'd once again caused Joe to lose control, a fact that gave her a surge of feminine power that had her smiling and unable to stop.

When she followed him, he glanced over at her and narrowed his eyes at her smile. This only made her smile wider and he shook his head—whether at her or him, she couldn't be sure, but she thought maybe it was at himself. Which she liked very much.

Inexplicably happy, she followed him and took in the sight of Eric. She hadn't seen him in years and he hadn't changed. He still looked like Gumby in cowboy gear, complete with hat and boots. When he turned from locking the back door of the gallery and saw them standing there, his eyes went straight to Joe and lit up like Christmas.

"Wow, dreams do come true," he said and gave Joe a slow look up and down.

Joe didn't blink, just gave Eric that patented bad-ass look of his, the one that would have had Kylie peeing her pants if it'd been directed at her.

"We'd like to ask you some questions," Joe said.

"Sugar, you can ask me anything you'd like."

Joe slid a look in Kylie's direction, bringing Eric's attention to her for the first time. He paused and then his entire face brightened, going from flirty to happy. "Kylie Masters!" he squealed. "Oh my God, is that really you?"

"You recognize me? This isn't even my own hair!"

"I know. I have that same wig. And with or without the hair, your smile hasn't changed and neither have your eyes." He pulled her in for a warm hug, which she returned with a sigh. So much for her disguise. She'd have to get better at that.

"It's definitely been too long," Eric murmured. "Way too long. I tried to contact you so many times after—"

She closed her eyes and he broke off. "I'm sorry," he said quietly. "Of course you don't want to talk about it."

He'd always been one of her favorites of all of her grandpa's apprentices and now she remembered why. She shook her head and hoped that Joe wasn't picking up on all the things that weren't being said, but she knew he was far too sharp for that. The fact was, she didn't want him to know. She didn't want anyone else to know her shameful truth.

"I heard you were working for Gib," Eric said to her. "That's awesome. He's doing so great with Reclaimed Woods. I always thought that you two might end up . . ." He gave Joe a quick glance and then lowered his voice. "You know."

"I work for Gib," she said. "That's it." There'd always been an unspoken belief amongst everyone at one time or another that she and Gib would end up together. And for the longest time she'd believed it too.

Gib was a good guy. But deep down she could admit that she'd always known he wasn't the *right* guy. She realized now that there was a huge difference between teenage love and grown-up love. In the past, she'd never really let herself think about being happy and in love. But sometimes in the deep dark of the night, she'd dreamed of what type of man she secretly wanted, and she always thought it'd be someone like Gib—kind, caring, gentle in spirit.

But lately she'd realized something. He was actually the complete opposite of what she needed, and *that* realization had absolutely nothing to do with her annoying attraction to Joe and everything to do with her own secret craving for love and acceptance.

Except . . . maybe it had a *little* to do with her attraction to Joe. Over the past week, he'd been there for her without question. In fact, he'd stepped up in a way no one else ever had. Whatever the two of them had going on, friends or maybe more or maybe far less, the fact remained that in a very short time, she'd come to trust him more than she'd thought herself capable of.

And there was more. In addition to the trust and the fact that she ached for his body, he allowed her to be her. Even when she was crazy, wearing a blond wig, insisting he learn how to carve.

And because of all of that, she couldn't seem to help herself. She wanted more.

A lot more.

"What are you doing out here in the back?" Eric asked. "I didn't see you inside. I would've loved to introduce you to everyone."

"We weren't inside," Kylie said. "We didn't have an invite—"

"Oh my God. Darlin', why didn't you get in contact with me?" Eric asked, horrified. "I'd have had you as a guest of honor!" He gave Joe another sideways glance. "And this tall, cool drink of water could have come with."

"His name is Joe. He's . . ." She met Joe's eyes and saw a flash of humor. She had no idea how to describe him and he knew it. ". . . Helping me. I've had a few—"

"*Very* excited to meet you," Joe interrupted her and pulled a small pad of paper and a pen from one of his pockets, leaving her wanting to go through his pockets sometime to see what she might find . . .

She came back from her brief and very naughty fantasy to hear Joe ask Eric for his autograph.

Eric fluttered in excitement. "Seriously? Oh wow. Sure thing, sugar, I'll give you my autograph. I'll give you whatever you want." He grinned and signed the pad with a flourish.

Joe looked at the signature and then at Kylie.

Her penguin thief wasn't Eric. "I have something to show you," she said and pulled out the Polaroid she'd gotten, the one with the table and bench. "I thought maybe this was your work?"

Eric looked down at the table with a frown. "That looks like your grandpa's, darlin'." The frown deepened when he took in the bench next. "But that isn't his, and it sure as hell isn't mine either. I don't do sloppy edges like that." He shuddered. "And I'd never have picked that color stain. What am I looking at?"

"An imposter. I'm trying to find the woodworker who made the bench."

"Huh," Eric said and looked closer at the photo.

"What?" Joe asked him.

"Well, I'm not sure but something in the workmanship reminds me of another woodworker I know."

"Who?" Joe asked.

"A couple of years back, some guy came by trying to sell a bench. It was supposedly done in the style of your grandpa. But it wasn't even close."

"What did you do?" Joe asked.

"I sent him on his way, but I did take his card." He flashed a smile. "I take everyone's card."

"I'd like to see it," Joe said.

Eric snorted. "That could take a while. Like I said, I take *everyone's* card and I never throw anything away."

"But you do still have it somewhere, right?" Kylie asked. "We really need to talk to him."

"Yes, I still have it, certainly. It might be tricky for me to get my fingers on it, but I will." He looked at Joe. "In the meantime, Kylie knows how to get ahold of me, handsome. Don't be a stranger." He winked at Kylie. "And you either! Let's lunch?"

"Absolutely," she said, and started to say more, but Joe grabbed her by the hand.

"We've gotta go," he said. "Have a good night."

"But—" But nothing because Joe had her in the truck and down the street before she could blink. "What was that?"

He tossed the pad of paper into her lap and kept driving. "Things to do."

"Was what we just learned enough to knock Eric off the list?"

"That, and the fact that he sold out tonight making furniture that isn't in your grandpa's style. Plus he's driving a Tesla Roadster."

"What does that have to do with anything?"

"It's an expensive car."

"So he's not trolling for easy money," she said.

"Exactly."

She sighed. "I thought you were just being rude, rushing me out of there."

He shot her a glance. "How about clever? Isn't it just as possible I was being extremely clever?"

"Maybe," she admitted. "But also rude. It wouldn't hurt you to be normal in social situations, you know."

He ignored this, which didn't surprise her. "It is interesting," he said. "Eric's yet another apprentice who's alluded to something that happened to you on the night of the fire."

She stopped breathing. "Of course something happened to me. My grandpa died."

He glanced over at her, his eyes sympathetic. "I know, and I'm sorry to bring up bad memories, but are you *sure* there's nothing else you want to tell me?"

"I'm sure," she said, staring straight ahead out the windshield. "And Eric's not going to find that card. At least not in time," she said, watching the night as it whipped past her.

"Be patient. Have some faith."

This had her looking at him again. "Be patient? Have faith? Are you kidding me?"

"You've got to leave emotions out of it or you'll react with them instead of your brain."

She snorted in annoyance and frustration. "Easy for you to say. You don't have to fight anything as messy as your emotions."

He spared her another glance. "You think I don't have emotions?"

"I think you don't very often give in to them."

He was quiet at that, concentrating on the road or who the hell knew what, and she thought it was done, conversation over. Until he pulled onto her street and put his hand over hers to stop her from getting out.

"The job taught me patience," he said. "And believe me, it came hard-won and I've paid the price for it. There were times when hiding my thoughts was the only thing that saved my ass, so yeah, I'm good at it. But don't mistake that for me not having emotions or feelings, Kylie. You've seen me lose it over you more than once now."

Yeah, and still, she wanted more from him. But she refused to ask for it.

Joe's hands slid up and down her arms in a caressing touch that had her wanting to close her eyes in sheer pleasure, but then he expelled a long, shuddery breath, let go of her, and got out to walk her up.

"That isn't necessary," she said.

"Someone's taunting you with a personal memory and they know where you live. They're just playing with you right now, but that could change. I'm walking you up."

She sighed. She hated that he was logical and reasonable when she couldn't be. "Fine," she said and relented. "And thank you." Then they got to her apartment, where she unlocked her door and froze at the sight of yet another envelope on the floor.

Chapter 13

#TheresNoCryingInBaseball

Kylie might have frozen at the sight of the envelope on her floor, but Joe didn't. In the doorway, he put one hand on her arm to indicate she should stay while simultaneously scanning their immediate area.

She had no idea what he saw, but she didn't catch anything out of the ordinary. Still keeping ahold of her, Joe shut the door behind them, engaged the locks, and picked up the envelope.

She started to say something, but he put a finger to his lips, scooped up Vinnie, who'd come running at them, and gently set him into her arms. Then he went through her place, flipping on lights, obviously clearing the apartment like she saw law enforcement do on TV, only even cooler.

"I don't think whoever it is actually comes in,"

she said, but Joe didn't respond, just continued to work his way through the apartment. Kylie cuddled Vinnie close as he licked her chin, ecstatic as always to have her home. She set him down and he immediately went running for a toy to bring her. Tonight he brought his current favorite, a miniature-size tennis ball.

She obliged him by tossing it. "Fetch," she said, ever hopeful he'd finally get it.

Vinnie pounced after the ball and . . . ran down the hallway with it and vanished. She was sighing when Joe came back to the living room.

"Open the envelope," he said, clearly getting that she was stalling.

Predictably, it was another Polaroid. This one had her poor penguin precariously balanced on a cable car, close to falling off into oncoming traffic, and her heart squeezed. "Dammit." She clutched the picture to her chest. "I've got too much crazy in my life. The photos, my missing penguin, *you*."

He let out a quiet, low laugh, taking the picture to look at it. "You started it with that kiss."

Her entire body reacted as if he'd just planted another one on her, which was annoying enough to have her go into full-court-press defensive. "I keep telling you, I barely remember what that kiss felt like," she said. "Or, for that matter, the second one."

"Really."

"Yes, really," she said, having no idea why she was baiting him. "Maybe you're not as good at kissing as you seem to think."

"Hmm," he said. "Hold this for a sec." He handed her back the picture.

She took it without thinking and then he tugged her into him and kissed her. He kissed her long and deep and deliciously hot, until she couldn't help the moan that escaped her, until she was remembering *exactly* how good he was with his mouth, until she dropped her keys and the picture and threw her arms around him to hold him close.

When they ran out of air, he made his way along her jaw and she found herself tilting her head to expose her throat to him, loving the feel of his lips and teeth running over her skin. He bit down gently and a shock ran through her body, all the way to her toes, just as Vinnie trotted back into the living room and dropped something at their feet.

Breaking free, Kylie started to smile, so proud. "Yes! You've finally learned to fetch—" She broke off in horror as Joe burst out laughing.

Vinnie had "fetched" her vibrator.

Face flaming, she bent and scooped it up and shoved it beneath a couch cushion. "I have no idea how he got ahold of that . . . lightsaber."

At that, Joe only laughed harder. He had to bend over and put his hands on his knees, and by the time he'd finished and straightened back up, swiping at his eyes, she was hands on hips, definitely cooled off . . . and so embarrassed she could hardly talk. "You have to go now," she managed.

"Because you don't need me since you have a vibrator?"

"Lightsaber!" She opened the front door. "Out."

He came toe-to-toe with her and, eyes on hers, reached out and shut the door. "Hey," he said. "If a person isn't at least having a one-some every night, then you're squandering your pre-apocalypse time."

She closed her eyes and moaned, and he laughed again. "Kylie," he said, clearly having to work hard to get ahold of himself. "I love that you have a . . . lightsaber. I love it so much I'm hoping you let me watch you play with it."

"Ohmigod." She shoved him away and covered her face.

He gently peeled her fingers from her cheeks. She met his gaze with effort. "I shouldn't have brought you in on this," she murmured. "Things really do seem even crazier now than they were."

She expected him to make fun of her and continue to tease her, but instead he shook his head. "We're making progress. You've just got to be patient."

She was *so* not good at being patient. The amused look on his face said he knew it too.

"And as for the crazy," he said and let loose a small smile, "maybe it's you. Maybe you're a crazy magnet."

"Yeah? Then what does that make you?"

He flashed a full-out grin now and blew the rest of her brain cells. Then he vanished into her kitchen. "Got popcorn?" he called out. "Hot chocolate?"

"Of course. They're both very important food groups. Why?"

"Because we're going to watch a movie."

"At the risk of repeating myself," she said, *"why?"*

"Because you're unsettled and you're not ready to be alone."

And he was going to sit here with her until she was ready. She tried not to let that warm her, but it was too late. Heart warmed. And other parts too, parts that had previously warmed only for her "lightsaber."

Five minutes later they were watching a *Fast & Furious* movie and eating popcorn and drinking hot chocolate, Vinnie sprawled in Joe's lap.

When the movie ended, Kylie turned to Joe. "You were a perfect gentleman. How come?"

"I'm trying to be good."

She stared at him. "Good isn't exactly what comes to mind when I think of you."

"I'm trying to be good for you," he said. "But sometimes I lose it."

"You do?"

"Yeah," he said on a small smile. "Have you seen you? A dead man would respond to you. And I'm not dead, Kylie." He stroked a finger along her temple. "At first I thought it might've been the wig. Hell, maybe it's your lightsaber."

"Ha ha," she muttered, patting her head. Damn, she was indeed still wearing the wig. Great.

He was smiling when he leaned in and kissed her, slow and deep. He groaned low in his throat, a heady, masculine sound, and she pulled back. "Are you still trying to be good?" she asked softly.

He stared at her mouth, eyes so hot she was shocked her clothes hadn't gone up in flames. "Yeah, but being good isn't my first nature so don't tease me." He tugged her up from the couch, took her to her kitchen table, and pulled something from his pocket.

"A lock?" she asked, confused.

"One last thing on the program for the night. You asked me to teach you basic B&E skills."

And here he was, following through on his word.

He paused, head cocked. "You didn't expect me to do what I said I would," he said, not sounding thrilled about that.

"Honestly?" She shook her head. "No, I didn't."

He shook his head, gestured her closer, and showed her the tool. He then picked the lock in about two seconds right in front of her and she still had no idea how he did it.

"Again," she said.

He went much slower, carefully and thoroughly explaining each move. When his phone buzzed, he took a quick second to glance at the screen.

"What?" she asked.

"I need to help Archer with something." But he stayed where he was, gesturing that it was her turn to work the lock.

She was on her tenth—unsuccessful—attempt and getting pissy all over again when he came up behind her to watch over her shoulder, making her screw up attempt number eleven *and* twelve. "Dammit!"

She felt his body contract in a silent laugh as he brushed a kiss along her jaw.

"Relax," he said in her ear.

With his solid, warm body pressing up against her back? Not likely. But not wanting to reveal how much he affected her, she continued to try to work the lock.

"Patience." He then slid his hands over hers, guiding her through the process until the lock clicked open.

His doing, not hers.

"Thought you had to go," she said quietly, feeling anything but quiet.

"I do."

Joe took the lock and the tool she still held and set them both on the table. Then he turned her to face him and pressed up against her. Her lungs stopped working as every inch of her went on high alert, quivering with need.

"Kylie," he said, voice thick with desire.

"Yeah?"

"I'm about to lose it again."

"Okay," she whispered.

"Okay," he whispered back and lowered his mouth to an inch from hers. They shared a breath before he closed the gap and kissed her, slow and intense.

Someone moaned. *Her,* she realized, and then he deepened the kiss, a hot, intense tangle of tongues and teeth that would've had her sagging backward if she hadn't been sandwiched between her kitchen table and Joe's hard, hot body. One of his hands moved to her hip, the other cupped the nape of her neck, pinning her to him as he continued to kiss her until she was clutching him, panting, whimpering for more. She wanted this—oh God, how she wanted it—but he was needed at work, so she put a hand to his chest and slowly pulled back.

He chased her mouth with his but she pressed on his chest until he opened his eyes and met hers.

"You've got to go," she whispered.

"Right." He pulled in a slow, unsteady breath before letting it out in a way that sounded suspiciously like a sigh as he rested his forehead on hers. "One of these days you'll have to explain to me how it is that you suddenly have all the power in this relationship."

She smiled and he shook his head at the both of them. "You're going to be okay," he said.

"I know," she said.

His smile faded as he watched her, rubbing his thumb along her jaw. He brushed a light kiss to her bottom lip and then lingered, kissing her again as if maybe he couldn't help himself. "Later," he murmured.

She nodded dumbly before realizing he'd vanished, locking the door behind him.

It was only then that she also realized he'd taken the latest picture and envelope with him.

Chapter 14

#MayTheForceBeWithYou

"And that's when Vinnie finally fetched something," Kylie said, regaling her friends with the story of the previous night's activities.

"He did?" Haley asked, thrilled. "Oh, what a good boy he is. I *knew* he could do it."

Elle, eyes narrowed on Kylie's face, shook her head. "Nope. That's not the whole story. What did he fetch? A pair of your socks?"

"Um," Kylie said.

"Panties!" Elle guessed and everyone laughed.

Kylie dropped her head. "Worse."

They were at the coffee shop, in line for their various choices of caffeine. Tina owned and ran the shop, a tall, dark-haired, dark-skinned stunning woman who had a love of everything big—big hair, big earrings, big shoes.

Kylie admired her commitment to fashion as her own style could best be described as "doing everything possible to avoid underwire."

Thankfully, Tina also loved baking muffins. Back when Tina had been Tim, there'd been no muffins at the coffee shop. Just coffee. But Tina was happier than Tim had ever been and that translated to the most amazing muffins on the planet.

"Could be worse," Tina said. "He could've fetched your vibrator."

Kylie moaned miserably and everyone burst out laughing.

"Oh my God," Haley said. "He did that really? He fetched your vibrator? You're my new hero!"

Kylie's face was flaming.

"Hey," Tina said, "don't be embarrassed. You're a woman with needs and now he knows you know how to meet those needs. Which means he also knows that you don't need no man. It puts more pressure on him to perform well or be replaced." She grinned. "Trust me, for a man, that's *always* a good thing."

"Don't worry, honey," someone said from behind her in line. Eighty-something Mrs. Winslow, who lived on the third floor of the building. The older woman smiled knowingly. "He'll appreciate your toys. But remember, it's all fun and games until someone loses the key to the handcuffs."

Tina reached over the counter to high-five Mrs. Winslow.

Pru, another of their gang, entered the shop wearing a workout tank and capris. "I hate it when I'm on the treadmill and accidentally hit the stop button and come to buy a muffin," she said.

"You're not supposed to work out on a full stomach," Elle told her.

"Right. So I can't work out. Ever." Pru smiled, suddenly a little nervously. "Or . . . for at least the next nine months."

Everyone gasped and jumped up and started talking at once.

Elle held up her hands for them all to shut up and looked at Pru. "You're *pregnant?*"

"Turned the stick blue," Pru said and blew out a breath. "I'm only slightly terrified."

They all hugged and squeezed and fussed until Pru stopped them. "Okay, okay, you love me, I love you, yada yada. We're in public making a scene and I'm not going to be that pregnant chick who makes it all about her."

"How's Finn taking it?" Elle asked.

Finn was half owner of the pub and Pru's husband. She grinned dreamily. "He's so happy."

"Good," Elle said. "But man, I'm glad it's you. Out of all of us, you're the one who could handle the whole getting fat, having to stay up all night singing lullabies, and other stuff like not drinking for nine months— What?" she said to Kylie, who was miming that she should zip it because Pru had gone pale.

"Oh my God," Pru whispered. "I'm going to get fat."

"No," Elle said, looking unaccustomedly panicked

and clearly trying to backtrack. "Well, maybe only a little. And hey, it'll be for a great cause, right?"

"Right," Pru said. "Except I'll have to stay up all night singing lullabies. And I don't know any!"

"We'll buy a book," Elle said. "And get a gym membership. It's going to be okay."

Pru had a death grip on Elle's hand. "You promise?"

"We all promise," Kylie said even though she hated going to a gym, and they all hugged again.

Willa came running in next, apologizing to everyone in line as she bypassed them to catch up with her group. "Sorry," she murmured. "Sorry . . . I'm not buying anything, I promise."

"Pru's pregnant," Elle told her.

Willa gasped and grinned. "I knew it!"

"You did?" Pru asked. "How?"

"Cuz after we ate that plate of wings last night, you had to unzip your jeans." Willa gave Pru a hug and her purse made a funny noise.

It was filled with three black Lab puppies.

Everyone peered in and let out a collective "awwwwww."

"I know, right?" Willa asked. "I'm babysitting. When I die, I want to come back as a black Lab pup."

"I'd come back as a German shepherd," Tina said.

"Tough, impenetrable, and loyal to a fault," Haley said and nodded. "Suits you."

"Thanks, sweetie." Tina smiled. "I think you'd make a great St. Bernard."

"Hey," Haley said, but then sighed. "But seeing as I accidentally punched myself in the face while trying to pull my blanket up this morning, I get it."

"No, it's because you're sweet, kind, loving, warm," Tina said.

"Oh." Haley smiled. "That works too."

"I think Elle would be a Doberman," Willa said. "Tough, badass, smart as hell."

"I can live with that." Elle looked at Willa. "You'd be a pit bull. All bark, some bite, but fiercely protective of those you love."

And then everyone turned to Kylie. They all looked at her for the longest time while she waited impatiently. "Well?" she finally demanded.

"A cat," they said in unison.

"Great," she said, tossing up her hands. "I'm picky, independent, and bitchy."

"No, you're loving, curious, playful, goofy, and adventurous," Elle said.

Okay, she supposed she could live with that.

"Muffins to go with the coffee, ladies?" Tina asked.

"We shouldn't," said Elle, the strong one.

Sadie walked by and shook her head. "The more you weigh, the harder you are to kidnap," she said. "Stay safe. Eat muffins. Plural."

So they ate muffins. Plural.

Later that day, Kylie was surprised when her mom stopped by the shop with takeout for lunch. "What's wrong?" Kylie asked, removing her apron and trying to dust off.

"Does something have to be wrong?" Her mom was in a sundress and a denim jacket open to reveal her ample, store-bought cleavage, paired with high-heeled sandals. Her hair added a good five inches to her height. As always, she was camera ready, looking thirty-five instead of nearly fifty. But today her eyes were sad.

"No," Kylie said on a sigh. "Of course not. It just usually is when we actually get together, that's all."

"Maybe a daughter should try harder to see her mama."

Kylie took her mom's hand. "Maybe she should. Tell me what's up."

"Nothing, honestly. I just wanted to see my baby for lunch, is all. Vinnie, darling, come over here and love me since my daughter won't."

Vinnie raced over there, butt wriggling, eyes warm and happy to see anyone who wanted to see him. Her mom scooped him up and loved up on him, her mouth curved in a glossy pout.

Kylie sighed. "Well, I'm not going to compete by licking your face or wriggling my ass in happiness," she cautioned.

"How about just a hug then?"

"I'm dirty," Kylie warned.

"I can wash up."

So they hugged hello, her mom smelling really great of some fancy perfume, Kylie all too well aware that she smelled like wood chips and probably lacquer.

They sat in the courtyard with Vinnie at their feet,

eating the deli sandwiches and chips her mom had brought. When they were finished, Kylie looked at her.

"What?" her mom said.

"I'm waiting for the other shoe to drop," Kylie said. "For the real reason you're here today."

"Maybe I missed you."

"I missed you too, Mom."

They smiled at each other and Kylie realized she *had* missed her mom. "It's nice to see you."

"It's been a few months," her mom said. "We tend to like each other better with a few months' distance between visits."

Kylie opened her mouth to deny that, but it was true and her mom laughed at the look on her face. "I'm right."

"Maybe," Kylie admitted.

"But I'm happy to hear you missed me."

"I did. But I'm sensing there's more to this lunch than I-miss-yous."

Her mom sighed. "I'm just in a little bind right now, that's all."

"What kind of a bind?"

"I'm in between bartending gigs, but I've got some irons in the fire. It's just that I could use a little help with my rent this month until they pan out. I'll pay you back with my next paycheck, I promise." She paused and sighed. "It's that or I'm moving in with you."

The horror of that thought had Kylie seriously considering the loan. Mentally calculating the balance in her bank account, she figured that even though she couldn't afford it, it was the only way to ensure neither of them killed the other. "I'll help you."

"Thanks, honey." Her mom lifted her soda in a toast. "To us never having to be roommates."

Kylie toasted her iced tea to that.

Chapter 15

#GonnaNeedABiggerBoat

Two days later, Joe woke up after a night of shitty sleep. The cause could be attributed to a lot of reasons, but the biggest probability was a light-brown-eyed vixen he couldn't get out of his head.

The night before, he and Kylie had eliminated another apprentice. He'd tried to go alone, but true to form, she'd insisted on going with him. She'd also insisted on once again disguising herself, a black wig this time, short and straight, with moody emo makeup that made it hard to concentrate, but she hadn't wanted to jeopardize his efforts if it came down to them needing her to be unrecognizable.

It would have been a lot easier if she'd just agreed to stay in the truck.

Or better yet, at home.

But Kylie wasn't very passive. Not in this and

not in life, as he'd learned by just watching her go at everything that was thrown at her with all she had. If he hadn't already learned it by watching her at work or with her friends, he'd have learned it by kissing her.

Kylie gave everything her all, *especially* passion.

It made him want her in his bed. And as explosive as he knew they'd be together, it wasn't all sexual. He'd known almost since that first kiss that she was someone worth going after. He'd been doing his damnedest to keep his emotions out of it, but he'd failed.

Spectacularly.

At this point, he was starting to realize that he was incapable of denying himself her. Or resisting her, proven by how she was the only one who could shake his legendary control. He was getting tired of fighting it.

But at the moment he had a job to do and nothing came before a job, which he said to anyone who asked how things were going. And people asked. Archer. Lucas. Molly. Everyone asked.

They were curious as hell about his feelings for Kylie. "It's business," he kept saying until he was blue in the face.

A lie, as nothing regarding his feelings for her was businesslike. This wasn't good, as he'd promised himself she was only a distraction, an amusing, fun, sexy distraction, but nothing more. But even if that had been true, he couldn't go there with her. She wasn't exactly the type to hook up with him for one night and release some of this undeniable tension.

And even if she was, they wouldn't act on it because things *would* eventually go bad—they always did—and that meant Archer would kill him. Assuming, of course, that Elle didn't get to him first.

Besides, he was busy cleaning up the streets of asshats and hopefully also cleaning up his karma while he was at it. He didn't have time for this.

He finally fell asleep just before dawn and then overslept. He hit the office at a run to find Molly in the staff room, making coffee. She handed him a mug along with a sympathetic look. "You're late. Again."

"I know," he said, willing the caffeine to kick in fast and give him grown-up manners.

"You must like having your ass chewed out."

"Yeah, I live for it," he said dryly and then turned and found Archer standing there, arms crossed, expression dialed to pissed off.

"Should I be rethinking you as my number two guy?" he asked. "Because if you can't program a fucking alarm, then we have problems."

Joe resisted rolling his eyes. "Sorry. Bad night."

Archer dropped his arms and his bad 'tude. "Your dad?"

"No."

Archer looked at Molly, who went palms up. "Not me," she said. "I'm good." She paused and then got a worried expression. "Is it Kylie?" she asked Joe. "Did she get another pic from that asswipe?"

"What asswipe?" Archer wanted to know. "And why don't I know about said asswipe?"

"She wanted it kept quiet," Molly said. "She had a family heirloom stolen. And now the guy who stole it is toying with her, sending her pictures of the thing in peril. Joe's on the case for her."

Shit. Joe sent his sister a *thanks a lot* glare because Archer hated it when his guys took side jobs without informing him.

"You need help?" Archer asked him.

Joe looked at him in surprise.

"It's Kylie," Archer said simply.

All of them cared deeply for Kylie. Well, maybe some of them more than others, Joe thought.

"She need anything from us?" Archer asked.

"I have some research to do, was going to do that after work here."

"Do it now." Archer turned to Molly. "Mark him as busy this morning and not to be interrupted."

Joe nodded at him. "Thanks."

"Help our girl. You know where to find me if you need anything."

Which was how Joe found himself glued to the computer in his office for the next few hours. He had a lead on their next apprentice, who'd moved to Santa Cruz. Sixty-year-old Raymond Martinez had changed his name to Rafael Montega, maybe to escape a mile of the bad debts left in his wake, including a bankruptcy disaster. Rafael wasn't woodworking anymore. He'd recently begun managing a little art gallery.

Joe sent Kylie a text that he was driving down there after work. "And five, four, three, two . . ." he murmured, smiling grimly when his phone buzzed a return text.

I'm coming with.

Of course she was. He texted that he'd pick her up after six o'clock.

But then he and the guys got held up on a job. One of their clients' cases had gotten moved up on the board as needing immediate attention. The client's very successful company had grossed close to fifty-five million dollars in the past year and was in the process of trying to sell itself to another entity.

Unfortunately their client discovered by accident that he was being embezzled. He'd been having lunch with a banker friend, who'd thanked him for opening a new business account at his bank and making such a large initial deposit.

The client freaked because he hadn't opened any such account. He'd immediately reported the embezzlement to the police, who'd been slow to mobilize. That's where Hunt Investigations had stepped in.

Yesterday, Archer had sent Joe and Lucas in to snoop around. They'd discovered the client's receptionist was opening the mail and passing client checks to her partner-in-crime. This partner then filed a fictitious business statement, which enabled him to open a bank account in the client's name and deposit the monies into his own account.

Joe had notified the bank and told them to let Hunt Investigations know when there was activity on the account. Almost immediately after, the suspect called the bank to ask why they'd not cleared a $55,000 check. Joe told the bank to tell the guy to come in and sign the check to get the funds. Joe and Lucas were parked outside the bank when the partner parked right next to them.

Unfortunately, somehow he smelled a rat, jumped back in his car, and took off, with Joe and Lucas in hot pursuit. Joe was driving and Lucas was on the phone with both law enforcement and Archer when the suspect started shooting at them.

Needless to say, the shooting ramped up police interest in a big way. They'd eventually caught up with the gun-toting rat and arrested him, but the incident had involved a lot of extra hours of reporting.

Joe hated reports.

In the good news department, the embezzler had been caught and Joe and Lucas had secured a very nice bonus for Hunt Investigations from the pleased and relieved client.

But it was nine o'clock that night before Joe got to Kylie's place. He stood on the porch and once again remembered the other night, how he'd felt watching Gib come out of her apartment obviously in possession of a key, and his own over-the-top reaction.

Because he'd wanted it to be *him*.

Just as he lifted his hand to knock—since *he* didn't have a damn key—he heard Kylie cry out from inside.

In five seconds he'd broken in and had his gun out. Sweeping his gaze across the room, he found

Kylie asleep on the couch, clearly in the throes of a bad dream. He quickly cleared the room and the rest of the apartment before coming back into the living room to crouch at her side. "Kylie," he said softly.

"Don't leave me," she whispered, voice thick with tears, and for a minute Joe's heart stopped because . . . she wanted him to stay?

He dropped to his knees and took one of her flailing hands in his. She squeezed it tight and pressed it to her heart. "Grandpa, please don't die."

Well, hell. All those years of living with his dad and then his own experiences in the military had taught Joe the dangers of waking someone up without warning. But this was Kylie and she'd been reduced to heart-wrenching whimpers, so he scooped her up into his arms and sat on the couch with her in his lap. "I've got you, Kylie." He brushed a kiss to her damp brow. "You're safe. Wake up now."

At the sound of his voice she instantly came awake. He could tell by the sudden stillness of her entire body and how she stopped breathing. Pulling her in closer, he kept his mouth at her temple. "You okay?"

She let out a shuddery sigh and relaxed into him, pressing her face into the crook of his neck as she nodded. He didn't believe it for a second, but sometimes one had to fake it to make it, so he let her have that one. "Bad dream?"

Face still buried against him, she nodded again. She had one arm around his neck, the other clutching something.

A photo.

Shit. He pried it from her fingers. It was the penguin, perched on the edge of a bonfire this time, tipped as if it was about to fall in. He started to get up, but she tightened her grip and he relaxed back into the couch, willing to give her whatever time she needed to compose herself. He held her close with one hand, using the other to pull out his phone to access the app that would bring up the feed of the security camera he'd installed outside her door the last time she'd gotten a delivery.

The camera recorded only when there was motion, so he could zip straight to any action, as he'd been doing two times a day since he installed the camera. He ran quickly through, pausing at the first action sequence—a cat chasing a bird.

And then a shadow arriving on the porch, time-stamped to several hours before.

Male.

Bulky.

He wore a hoodie sweatshirt and kept his face averted as he shoved the manila envelope into Kylie's mail slot before vanishing into the night.

"I got a new pic," she murmured, face still planted against him.

"I see that," Joe said calmly, but he wasn't actually calm at all. He was furious—for her.

"It upset me," she said.

"Of course it did."

"No," she said, and then paused. "I mean it upset me because it showed the penguin near a fire."

And he got that too. "Because of the warehouse fire."

"Yes. It's the setup. It's a play on how he died."

"But he didn't die in the fire," Joe said. "He died two days later when he succumbed to his injuries in the hospital."

She blinked in surprise. "How do you know that?"

"Because I researched it."

"Wait." She stared at him. "You researched him? Did you research me too?"

"I research every job I take. It's why I'm so good at what I do."

"Right." She nodded, scooting back away from him, making herself comfortable in a small ball on the far end of her couch. "I'm a job. Somehow I keep forgetting that."

"Okay, not what I meant."

"You researched me," she whispered to herself.

"Yes." Joe drew a deep breath and held eye contact as he gave her the rest. "And there's something else. I put a security camera outside your front door. Motion sensor detection."

She gasped. "You *what?*"

"I wanted to make sure you were safe and also hopefully ID whoever was doing this at the same time."

"And?"

"And what?" he asked.

"I thought maybe you'd want to apologize for the camera thing."

"No, because I'm not sorry," he said.

She stared at him and he blew out a breath. "Okay, I'm sorry I didn't tell you," he said. "But not for the camera itself."

She studied him and then nodded. "Did you get anything?"

"Not until tonight." He showed her the feed. "Recognize him?"

"I can't tell." She shook her head. "He's smart. He kept his head down and the hoodie up." She slid him a look. "What did you learn about me? When you did your research?"

"Mostly stuff I already knew." That she'd been raised primarily by her grandpa because her parents had been teenagers when they'd had her and hadn't been up to the task. A fact that'd been proven the time that a four-year-old Kylie had been found in the street in the middle of the night, having walked out the front door after being scared awake from a bad dream and finding out that she'd been alone in the house. Her dad hadn't been in the picture by then and her mom had gone out for the night.

That's when Kylie's grandpa had stepped in and taken her. She'd grown up and attended an art high school where she'd shown big promise. The tragic warehouse fire had happened the summer following graduation.

Afterward, she'd taken a year off from school, then gotten her AA before entering in her chosen field. She'd worked for herself on her own for a short time before going to Reclaimed Woods.

She was looking at Joe and then suddenly she

broke eye contact. "The dream I just had . . . it re-minded me that there's something I haven't told you about, either. Something I wasn't sure I was going to tell you at all."

"Okay." He tried to meet her gaze, but she wasn't having it.

"It's something I've never told anyone," she said.

He got up and moved closer, sitting right next to her, and ran his hand up her back and into her hair, trying to soothe her. "You can tell me anything."

She gave a mirthless laugh.

"Anything, Kylie."

She shook her head. "You're going to think different of me after you hear it."

Gently he pulled on her ponytail until she looked at him. "Listen to me," he said. "I've done and seen shit that would make your hair curl . . ." He spared a glance for her wavy hair and smiled. "More than it already is."

She gave him a small smile but shook her head. "You don't understand."

"I do understand," he said. "I was an asshole punk when I was younger. And then in the military . . ." It was his turn to shake his head. "So trust me. There's nothing you can tell me that would change my mind about you."

"It's my fault." Her eyes filled with tears, but not a single one spilled over. "It's my fault my grandpa died."

He shook his head. "The fire was deemed an accident by the arson investigator," he said. "It's believed that possibly a soldering iron caught fire. Your grandfather was soldering some copper pieces onto a dresser but no one was listed as at fault."

"I was the last one to use the soldering iron," she said. "Which makes the fire my fault."

"That wasn't in the reports," he said.

"No, because when my grandpa was transported to the hospital, he was awake. He told the police and firefighters that *he* was the last one to use the iron. I don't know why." She closed her eyes. "It was me. Which means the fire was all my fault."

His heart squeezed tight. "Kylie, no. It wasn't—"

"Yes! It was!" She jumped off the couch and scrubbed her hands over her face. "And on top of that, I lost everything that was his. I have nothing of my past except that penguin, and I want it back." She grabbed a sweatshirt and yanked it over her head. "You said you had a lead on another apprentice. We doing this or what?"

"Yes," he said carefully. "But it's late and you're upset. Maybe we should try this again tomorrow—"

"No," she said. "Nothing matters except the penguin. I want to know whatever the hell you've found out."

All he wanted to do was haul her back into his arms and hold her, but that yearning was his own problem. He'd bent his rules, changed his ways for her from the very start. They should probably talk about that, but she'd had enough emotional upheaval for one night. "I located Raymond Martinez," he said. "He's changed his name. He goes by Rafael Montega now and he's managing a small gallery in Santa Cruz."

She blinked. "Why would he change his name?"

"Let's go find out."

Chapter 16

#BondJamesBond

The drive took an hour and Joe spent that time dividing his attention between watching the road and Kylie, who stared out the window for a long time, lost in her thoughts. Then she unexpectedly turned to him and out of the blue asked, "Have you never been in love, not even once?"

He glanced over at her in surprise. "So *now* you want to talk about feelings?"

"Do you ever just answer a question?"

He used the excuse of going around a slower vehicle to give himself a moment. "I've been in lust," he said carefully. "I've been in like. And maybe a few of those might've eventually led to love, but I bailed before they could."

"Why?"

"Because loving someone comes with a price."

"One that you're not willing to pay?" she asked.

"One that I'm not willing to let someone *else* pay," he corrected her. It began to rain and he flicked on the windshield wipers. The rhythmic swooshing back and forth was the only sound in the truck for a long moment. "And you?" he asked against his better judgment.

"Me what?"

"You know what," he said. "You ever been in love?"

She was quiet so long that he wasn't sure if she planned on answering or not. Then she finally said very softly, "I'm not real good at love."

Because her mom had always put men before her? Because her dad didn't appear to care enough to check in with any regularity? Because her first crush/love had been oblivious for too long?

The insane thing was, she deserved love more than anyone he knew. "You don't have to be good at it but the one time," he said.

She laughed. *Laughed.*

He glanced over again. "What's so funny?"

"You," she said, shaking her head. "Giving *me* love advice."

He thought about it and had to laugh as well. "Okay, so that was a definite stretch for me." But it'd been nice to hear her laugh.

"My mom once told me to fall for someone who makes me feel like I do when my phone's at three percent and I just found a charger." She paused. "But my problem is that I never let my phone get to three percent."

He smiled. She matched it, but then sighed. "We're both pretty messed up. You realize that, right?"

"In a very large way," he agreed.

They were silent for a minute. "I never got to ask you," he said. "What happened with Gib after I left the other night?"

She paused. "Does this pertain to the case?"

"No," he said honestly.

She absorbed that for a moment. "Interesting," she said. "Given your relationship stance of not liking anything too relationship-y."

"It's not that I don't want a relationship," he said. "It's that I can't be serious with anyone right now." Or ever . . .

"Also interesting, given the intensity of the kisses you've laid on me."

He let out a breath. "I never said I didn't want you."

She bit her lower lip. She wanted him too, something he already knew but didn't mind being reminded of.

"So if we gave in to that wanting, this would be what?" she asked quietly. "Just a physical relationship?"

"We're also friends. And at the moment, coworkers." He paused, knowing damn well that no matter what he might want, she couldn't agree to just a physical relationship. She was a woman who needed—and deserved—more, the very least of which was an emotional connection. Something he couldn't afford. "I'm sorry," he said. "But that's all I've got to offer."

Joe would've sworn there was nothing that could

surprise or shock him, not anymore. Not when he'd seen or done it all, which had left him jaded and cynical to say the least.

But Kylie had managed to put him off his axis more than once and she scored again.

Staring out the front windshield, she said, "I'm okay with that."

They drove in silence for a few minutes, him because he was stunned and turned on and also wishing she'd said so before they'd left her place so they might have been able to get started on that physical relationship. He had no idea why *she* was so unusually quiet though.

She didn't say anything else as they drove into Santa Cruz. "Almost there," he said.

Kylie took a wig from her bag and set about putting on her disguise, God help him.

"I know you think the disguises are silly," she said quietly, seriously. "I guess I just get into the excitement of it."

Here he'd been planning his route to getting her naked and she was thinking about the job. *How times have changed,* he thought ruefully and ordered himself to get his head in the game. "This isn't exciting," he said. "It's dangerous."

She nodded, though he was pretty sure she didn't get it. And why should she? She didn't wade knee-deep through the scum of the population for a living.

"So . . . a redhead?" he finally asked.

"You've got a problem with that?"

"No." She looked sexy as hell. He parked and got out of the truck. "Let's do this, Red."

She rolled her eyes, but followed him toward a gallery on a small narrow street with a bunch of other galleries and shops designed for foot traffic. It was a mix of business and residential, but at this time of year, the sidewalks rolled up early.

Everything was closed, including the shades on the windows, so there was no checking out the interior. Joe led the way around back and down the alley, standing a few doors away behind an electrical unit so he could get a feel for things. But all he was getting a feeling for was Kylie in that pixie wig, which in the dark was like a beacon, both to anyone passing by and to his own libido.

"We going to break in and take a look at the inventory?" she whispered, staring at the gallery's back door.

"That's illegal."

She snorted. "Since when have you let that stop you?"

Good point. But they were more out in the open here and the buildings were all close together, the ones on either side of the gallery lit up. Which meant people were nearby. "I can't break in here with you. If we got caught—"

"You don't get caught. You're too good."

"Flattery will get you everywhere." He pulled out his tool kit. "You're going to do exactly as I say."

She nodded eagerly.

He didn't buy it. "If I say move," he told her, "you

put it in high gear without question. You get the hell out of here and don't look back. You got me?"

She stopped nodding eagerly and changed to shaking her head. "I'm not going to leave you behind, Joe."

He looked down into her determined, fierce face and . . . felt his heart slowly roll over in his chest and expose its underbelly. "Yes, you will," he said. "You're going to have to trust me that I'll be fine."

"I'm not leaving you," she repeated in that firm rhino-tone that told him he'd have better luck shifting the moon out of its orbit.

He pulled her back into the shadows and did some reconnaissance, searching for cameras. There weren't any so he moved back to the door and . . . found it unlocked.

Kylie was right at his side. "That's never good when it happens on TV," she whispered.

"Stick to me," he said.

She nodded earnestly, her red bangs in her eyes.

"Like glue, Kylie."

She held up two fingers like she was making a Boy Scout oath, which cracked him up in spite of himself. He nudged the back door open and they looked into a very tiny kitchen. "Hello?" he called out, stepping inside—with Kylie right on his ass.

No one answered.

They moved to the interior door and found themselves in a hallway with several doors.

"That one goes to the retail area," he said, flicking his penlight directly in front of them. He opened that door and found . . . "Stained glass," he said in surprise.

The entire shop was stained glass. Doors, windows . . . everything was stained glass, including the furniture. *This guy isn't our guy.*

"It's not him," Kylie whispered just as he thought it. He started to tell her to turn around and go, but a sound came from behind them.

Someone was coming in the back door.

Adrenaline was second nature to Joe, but she had no training for this, no experience to get her through, and why would she? Criminal behavior wasn't exactly a skill that normal people acquired.

Oh my God, she mouthed to him, eyes wide.

Only one thing went through his mind. She trusted him. She probably wouldn't admit that, but she did. It was in the way she looked at him. It was in her kiss, and how she touched him. Whether she wanted to admit it or not, she was depending on him to keep her safe and there was no way in hell he was going to let her down. He opened one of the hallway doors to the left, hoping . . . *Yes.* A closet, although a very small one. He shoved Kylie into it ahead of him, followed her in and shut the door.

The space was small and messy, lined in the back with boxes. Clothing hung haphazardly down over the top of them, leaving just enough room to stand up against each other. Considering what their limited options had been and the far worse situations he'd found himself in over the years given his career choice, he couldn't have asked for much more.

But Kylie was making small, panicked noises in her throat and that's when he remembered—she was claustrophobic. "It's okay," he murmured, reaching for her. Not that he had far to reach.

"It's not okay!" she whispered. "I'm going to puke!"

Chapter 17

#ETPhoneHome

Great, Kylie thought. She was in yet another tight space with Joe, in the dark, about to get caught for breaking and entering and go to jail, and she didn't look good in orange jumpsuits.

"Just breathe," Joe whispered. "You've got this, Red."

What the hell did that mean, she *had this?* She *so* didn't have this! "I'm not kidding about the puking," she whispered. "And I'm not a pretty puker either."

"You're not going to puke."

"Because it'll give us away?" she whispered.

"No, because these are new work boots I'm wearing and I like them. I've gotten them broken in just right."

She might've told him what she thought of his boots and where he could put them but since she was no longer speaking to him as of right this very moment, she settled for flipping him off. She then squeezed her eyes shut to concentrate on swallowing compulsively in order to keep the bile down. She'd had popcorn and wine for dinner à la Olivia Pope and that wasn't going to be pleasant. *Be cool,* she told herself. *You are not going to throw up on the hot guy.* But it was difficult to control herself while simultaneously trying not to hyperventilate. Dammit. Damn him.

Except . . . this wasn't Joe's fault. She'd insisted on coming along. So damn *her* and her impulsiveness. And . . . dear God, were they running out of air in here? Yeah, they were. They were totally running out of air—

"Hey," Joe murmured softly, running his hands up and down her arms. "It's okay. I've got you."

"Yes, in a dark, teeny, tiny closet!" she hissed as panic gripped her, and oh perfect, now the walls were closing in on her as well.

"Shh," Joe breathed, holding her upright because apparently her legs were done working. She lifted her head to his and he set a finger against her lips.

Yeah. She got it. *Don't make a sound. And preferably also don't get sick . . .* But seriously, the closet really was getting smaller by the second.

"I'm not going to let anything happen to you," Joe whispered, his lips brushing her earlobe and making her shiver.

She really wanted to believe him, even tried to take solace in the fact that he hadn't yet made any promises he hadn't kept, but panic didn't care about logic.

"Good," he whispered against her ear. "You're doing great. Now I'm just going to—"

She clutched at him as he started to shift away. "No," she whispered.

"I have to take a look, Kylie, but I'm not leaving you. I wouldn't leave you behind either. Ever."

She met his gaze and nodded, and in the cramped space they had, he turned away from her to peek out the door.

Unable to refrain, she plastered herself up against him and dropped her forehead to his back as she held her breath. Next time she was going to listen to logic and consider staying in the truck.

Except she knew she wouldn't. She knew that she'd choose the exact same thing again, which meant she had a lot more of her mother in her than she would've liked to admit.

"Okay," Joe whispered. "Don't freak."

Oh, God. "Too late. What is it? What's happening?"

"Rafael's here."

Oh shit. She'd not known Rafael real well. She remembered him as being in his forties and a terminal bachelor due to his curmudgeonly personality. Mostly he'd avoided her like the plague. At the time she'd thought maybe girls weren't his thing, but it'd turned out that *teenagers* weren't his thing.

"Apparently he also lives here," Joe murmured. "He just opened the door at the end of the hallway and it's a converted bedroom." He paused and she didn't think it could be for anything good. "We're going to have to hang here for a bit," he finally said.

Nope, nothing good. She did love being right, but this one time she could've handled being oh-so-wrong. "How long is a bit?"

"Until he leaves or goes to sleep."

"Oh my God."

Joe sent her a considering look over his shoulder, the picture of unflappable, impenetrable, tough, stoic male. He was always like that, which was a good thing because she was about to make a caffeinated squirrel look mellow.

"Joe," she said, her voice higher than usual as she worked hard at reining in her growing panic *and* keeping her voice down. "What if he finds us?"

"He won't."

"But what if he does? What if we get caught?"

"I don't usually get caught."

She gripped the back of his shirt in two sweaty fists. "Usually?" she squeaked. "*Usually?* Oh my God." Again she dropped her forehead to his back. She was starting to sweat in some very uncomfortable places.

"Deep breaths, Kylie."

"I really hate it when people tell me that!"

Reaching back, he hooked an arm around her, holding her close to him. "I need you to relax."

She let out a soundless half laugh, half sob. "Not my strong suit."

"Work on it, because it gets worse."

She lifted her head. "How? How can it possibly get worse?"

He pulled her in front of him so she could see out the crack in the door, which was a relief. And hold up, there was an additional benefit as well, one that just might have the power to take her mind off the fact that she was going to die in this closet. Because now Joe was pressed up behind her, up close and personal.

Very personal.

Suddenly she couldn't concentrate on the fact that she couldn't breathe. She couldn't concentrate on *anything* but the feel of his big, strong body perfectly aligned with hers.

Everywhere . . .

He'd offered her a physical relationship. She knew that she shouldn't be intrigued but she was because the idea worked for her. It really did. Even just thinking about it put her body on high, hopeful alert. Doing her best to shake that off, she peered out the crack. She could see down the hallway into a room. Raymond, aka Rafael, stood there looking much as she remembered. Still rounder than he was tall, but older. He was frowning at his TV.

"He's in for the night and— Shit." He put a hand over her eyes.

"What are you doing?"

"Protecting you," he whispered. "Rafael just stripped down to his twig and berries. I'm seeing things that I do not need to see."

She grimaced at the mental visual. "Is he going to sleep?"

"No, he's sitting on the edge of his bed flipping through TV channels like it's his job. Luckily he's also half-deaf, given the decibels he has the volume up to." Still behind her, he brushed his lips along the column of her throat. "I liked you as a blonde," he murmured. "I liked you dark, too. But I *really* like the red. It matches your temperament." Every word had his mouth brushing against her bare skin and she felt his laugh when she elbowed him in the gut, not that she could possibly hurt him.

"I almost forgot I'm not speaking to you," she said. But it was without a whole lot of heat because the feel of his mouth on her was making her shiver, and she learned something about herself that she hadn't known. It turned out that she could feel only one overpowering sensation at a time. The terror and claustrophobia retreated enough to let in a wave of desire.

Which meant she'd lost her ever-loving mind. "Are you coming on to me in a closet on a stakeout?" she whispered incredulously.

"Do you want me to be?"

Of course she wanted him to be. But she also wanted him to work for it. "Keep going," she said, "and I'll let you know."

There was a smile in his voice when he spoke, his mouth still at her ear. "Do you realize that every time I've tried to protect you, you've managed to hold your own? And damn if that's not sexy as hell, Kylie."

With a rough laugh, she closed her eyes to concentrate on the feel of him and he pressed into her. "*Joe.*"

"Don't worry. It's not going anywhere. I can think with two body parts at the same time."

Well, thank God one of them could.

"Although," he murmured, "the things I want to do to you in this closet . . ."

She shivered and then gasped when he sank his teeth into her earlobe, tugging lightly, playfully.

Only it didn't feel playful. It felt like if she didn't have him inside her soon she might expire on the spot. He must have felt the same because he whipped her around to face him and slid his fingers into her hair, tugging her face to his. When his mouth touched hers, all of it—Rafael, the pictures, her grandpa's death, *everything*—disappeared in the heat of the moment and they were back into the flames until it was to the point that they had to stop or go at it right there in the closet. She wasn't sure about Joe but she wasn't prepared to go there, so she pulled back. She felt him take a deep, shaky inhalation before very purposely letting it out again.

They stood like that for a moment, thighs-to-thighs, chest-to-chest, and everything in between. And everything in between included some of her favorite parts, especially as he was hard. *Everywhere.*

"What's he doing now?" she asked.

Joe took a look. "Lying on his bed, lights and TV still on—but his eyes are closed. I think he's asleep." He still waited a full five minutes, which she knew because she counted the seconds. "Stay at my back," he said, "and don't make a sound." Keeping a tight hold on her hand, he led her silently out of the closet and out the back door into the night. Then they ran for his truck and took off.

Joe usually drove like he did everything else—utterly calmly and in control. Not today. The set of his shoulders and the tightness of his mouth gave him away. Did he realize he was starting to show her the man beneath the cool, calm façade he showed everyone else? Or how thrilling that was? "You're mad at how it went down," she said into the tense silence of the vehicle's interior.

"I didn't like you being in that situation because of me."

"I was in that situation because of me," she corrected him. "But I did good."

A small smile crossed his lips. "You did great."

"Then what's the matter?"

Without taking his gaze off the road, he reached for her hand and brought her palm to his mouth. "Kylie, you did so good, I'm hard as a rock. I told you, watching you handle yourself gets me every time."

Their gazes met briefly and she felt the heat rise in her. Again. Heat, and a need. He kissed her palm once more and then, his hand still in hers, set it on his thigh. "I want to take you home," he said.

A thrill went through her at that. "Then do it. Take me home."

They didn't talk after that. Just drove through the dark night with Joe seeming to go as fast as he could without killing them while simultaneously using every second of the ride to torture her with knowing touches. By the time he parked at an inviting-looking duplex in Inner Sunset, she was so worked up she could barely breathe.

He turned off the engine and looked at her, and she could see that for as out of control she felt for wanting him, he felt the same. It was in the heat of his eyes, the tense lines of his gorgeous body, the way he touched and spoke to her. It all added up to a sense of need and hunger and desire, for *her,* the depths of which she'd never felt from another man.

So much that the air seemed to crackle between them. She actually *ached* and if he so much as reached out and touched her, she was going to jump his bones right here in his truck. Yes, there was a little niggling in the back of her mind that she was getting too far gone over him, that she needed to hold herself back from going all in, but she ignored it because she couldn't hold back. Not with him. But still, something of her brief hesitation must have shown on her face.

"Say the word, Kylie, and I'll take you back to your place."

She met his gaze, knowing her own was surprisingly steady. She wanted this. She needed this. "What word do I say if I want to go inside with you?" she asked. "Or want you inside me?"

He had her out of his truck so fast her head was spinning as they practically ran up the walk. He was working his key into the lock when she pressed up against him, going up on tiptoe to whisper in his ear, "What's taking you so long?"

He shoved the door open and within seconds had her inside, the door kicked closed, and her entire body pressed between his and the wall. Then his mouth was on hers, their tongues touched, and she moaned. She couldn't help it. All the heated looks, the kisses, the lingering touches that they'd shared up to this point combined, multiplied exponentially, leaving her shaky with need and just about panting for him. A situation not improved as his fingers slid up her belly, finding their way beneath her shirt. As his lips made their way back to her mouth, he palmed her breast, his thumb rasping across her nipple.

"Joe." As she was a puddle of need, it was still all she could get out, but he heard her, heard the obvious desperation behind the single word, because he groaned and pulled her tighter into the cradle of his thighs.

Perfect, since her goal was the bulge between them. When she rocked into it, he groaned again and tightened his grip on her with a low laugh. "I've got the muscle," he said. "But you've got all the power. I can never seem to resist you, Kylie. Even when I know I should."

"Maybe you should stop trying."

This got her another low laugh. "Already have." He took her mouth with his and the night caught fire. Mouths, teeth, tongues, hands, bodies, all strained to get even closer. Joe appeared to try to devour her, which was fair game since she was currently attempting to consume him right back. Both of them together made the air heat and close around them like a dark vacuum, sucking away all thought except this, him, now. "Joe."

He lightly bit down on her lower lip. "Changing your mind?"

Hell no she wasn't changing her mind. She'd be crazy to. He was watching her think, his eyes burning dark with heat. It had her legs turning to jelly and she wobbled before somehow managing to lock her knees. "I'm not changing my mind," she murmured.

"Good. Because I have plans for you." And then he kissed her slow and deep.

With a moan, she rocked into him until he lifted her up so she could wrap her legs around his waist, her nails digging grooves into his shoulders to hold on. He braced one hand on the door frame and the other had a firm grip on her ass as they kissed and ground into each other until they were both half-gone.

"Now," she gasped. "Oh, please, Joe. *Now*."

Equally breathless, he jerked her closer. "You're not ready yet."

"If I was any more ready, I'd be in flames!"

At that, he flashed a wicked, bad boy grin just before lowering his head and kissing her again. In the next beat her shirt was gone and then so was her bra. And then that hot, talented tongue of his rasped over first one nipple and then the other before he dropped to his knees in front of her and stripped her out of her boots and jeans. "Nice," he said of her lacy panties and then slowly slid them down her thighs, leaving her bare-ass naked except for her boots, which he left on. "Oh, Kylie," he whispered, voice gruff, his heated gaze taking her in. "Open for me." Before she could move, he lent his hands to the cause, his big palms nudging her legs apart, his calloused thumbs slowly teasing her damp flesh.

By the time he finally leaned in and put his mouth on her, she was already trembling, her toes curling. Then, hands on her hips to hold her upright, he took her to a whole new place, showing her things she'd never known she could feel.

Twice.

When she was still gasping, still shuddering, he rose to his full height, bared his essentials—and *oh my goodness she did love his essentials.*

He pulled a condom from somewhere and she once again wrapped herself around him, crying out when he slid home. The sound seemed to finally unleash the beast within him. He was still holding her face in his hands and she could feel his fingers curling into loose fists in her hair as she moved with him, meeting every thrust, spurring him on as the deep sensations pulsed and spread through her until she couldn't contain herself.

As she came, crying out, clutching at him, he roughly groaned her name and buried his face in the crook of her neck, following her over and into the abyss.

Chapter 18

#NotInKansasAnymore

They ended up on their backs, boneless and sated on the hardwood floor. At least, Joe was boneless and sated. He hoped like hell that Kylie was too. As soon as he could find his limbs, he'd make sure of it.

After what might have been five minutes or maybe even a year, he felt her shift, throwing an arm over her eyes. A little sigh escaped her and at that tiny sound, he managed to stir. He rolled to his side and brushed a kiss over her shoulder, his lips curved in a smile because she was still wearing the wig. "Hey, Red."

She stared up at him, going still. "Oh my God, don't tell me I'm still wearing the wig."

"Okay, I won't tell you."

She touched her head. "Dammit."

He smiled. "Your boots too. Love those boots, Kylie."

She moaned and he laughed. Laughed, while naked on the floor with a woman. Shaking his head at that, he had to laugh again. "Didn't see you coming, Kylie."

"Hmm," she murmured, which he hoped meant she knew the feeling.

He came up on one arm, using the other to tug her into him. "'Hmm' good, right?"

She let out a rough, mirthless laugh. "Fishing for compliments?"

He stroked a finger along her jaw, his mouth curved. "Yeah, well, you're a hard woman to read."

She met his gaze. "All you have to do is look in the mirror at the ten nail indentions in your back."

He chuckled and rubbed his finger over the brow she'd furrowed. "But something's bothering you."

"But . . ." She paused with a rueful smile. "I have to admit . . ." She looked around them. "I feel a little bit like I just turned into my mother, boinking against the wall to scratch an itch. I mean, what the hell was that?"

"Adrenaline," he said. "Sometimes after a mission's over, it all builds up and you need to release it somehow. A good fight works, but sex works better."

She just stared up at him.

"It's totally normal," he said, meaning to soothe and comfort. "It happens."

"Oh really. It happens," she said.

He hesitated at her suddenly overly careful tone, replaying what he'd just said and wondering how he'd screwed up so that she'd misconstrued his statement.

"Not to me, this doesn't happen," she said and sat up.

"Kylie—"

"No. I get it. Please don't explain it again." She got to her wobbly feet, moving around, picking up pieces of clothing and pulling it all back on.

"Kylie. Wait." He got up as well, reaching out for her, but she pushed his hands away.

"I've got it," she said.

His phone buzzed an incoming text. He glanced at it and grimaced. "I'm sorry," he said. "But it's my dad. I have to look at it."

She nodded and he assessed the text.

I've been followed.

Oh, shit. His dad was going off the rails again. He hit his dad's number. "What's wrong?" he asked, relieved his dad picked up. He didn't always because cell phones could be traced and he was paranoid.

"They're tracking me," his dad said. "Through the walls. They're banging on the damn walls."

Joe looked at the common wall between his place and his dad's. The wall he'd just taken Kylie against. He closed his eyes. "Dad, no one's tracking you. It was . . ." Hell. "The wind."

"There's no wind tonight."

"Okay, then it was me." Joe grimaced. "I was . . . hanging up some pictures."

Kylie stopped straightening out her clothing, pivoted and gave him a brows up.

"You don't have any pictures," his dad said in his ear. "And it's almost midnight. I'm telling you, someone's coming to get me."

"Dad, listen to me," Joe said, pinching the bridge of his nose. "No one's coming to get you. I'll be over in a minute. Do not do anything until I get there." He shoved the phone into his pocket and turned around to find Kylie standing in front of his living room window, hugging herself, looking out into the night.

"Hey," he said, coming up behind her, enveloping her in his arms. "I've got to—"

"I know." She stepped away. "I've got to go too. I've got an Uber coming."

She started to walk out the door, but he caught her by the wrist and reeled her back in. "What's going on, Kylie?"

She tried giving him an innocent look. "What's going on is that you've got to go."

He pulled her around to face him and bent his knees a little to look into her eyes. "It seems like maybe it's *you* who has to go."

She turned her head away and he gently turned it back. "My dad lives right next door," he said, "on the other side of this duplex. Unfortunately, he needs me to stop by right now, but I thought I could make us a late dinner. Us, as in you and me and him."

"It's nearly midnight," she said.

"So everyone keeps saying, but my stomach doesn't tell time. It just tells me when it's hungry. My dad and I often eat really late. You in?"

"You cook?" she asked in surprise.

"I'm an awesome cook," he said, not above wanting to impress her with his skills. He'd learned young that if he didn't want to eat out of a can, he had to make his own food. He'd gotten good at it, and then even better once he'd hit puberty and realized how much girls loved the fact that he could cook for them. He'd gone on to use that knowledge ruthlessly to his advantage with women for a lot of years, but this would be the first time he'd ever cooked for one and his dad at the same time. Which meant that Kylie was different, a fact he already knew.

She was looking at him now, studying him with a slight furrow to her brow.

"What?" he asked.

"You're like this really big puzzle. One of those with a thousand-plus pieces, and I'm not only missing a bunch of those pieces, I don't even have all four of the corners."

He had to laugh. "Yeah. And I don't fit into a box very well either."

At his smartass comment, the corners of her mouth curved in a very small smile that said not only did she have his number, but she also got him, as in all the way to the heart and soul got him, and it made his breath catch. He pulled her in for a hug, needing the contact in a way he couldn't have articulated if he'd tried. But luckily he didn't need to. She willingly snuggled into him as well, as if maybe she had the same need. Brushing a kiss to her temple, he closed his eyes and held on. He had no idea what he was doing, which was a hard thing to swallow since he made sure to *always* know what he was doing. But one thing he did know—he wasn't sorry. And something else—he wasn't ready to let her go yet.

She dropped her head to his chest. "I'm worried," she murmured and his heart stopped. Because this was probably where she told him what he could give her wasn't enough for her and then she was going to dump him—

"We're getting nowhere," she said, "and I have less than a week left before I've got to authenticate those pieces or lose the penguin forever."

He let out a breath of relief. She was giving him a stay, a reprieve. She wasn't dumping him.

Yet.

"You're not going to have to do that," he promised. "We'll find the penguin."

"I want that to be true," she said.

"It *is* true."

Kylie nodded and held on to him for another minute. She was fierce, she was strong, she wasn't easy, and she always had something to say. She had flaws and he loved that. But he thought maybe his favorite thing about her was that when she got knocked down, she got right back up again. Something he could relate to, not that he'd planned on relating to her at all.

Chapter 19

#ShakenNotStirred

Kylie waited as Joe pulled some things from his fridge. Then he took her by the hand and walked her outside and around to the other side of the duplex. Not ten minutes ago, she'd been naked on his floor with him, a big deal for her. Normally right about now she'd be running for the hills, needing some time alone to process and assimilate. And to distance herself.

So the fact that she was actually still here and preparing to meet Joe's dad staggered her. "Won't he think it's odd that I'm with you at this time of night?" she asked.

"My dad doesn't keep track of time unless I'm late or he needs something," he said. And then he paused. "But there's something you need to know about him. He's . . . different."

Kylie smiled. "And you're not?"

"Smartass," he said with an answering smile, but then he hesitated again. "Listen, if he says any weird stuff, just ignore it, okay? He doesn't mean anything by it."

"What kind of weird stuff?"

"He's not always 100 percent present," he said. "He came home from the Gulf War with some injuries, not all of them physical."

Her heart softened and she met his gaze. "And you and Molly take care of him."

"Yeah. And he doesn't like anyone else, ever, so don't be insulted if he ignores you." Joe knocked on the front door, four hard raps, then a pause, and then one more. "Dad?" he called out. "It's me." He unlocked three dead bolts and then knocked again in the same pattern as before as he opened the door. "Dad? You hear me?"

"Of course I do," came an irritated male voice. "I'm not deaf."

Joe didn't step over the threshold. "And you're also not armed, right?"

Kylie shot Joe a worried look. *Armed?*

Joe smiled reassuringly at her. "Don't worry. He doesn't have any bullets right now."

Oh good. That made her feel all better.

"But he likes to hold his gun," Joe warned her softly. "Just ignore that too."

Kylie nodded, thinking she was doing a most excellent job of hiding her nerves until Joe squeezed her hand and smiled reassuringly.

"What's taking you so damned long?" his dad yelled.

Joe stepped inside first, making sure Kylie was behind him. He took a quick look into the dark room and apparently saw something she couldn't, because he sighed. "Dad, where are your pants?" He shifted, and then there was a click and a light came on.

The place was small and extremely neat, not a thing out of place. Well, except the man in the wheelchair in the doorway wearing only a wifebeater and boxer shorts.

Oh, and a shotgun, which was lying across his knees.

In spite of his dark hair liberally streaked with gray and his equally dark eyes surrounded by a web of weathered wrinkles, Joe's dad looked very much like Joe, and far younger than Kylie expected. The Gulf War had been nearly thirty years ago. She tried to do the math in her head, guessing that he had to be fiftyish.

"Pants are stupid," he said.

"Yes," Joe said. "And so is greeting visitors with a shotgun and no clothes and yet you do it. Put your gun away."

Joe's dad looked beyond Joe to Kylie. "Who's that?"

Joe turned to Kylie. "This is—"

"Not you," his dad said. "Her. I asked her."

Kylie smiled at him. "My name's Kylie Masters."

"Huh," he said. "I had a Masters in my platoon. Jeremy Masters. He was a class-A asshole. Is he your father?"

Joe shook his head. "Jesus, Dad—"

"No, it's okay," Kylie said to Joe, but kept looking at his dad. "My dad *is* a class-A asshole, Mr. Malone, but he wasn't in the military. At least, I don't think so."

"You don't know for sure? How come?"

"Because he walked away when I was young and hasn't always kept in touch."

Joe's dad stared at her and then nodded. "You can stay." He turned to Joe. "What's for dinner?"

"Nothing unless you're going to be nice."

"I'm always nice."

Joe snorted and passed him and went into the kitchen.

"Thinks he knows how to cook," his dad said to Kylie.

"I do know how to cook!" Joe yelled from the kitchen.

Joe's dad lifted his forefinger and thumb about an inch apart.

Joe stuck his head out of the kitchen. "How about you call for takeout if my food sucks so bad?"

"And he's as sensitive as a girl," his dad said.

"Boys are just as sensitive as girls," Kylie said. "Maybe more so. So probably you meant to say he's as sensitive as a *boy*."

Joe's dad paused and then tipped his head back and laughed out loud. "Son, you went and did it now," he yelled. "This one's going to give you a run for your money."

Joe didn't respond to this, but Kylie could hear

him banging stuff around in the kitchen. She told herself it didn't matter that he didn't agree with his dad about her giving him a run for his money. Because what they *did* agree on was that this was merely a friendship and a working relationship with a bit of holy-cow sex on the side. Which was fine. Because *maybe* there were some feelings developing for him deep down, but since she had no idea what those feelings were exactly, or what to do with them, it didn't matter.

But she couldn't deny that a small part of her would've filled with warm fuzzies if Joe had agreed with his dad about her at all instead of radio silence.

His dad rolled himself past Kylie and checked all the front door locks. He checked each of them exactly four times, paused, and then checked them a fifth time.

The same pattern Joe had used to come inside.

Kylie watched this with a sudden lump in her throat, understanding now exactly how much Joe cared about his family. And—whether he realized it or not—just how big a capacity he had to love.

Joe's dad finished at the front door and grunted in satisfaction before wheeling to the windows, checking each of those four times as well. And then a fifth. There was one window that was too high for him in his chair so Kylie crossed to it herself and checked the lock. She did it four times. Then paused and checked it a fifth time.

When she turned around, Joe's dad nodded in satisfaction. "Yeah," he said. "You'll do."

She looked up and found Joe watching them both, his expression unreadable. "Kitchen," he said, and vanished.

She and his dad exchanged a look.

"He's probably getting his period," his dad said.

Something slammed in the kitchen and his dad grinned. "Yeah, definitely he's getting his period. Maybe we should buy him some of that shit, what's it called? Midol."

There was another bang in the kitchen.

Joe's dad laughed. "For such a tough guy, he's an easy target."

Kylie bit her inner cheek. "You're messing with him."

"Well, of course I am."

"Why?" Kylie asked.

His dad shrugged. "I cheated on Joe and just finished a season of *Pretty Little Liars* without him. I'm bored."

Joe stuck his head out of the kitchen. "Hey, *PLL* was supposed to be our dirty little secret."

Kylie was smiling. "You watch *Pretty Little Liars*?"

Joe scowled and vanished back into the kitchen.

"Told you," his dad said, grinning at her. "He's sensitive as a little . . . boy."

"Food," Joe yelled. "Come and get it or I'm eating it all myself."

They entered the kitchen. Joe's dad went straight to the sink and jabbed a finger at the stack of dirty pots and pans. "What's that?"

"Dinner first," Joe said. "I'll do dishes after."

"Around here, we always do dishes first."

"Not tonight, Dad."

"Since when?"

"Since it's midnight and I'm tired and you're being an asshole. On purpose." He jabbed a finger in the direction of the table. *"Sit."*

"I'm already sitting," his dad said, sounding irritated, but when Joe turned his back, the guy winked at Kylie, in that moment looking very much like his son.

Joe served pasta and sauce and a salad. Kylie smiled when she saw that the pasta was little noodles in the shape of the alphabet.

"Hey," his dad said, poking at it. "This isn't Chef Boyardee."

"Nope," Joe said.

His dad pushed away his bowl. "You know that I only eat my SpaghettiOs from a can. That's how I like 'em."

Joe pushed the bowl back at him. "We've been over this. The stuff in a can that you ate all through the eighties like it was going out of style has way too much sodium. Your doctor said you have to cut back. And it'd be a lot easier to feed you if you'd agree to eat something other than pasta."

His dad picked up a fork. "You know what you are? You're a pants-wearing, sodium-hating commie."

Joe nodded. "Impressive. You managed to fling insults without using the F-bomb."

"My PT and nurse both threatened to quit if I didn't stop saying it," he confessed. "They gave me a book on how to swear without swearing. I don't give a shit what Nurse Ratched thinks, but my PT's alright."

"Well look at you, learning to be social," Joe said.

His dad snorted, but still only poked at the food.

"Dad, just try it."

"Fine." He took a bite with exaggerated caution.

"Well?" Joe asked.

"Eh." He chewed. Swallowed. Took another big bite. And then another. "It's nothing you'd see on *Iron Chef* but it's okay."

Joe rolled his eyes. "Gee, thanks. Do you remember that time the power went out and in order to eat we had to heat cans over a fire pit we made in the backyard?"

His dad took another bite. "The power didn't go out. It was turned off because those fuckers—er, I mean those *effers* didn't tell me that my check had bounced. And since you couldn't find a can opener, you used a battery-powered screw gun from the garage and poked holes in the can. And also in your own damn finger. Bled like a fire hose. It was so bad we couldn't tell the difference between the sauce and the blood."

"Needed stitches," Joe said fondly, as if proud of this moment. "We used superglue, remember?"

"Hell yeah, I remember. We saved hundreds of dollars in ER bills."

Kylie stared at the two of them laughing together over this rather horrifying memory. She was starting to realize just how much responsibility Joe had on a daily basis. How much responsibility he'd *always* had, starting from way too young an age, taking care of both his little sister and his dad.

She might not have had her parents, but she'd had her grandpa. He'd taken care of her, always. She'd never felt the weight of the world on her shoulders as surely as Joe had felt it. *Still* felt it.

When his dad's bowl was empty, Joe nodded in approval and rose, collecting all the dishes, ruffling his dad's short hair as he moved to the sink. It was a small thing, a quick little gesture, but it portrayed such love and acceptance that Kylie felt her throat go tight.

Joe's cell buzzed an incoming text. He glanced at it and his expression went grim.

"What's up?" his dad asked. "Work?"

"Yeah. I've got to go back in. We've got something going down tonight."

"Kick ass," his dad said.

Joe opened a drawer filled with prescriptions and pulled out a notepad to check the entries.

"I've been taking everything," his dad said. "Jesus. I'm not a baby."

"Taking them as in actually swallowing them," Joe asked, "or taking them to flush them?"

"I don't flush them anymore. They cost too fucking—er, effing much."

Joe nodded, put the pad away, and looked at Kylie.

"Don't worry about me. I told you, I'm a delight," she said. "I can Uber home from here."

"I'll drop you off."

She didn't bother to argue with him as they left. She waited until they were in his truck and on the road. "Your dad's pretty great," she said.

Joe snorted.

"He *is*."

Joe reached over and grabbed her hand, bringing it up to his mouth. "Thanks. You handled him well, so thanks for that too."

"There was no handling anything. It was nice to meet him."

He slid her a glance that she couldn't read.

"What?" she asked.

"I told you, he doesn't usually talk to anyone except people he knows and is comfortable with. But he talked to you. He liked you."

"A lot of people like me," Kylie said and made him laugh, which in turn warmed her because she felt like he needed the laugh, and also . . . it felt good that she'd given it to him.

The next day after work, Kylie walked into the pub and found some of the gang at the far right side of the bar, where they always hung out. Pru, Elle, Willa, and Molly. Kylie took the only empty barstool and paused when they all stared at her.

"What's up?" she asked, looking down at herself. "Am I trailing tissue paper on my shoe or something?"

"Yeah, you're right, Willa. She's most definitely sleeping with him," Pru said and slapped a ten down on the bar. "She's got the postcoitus glow."

Molly grimaced. "Come on, guys. I can't take that bet."

"I can," Elle said and dropped her ten. "Kylie's smiling with way too many teeth. Plus we all know Joe's hot as hell. And those abs—"

"Hey," Molly said. "My brother, remember? And anyway, it's what's on the *inside* that matters, not the outside."

"Not in the beginning," Elle said. "Be honest. It's all about first visual impression and chemistry."

Molly shook her head. "Not always."

"Give me an example," Elle said. "Even one example where in the first two seconds what's on the inside is more important than the outside."

"Uh . . ." Molly sighed and shook her head. "Dammit."

"Refrigerator," Sadie said as she came and sat down to join them.

Elle laughed. "Okay, I stand corrected."

"You don't get to talk," Molly told her. "You're with Archer, who looks at you like I look at fully loaded pizza. If a man looked at *me* like that, I wouldn't worry about first impressions at all."

While they went on to debate this, Willa turned to Kylie. "So are you?" she asked quietly. "Sleeping with him?"

"Technically? No."

Willa grinned. "And untechnically?"

Kylie bit her lower lip and Willa laughed. "I knew it. How was it?"

Magic . . . "We're not together like that," she said. "We're just friends." Sort of. "It's complicated."

"Honey, why would you want to be just friends with a perfect male specimen like Joe?"

"He's . . . not my type," Kylie said. *Lame.*

"How is hot and sexy not your type?" Sadie wanted to know.

She turned around to find everyone listening. Great. "Well," she said, brain whirling. "He's pushy. And arrogant. And . . ." And smart. And sexy. And he liked to kiss everything, and she did mean everything. Which wasn't exactly a fault . . .

Molly was watching her carefully and raised a brow.

Kylie swallowed hard and shook her head. "He's bossy." She tossed up her hands. "And okay, maybe just a little bit *really* hot and sexy." She strained to think of more insults to cancel out the hot and sexy but realized that suddenly every one of her friends had gotten an identical funny look on her face. *Crap.* "He's right behind me, isn't he."

"Yep," Willa said cheerfully.

Kylie closed her eyes briefly before swiveling in her barstool.

Joe was indeed standing right there. "I wouldn't say we're just friends," he told her.

"What would you say?" Willa wanted to know. "For the record."

"For the record . . ." He wrapped his fingers around Kylie's hand. "I'd say none of your business."

Willa sighed as Joe tugged Kylie outside.

Chapter 20

#IllHaveWhatShesHaving

Joe pulled Kylie along with him through the court-yard, past the water fountain, and right into the alley.

Old Man Eddie was sitting on a crate, feet up, head tilted back, watching the stars. At the sight of them, he sat up straight and waved.

"Need to borrow the alley for a moment," Joe said and slid him a twenty.

Eddie grinned, pocketed it, and saluted him. "Take as many minutes as you need, soldier."

And then they were alone. Joe watched as Kylie went through her bag of tricks and pulled out the red wig.

"What's that for?" he asked as she put it on.

"It's my superhero cape," she said. "I'm a little brave, but Red's *all* the way brave. She can handle anything. If we're going to talk about what just happened, I really need my superhero cape. I mean, I'd rather have an invisibility cloak, but beggars can't be choosers."

She was crazy. In the very best way, and he let out a low, rough laugh.

"Are you laughing at me?" she asked.

"With you," he said. "Always with you."

"But I'm not laughing."

He did his best to dial the good humor back. "Kylie, given what I do for a living and my family life, how many times a day do you think I actually laugh?"

"I . . ." She sighed, dropped her 'tude, and shook her head. "I don't know."

"Approximately never," he admitted. "Unless I'm with you." And that was the *real* admission. "So I'm not going to apologize for enjoying the hell out of your company."

"Even though I said you were pushy and arrogant? And don't forget bossy."

"Yes, but you also said I was hot and sexy."

"I did, but if you must know, it's really annoying," she said.

He laughed because she didn't look annoyed at all, and he stepped in to her so that even a sheet of paper couldn't have fit between them, palming the back of her head to protect her from the brick. He couldn't stop himself from touching her. And now that he'd had her naked and writhing for him, he knew he wasn't going to be able to get her out of his head either.

Deep down he knew he shouldn't have done it, shouldn't have slept with her. He'd known this, but he'd wanted her so badly she'd become way too big a distraction to ignore. Stupidly he'd assumed that would end immediately after.

Nothing had ever backfired on him quite so spectacularly, because now he wanted her more than ever before. Even just standing here with her in that wig flashed memories of her he couldn't control. Her lips on his skin, her breath hot on his neck, her legs wrapped around him, her hardened nipples pressing tight against his chest as she arched up into him. And her gasp when he'd moved deep inside her . . . *God.* The low, sexy sounds she'd made as she'd come had been his complete undoing, and the memories combined with what she'd said about him in the pub had him turned on all over again.

"I thought we weren't going to do this," she murmured, her eyes her own twin pools of fathomless emotion. "Give in to any real feelings. Thought you couldn't."

He was an inch from saying *screw that* when someone spoke behind them.

"I know I was supposed to vanish," Old Man Eddie said apologetically, "but I went around to the other alley behind Reclaimed Woods and there was an envelope leaning up against the back door with Kylie's name on it. Thought she'd want it."

Kylie stared at the envelope without moving, maybe without breathing, so Joe took it from Eddie. "Did you see who left it?" he asked.

"Nope, and it's wet from the rain like maybe it's been there a while. I didn't want it to get ruined." Eddie's smile faded as he took in their expressions. "What's wrong?"

"Nothing," Joe said. "Thanks for thinking to bring it to her."

Eddie, not taking his gaze off Kylie, nodded. "You got it." He slid a look at Joe, brows up, silently asking if Joe was going to take care of their girl. Joe nodded and Eddie backed out of the alley.

"Open it," Kylie said.

He did and revealed a pic of her penguin on a workbench, with someone holding a lit Bic at the penguin's feet. On the back of the pic were a few scribbled words.

You're running out of time.

"I am," Kylie said. "Running out of time."

"We're going to get your penguin back," Joe said firmly. "Before the deadline."

She looked up at him with those melting eyes of hers and he found himself cupping her jaw, stroking her skin with his fingers. "We will," he said firmly, wanting her to believe.

Eyes still locked on his, she nodded.

He nodded too and then took her by the hand to walk her through the courtyard. Kylie slowed at the fountain and looked into the water.

"What are you doing?" he asked.

Instead of answering, she pulled a coin from a

pocket and closed her eyes for a moment, about to toss the coin into the water.

Joe stopped her. "What are you doing?"

She looked at him. "Do you know about the fountain's myth?"

It wasn't a secret. The myth went that if one wished for true love with a true heart, they'd find it. Good thing Joe didn't have a true heart. Or a heart at all, at least not a working one.

"So you do know," she said, watching his expression carefully.

"Something about true love, blah blah blah," he said with a shrug. "Why?"

She let out a small smile, and this brought a reluctant one of his own because she never failed to make him feel things, whether he wanted to or not. "What does the fountain have to do with your penguin?" he asked.

"I'm going to wish for its return."

"Yeah, I'm pretty sure it doesn't work like that. It's about love."

"Well, I love that penguin," she said stubbornly and tossed the coin, which hit the water with a soft *plop*.

"So you wished for the penguin?" he asked cautiously. "Not for love for yourself?"

She went brows up and he knew he'd given himself away.

"Are you *afraid* of the myth?" she asked incredulously.

"Of course not." Actually, he was terrified. Because

not one, not two, not three or even four, but *five* people he knew had been bitten by the love bug in the past two years and *all* were directly linked to wishes from this very fountain. He stared at the coin she'd tossed, shimmering beneath the water's surface, mocking him. "Just tell me that you really did wish for the penguin," he said, because out of everyone he knew, she had the truest heart of them all. So if she'd just wished for love, they were both screwed.

She smiled, and he had one thought. He was so screwed.

"You were taking me somewhere," she reminded him, stepping closer. "By the way you dragged me out of the pub, you were clearly in a big hurry, too."

He gazed down at her in that red wig, unable to keep his hands from going to her hips in order to hold her to him. "We had unfinished business," he said.

"So finish it," she dared him.

His heart skipped a full heartbeat as he tightened his grip on her hand to lead her up the stairs to the second floor, where he disarmed Hunt Investigations' alarm and let them into the dark offices before resetting the alarm.

His office was the first door on the right. He could've found it with no light at all, but there was some ambient glow coming in through the closed shades on his window. He shut and locked that door and then turned to Kylie.

She was unbuttoning her coat. After letting it fall to the floor, she hoisted herself up onto his desk. "Nice work space," she said casually, looking around, as if she hadn't just laid herself out like a buffet for a starving man.

He moved to stand between her legs and placed his hands flat on the desktop on each side of her hips. "If I'd known we might end up here," he said, "I'd have cleaned it up."

She smiled and wrapped her legs around him, locking her ankles at the small of his back. "Liar. You don't care what anyone thinks of you."

That was true. He'd never cared what anyone thought of him. But he found he did care what *she* thought. With one hand, he swept his things to the floor. The other moved to her ass to anchor her to him.

A sound escaped from deep in her throat. She'd enjoyed the Neanderthal move and that did something to him too. With her, he could be himself— good mood, bad mood, riled-up mood, whatever. He didn't have to control himself for her. Ever.

Yet another huge turn-on.

She tilted her face to his, but then, just as he leaned in to kiss her, she pulled back an inch.

"What?" he whispered, fascinated by her, all of her.

She gave a single shake of her head. "I was pretty determined not to like you. But I keep learning new things about you. Things I like."

He half smiled. "Even though I'm pushy and arrogant and . . . what else was it you said? Bossy?"

Her lips twitched. "Definitely bossy. Maybe you should repeat them out loud every day to work on them."

"Sure," he said easily. "If you say something out loud for me."

"What?"

"My name." He nipped her ear and whispered into it, "I'm going to make you scream it, Kylie."

He heard the breath stutter in her chest. "I'm not much of a screamer," she whispered.

"A challenge." He slid a hand beneath the hem of her shirt and encountered warm, creamy, smooth skin. He stroked his way north until his fingertips brushed lace. Picking her up, he turned to the couch against the far wall.

"What are you doing?" she asked, clutching at him.

"I want to be horizontal this time."

"But . . . here?"

"Most definitely here."

"Your desk phone," she gasped. "You knocked it off the hook."

"Later."

"You have a candy bar. It's on the floor too, which seems like a big waste of a really good candy bar—"

"It's okay," he said. "I know something that's going to taste even better than a candy bar." He licked the sensitive skin beneath her ear and she let out a shuddery moan. Dropping her to the couch, he reached for her shirt, tugged it up, and pulled it over her head to reveal the chocolate brown lace of her bra. "Pretty." In another second he discovered that her barely-there panties matched.

No chocolate required . . .

"Hurry," she whispered, her voice a soft plea as she reached up for him. He was lowering himself over her when from his back pocket, his cell vibrated. He dropped his forehead to her gorgeous breasts and gulped in a breath.

"It might be urgent," she said, her hands in his hair.

No doubt. But it'd been a text and not a call, so he decided it couldn't be that important. "I don't care." Unhooking her bra, he drew it away from her, feeling his heart quicken at the sight of her sprawled beneath him. "Everything else can wait a minute."

She put a hand to his chest. "And if I need more than a minute?"

"You get all the minutes you need." His hand slid down to grip her sweet little ass, pulling her closer into the cradle of his thighs.

"Mmm, you want me," she said breathlessly, squirming against the part of him that wanted her the most of all. Her eyes were shining with triumph, humor, and her own need.

Damn, he was such a goner for her. "I do." He lifted his head to brush a kiss over her bare shoulder and then the underside of her jaw. "And I want you bad, too."

With a dreamy sigh, she tipped her head back, humming in pleasure as he trailed his mouth down her throat. Over her collarbone. The tip of her breast, which he drew into his mouth, making her arch up with a gasp as his tongue rasped her nipple.

Her hands slid into his hair, tightening on the strands. "Don't stop."

Never was his first thought, his fingers teasing her through her panties until they were wet. Then he hooked his thumbs into the straps. "You're not going to be needing these," he said and slowly drew the tiny scrap of material down her legs.

"Your clothes too," she panted. "Off."

"And you think *I'm* the bossy one." He rose to his knees over her naked body and peeled his T-shirt over his head while her fingertips skimmed his chest and stomach, wreaking havoc on his self-control. Knowing she had to touch him every bit as much as he had to touch her drove him crazy in the very best way. Bending over her, he took a nibble of her hip, then a rib, making her squirm. Gently, he closed his teeth around her nipple and tugged, and she tightened her grip in his hair. That made it difficult to remove the rest of his clothes but he managed, kicking everything off.

Kylie came up on an elbow to watch and reached for him the minute he was finished, her legs parting for him. And as he first protected them both with a condom and then made himself comfortable between her thighs, he felt a deep sense of . . . coming home. There was no other way to describe it as he slid into her.

"Kylie," he said, staring down at her. "Look at me."

She opened her eyes and revealed so much emotion that he felt his throat go tight. He kissed her then, hungrily drinking in the little noises she made in her throat as he began to move deep inside her. He tried to hold it together, but she was so tight, so wet, so hot that he thought he was going to blow right then. But somehow he managed to hold on through her first orgasm. He barely reined it in, but he didn't want this to be just a release like the first time they'd been together. He wanted to show her what was in his heart.

Except his heart had way too many walls up for that, even now, so he had to settle for showing her how much she pleased his body. And he thought, given the way she clung to him after, that maybe he'd given her that.

Much, much later, Kylie rolled over in her dark bedroom and heard a soft growl. "Oops, sorry," she whispered to Vinnie and rolled the other way, this time coming up against a different roadblock, one of the human variety. She reached out with a hand. Yep. A naked, hard, warm human body.

"Mmph," said that naked, hard, warm body, the one that had taken her to new heights and back. It reminded her that Joe had brought her home after they'd . . . well, decimated his office. No other word for it. And afterward, still hungry for each other, they'd ended up here, in her bed.

Now Joe reached out and wrapped his arms around her. She thought he'd get up, pull his clothes on over that amazing body, and walk it out her door.

But he didn't. Instead, he pulled her in close, pressed his face into the crook of her neck, and sighed heavily, his entire body relaxed. Sated.

"I didn't think you'd stay," she said.

"Tired."

She bit her lower lip because she didn't want to

mistake this for more than it was, something she could all too easily do if she let herself. "Thought maybe we were going back to separating church and state after, like last time."

"I can keep it in my pants if that's what you want," he said, voice low and husky.

"But you appear to sleep naked."

He let out a low laugh, but didn't move to get out of the bed. In fact, he didn't move at all. Vinnie did though. He came in hot and plopped down on top of them both, making his way to a spot in the crook of Joe's neck. It was a good choice. Kylie herself loved that spot. Rough with stubble, scented like a man, warm . . . With a smile, she closed her eyes and let herself drift off to sleep, safe and warm and wearing a ridiculous smile.

The next morning Kylie was in the shower when she felt the air pressure change. Then a hand, much larger than her own, took control of her washcloth. Joe's hands were slow and knowing as they glided over her body, making her heart pound as she melted into him.

Abandoning the washcloth, his slightly calloused fingers stroked her belly, and she shivered in spite of the hot water. When she tried to turn to face him, he held her still while continuing his delicious torture with his knowing fingers, until she'd flattened her hands on the tile in front of her, dropped her head back onto his shoulder, and let herself go. She was still shuddering when he pulled her hips back and entered her from behind, doing what he'd done the night before.

Taking her to heaven and back.

She was still in the afterglow when she finally showed up at work. Gib took one look at her face and closed his eyes.

"What?" she asked.

"So you and Joe *are* a thing."

"No," she said.

He gave her a *get real* look. "You decide that before or after you fucked him?"

She narrowed her eyes, some of her happy glow dimming. "You don't get to go there, Gib."

"He's going to hurt you, Kylie. He's not the right guy for you."

"I don't want to talk about it, not with you."

He looked pained. "Look, I screwed up, okay?"

She tossed up her hands. "What does that even mean?"

"It means I should've made my move sooner," he said.

"No kidding!"

He grimaced. "There was just never the right time—"

She laughed. Like really laughed, even when this caused Gib to frown.

"I don't see what's so amusing," he said.

"You had *years*, Gib."

"We were kids," he said. "And your grandpa did so much for me that I couldn't allow—"

"Come on," she said. "Be honest at least. When

push came to shove, you just weren't that into me. And no matter what I told myself, it was the same for me or I'd have made a move on you." She sighed and then reached for his hand because she didn't want to lose him from her life. She really didn't. He'd been an important part of it for a long time and life was too short. "It's okay," she said. "We're okay and we're going to stay okay. But this subject's closed. I'm going to get to work."

And that's just what she did. She went into the back and put her head down and concentrated on the mirror she needed to finish before Molly's birthday tomorrow, instead of dwelling on the fact that she had only a week left to find her penguin, one week until playtime—or until whatever she and Joe were doing—was over.

Chapter 21

#YouCantHandleTheTruth

The rest of the day was a blur for Kylie because she was so swamped with work. Whether due to guilt or otherwise, Gib had once again passed some new jobs on to her, leaving her in the throes of no less than five different projects. It was both wonderful and overwhelming but at least things were status quo between them.

By lunchtime, her brain was flatlining, so she took off her apron, dusted off as much as she could, and grabbed Vinnie, heading out to the courtyard to clear her head.

At the fountain, she sat on a bench. Vinnie lifted his little leg on a bush and then came to sniff at the water.

"Careful," she warned him. Not too long ago he'd gotten brave and had jumped in. Only problem was that because of his squat build and heavy head, he couldn't swim. Panic had ensued until she'd rescued him.

But smart and bright as he was, he was also over-confident and believed himself invincible—hence the reminder. "No swimming," she said.

He snorted and then ran in circles for a solid two minutes, doing his best roadrunner impression until suddenly he ran out of gas and flopped at Kylie's feet, panting in exhaustion.

Kylie shook her head and stared at the fountain. As she'd told Joe the night before, the legend was clear. Wish for love with a true heart and love would find you.

But legends were made up. Fantasies. Except . . . there really had been a lot of love stories to happen right here in this building in the past few years, several of them involving her good friends, and all could be traced back to wishing on this very fountain.

Last night when she'd wished for her penguin, she'd actually been tempted to wish for something else altogether, and how scary was that? She would've liked to wish for Joe to openly look at her the way he sometimes did when he thought she wasn't watching, his warm gaze making her hot and mushy at the same time, his expression telling her she was more than just sex to him, that maybe there *were* real feelings, feelings that could go deep, deeper than she'd ever allowed before.

Not that she'd wish away the sex though, especially since thoughts of that alone could give her a hot flash. The images were implanted, his just-for-her smile barely curving his lips, that hard, honed body taking hers however he wanted—because let's face it, any way he wanted had been pretty damn amazing so far, especially when he used his tongue to—

"Now see, you gotta actually toss in a coin," came a craggy voice, and something hit the water. A coin.

Kylie's head whipped around to stare at Old Man Eddie. He grinned at her. "Hope you wished for something good, darlin'," he said. "Would hate to see that penny go to waste."

"I . . . I can't believe you did that."

He shrugged. "You were standing here in indecision for so long that Vinnie fell asleep." He pointed to her dog, who was still curled up on the sun-warmed cobblestones at her feet, snoring like a buzz saw. "What did you wish for?" he asked.

Oh good God. She'd just wished for more wild sex with Joe. She stared at Eddie and he gave her a slow, sly grin.

"So it's like that, is it? Who's the lucky fellow?"

"No. No, no, no," she said. "It doesn't count since *I* didn't throw the coin. You did."

Old Man Eddie just smiled.

"Oh come on," she said. "Surely there are rules!"

"Don't know, darling." He shrugged. "I'm not much of a rule man myself."

"Well, I'm certain there are rules, lots of them." She told herself not to panic. "And anyway, the legend is about true love and that's not what I was thinking about, so it's not going to happen. Right? *Tell me I'm right.*"

He laughed. "I don't know that either, but I'd give more than a penny to know what you wished for to put that look on your face."

"Oh my God." She whirled back to the water, determined to climb in and remove the penny. Only . . . there were a bunch of pennies in there and she could no longer remember exactly which one she'd seen Eddie toss in. And what if she removed the wrong one? What then? Would that mean she'd erase someone else's wish? She couldn't do that. She couldn't live with herself if she did that. "Which one was it?" she demanded, stepping closer to the fountain. "I'm not sure . . ."

"What isn't she sure about?"

This was from Molly, who was walking by with Willa and Elle, all three carrying bags from O'Riley's Pub.

"Welp," Eddie said, rocking back on his heels, flashing Kylie a mischievous smile. "I believe our Kylie here just made a wish that she's second-guessing right about now."

Kylie stared at him. "But you're the one who tossed the coin!"

"Details," he said on a shrug. "Fact is, a wish was made, and it had you blushing big-time too. I'm thinking it must've been about someone whose name rhymes with—"

"No!" Kylie rushed to say, not wanting to go there.

Eddie grinned. "Exactly. His name rhymes with *no*."

Willa and Elle laughed. Molly looked speculative.

Kylie sighed. "I'm walking away now."

"Kylie."

She turned back to face Molly, who held out one of the brown bags. "I was going to drive this out to Joe, who's stuck babysitting a witness and is starving. But I've got a meeting. Maybe you wouldn't mind?"

Kylie looked at Elle and Willa, who were both suddenly very busy on their phones. "Um—"

"Great, thanks!" Molly said, and then before Kylie knew it, she was holding the bag and a hastily scribbled address on a napkin.

"What just happened?" Kylie asked Eddie when the women were gone.

Eddie laughed. "I think it'll be much more fun watching you figure it out."

The address on the napkin was a building only a few blocks away, so she and Vinnie walked. Or rather, Kylie walked, carrying Joe's lunch *and* the lazy Vinnie.

She ended up in front of a building in Pacific Heights that appeared to be a large Victorian home divided into four residences. Just outside the main entrance was Joe's truck.

With Joe in it.

He wore dark mirrored shades and a backward ball cap and—thanks to that and the window tinting, it was hard to see his expression as she walked up to the front of the vehicle. She hesitated, unsure whether to go to the driver's side in the street or to the passenger side. She didn't want to impose. She just wanted to drop off his lunch.

Oh, who was she kidding. He looked hot as hell

and she wanted to climb into that truck and onto his lap and—

He leaned over and opened the passenger door for her. Shaking off her fantasy, she walked over to him.

He was in his usual work gear of cargos, a Hunt Investigations T-shirt and a windbreaker, which she now knew was mostly to hide the guys' weapons and make them seem less threatening.

In Joe's case, it only made him look all the more badass.

"You busy?" she asked.

"Babysitting a witness as a favor to an attorney we do a lot of work for," he said. "The guy's not in any danger, except he's a flight risk. Lucas is in the back alley watching the only other exit. No one ever slips past Lucas. Get in."

She'd discovered she didn't much like him telling her what to do—unless she was naked—but she got into the truck with Vinnie and handed Joe the brown bag. "From Molly," she said.

He went brows up and ignored the bag, reaching for Vinnie instead, holding the dog up so that they could look at each other nose-to-nose. Vinnie panted in sheer joy and bicycled his little legs in the air, trying to get closer to lick his new favorite person.

One hundred percent, Kylie understood the urge.

Joe set Vinnie in his lap, where Vinnie turned in three circles—making Joe wince at the paw placement—and plopped down for a happy snooze.

Then and only then did Joe look inside the bag. "Chicken wings and fries. Nice."

"Molly said she was supposed to bring you lunch."

Joe stared at her and then pulled out his phone. He didn't greet whoever answered, just listened for a moment before saying, "You're going to want to watch your back. Paybacks are a bitch."

"Paybacks are a bitch?" Kylie repeated when he disconnected. "Who was that?"

"My meddling sister."

"Your . . ." She stared at him. "Are you telling me that they set me up?"

"They?"

"Molly and Elle and Willa," she said. "And Eddie and the damn fountain!"

This was the second time he'd looked alarmed at the mention of the fountain. "Come on," she said. "Stop kidding me about being afraid of that thing."

"Who's kidding?" he asked, sounding genuine. "And you should be afraid too. You know the stories. Finn and Pru. Willa and Keane. Max and Rory. Spence and Colbie. Archer and Elle." He shook his head. "And Archer is the badass of all the badasses. If he didn't stand a chance, *no one* stands a chance. No one, Kylie."

Now that she knew he was serious, some of his concern began to seep into her. Okay, *all* of his concern. "It was only a penny. A penny! You can't even buy anything for a penny these days, so—"

"Are you telling me you really made a wish for true love with me?"

"No!" She bit her lower lip. "Not exactly, anyway."

"Then what exactly?"

"It was a fantasy, okay? Sheesh!" She tossed up her hands. "And I didn't even mean to!"

"Kylie, what did you wish for?"

She blew out a breath. "Sex. With you. You happy now?"

His eyes softened with good humor *and* heat as he smiled. A Big Bad Wolf smile. "Very."

"Don't let it go to your head," she warned without thinking. "Wait. I mean—"

Too late. He laughed his rare, full-on laugh, the one that never failed to make her smile.

"Oh, forget it," she said on a sigh and opened the O'Riley's bag. "Since this whole lunch thing was a complete sham, you're going to share."

They ate in easy companionship while Joe kept one eye on the building he was watching for work. After a few minutes, a bunch of kids poured out of a school a block down.

"Were you a good student?" she asked, wanting to know more about him.

He snorted. "No."

"What was your favorite class?"

"Recess."

"Did you go to college?" she asked.

He slid her a look. "We playing twenty questions?"

"I'm trying to get to know you."

His mouth quirked. "You know me."

She rolled her eyes. "I know your *body*."

"And you like it," he said, smug.

Actually, she loved his body, every single hard, toned, perfect inch. And he knew it, too. But fine, if he wanted to go there, she'd go there. "How about an easier question. Like, what's your favorite sexual position?"

He cut those eyes to her, an intimate smile playing on his lips now, and she poked his arm. "Come on, surely you know this one. I'll tell you mine if you tell me yours."

He leaned in and dropped his voice to a pitch that sent tingles down her spine. "I already know yours."

She felt her face heat and broke the eye contact first. Scrambling, she tried to think of a new question, one that would knock that predatory expression off his face before she did something stupid—like jump his bones.

"I was an okay student," he said, surprising her into looking at him again as he answered her earlier question. "It wasn't that the work was hard. I got A's on the tests, but I didn't do the homework, which brought my grades down." He paused. "And recess wasn't really my favorite class. It was science."

"Yeah?" she asked. "Why?"

"Because I had a crush on my hot-as-hell teacher. Mrs. Jones." He smiled in fond memory and she actually felt a little jealous, which made him laugh and tug at a strand of her hair.

"We going to check out the last apprentice on our list tonight?" she asked, desperate for a subject change.

"Yes," he said. "I'll call you."

She nodded and reached for a sleepy Vinnie, her fingers grazing Joe's thighs as she did. He met and held her gaze while she scooped the dog, doing her best not to look like she enjoyed it. "See ya," she said. She'd meant to say it breezily but it came out embarrassingly breathless.

She'd walked all the way back to work before she realized she still had no idea what would happen once they found her penguin, if they even did.

Would they take this thing wherever it led them?

Or would they go back to ignoring each other?

And which did she want? Okay, so she knew what *she* wanted. But given how she knew he felt about relationships, hell if she'd ask for it.

Chapter 22

#StupidIsAsStupidDoes

The rest of the day turned out to be interminably long for Joe. After his surprise lunch with Kylie, he'd had to put out fire after fire at work. He'd begun his day at five a.m. that morning and he didn't head out until seven that night. He figured he'd grab some food and Kylie, and then they'd check out the last apprentice.

But Archer showed up in his doorway, dressed to go.

Dressed meaning armed to the teeth.

And Joe knew he was not done with work.

"Need you," Archer said.

Which was how Joe found himself also armed to the teeth and heading out with the guys. The client they were serving was a big commercial property contractor who'd hired Hunt Investigations because expensive pieces of equipment kept going missing from a renovation project in a financial district building. A week ago, anticipating the next heist, Joe and Lucas had hidden a transmitter on each of the remaining expensive pieces of equipment at high risk of being stolen.

Sure enough, tonight the transmitter had alerted them to a piece of equipment on the move when it shouldn't have been. They raced to the job site, where it all went down surprisingly fast but dirty. They found the equipment foreman himself stealing the small backhoe loader by literally driving it off the job site. They hauled him out of the machine, but at the last moment he must've realized this was the end for him. He objected by pulling a knife from nowhere and nearly gutting Joe. When that didn't stop the takedown, the dickwad then produced a grenade.

A fucking grenade.

Joe and Lucas both dove for it. Lucas shoved him out of the way and opened the trash chute. Joe was able to grab the grenade and throw it in. The explosion was contained—well, mostly. Neither Lucas nor Joe got fully clear and took unintended twin twenty-five-foot flights through a sheet of drywall, landing hard on a stack of demo wood.

All of which had to be explained to more than one responding agency, and that ate up another few hours.

After, Joe sat shirtless on the table in the staff room of their office with Archer checking him over to get a better look at the knife wound in his side.

"This needs stitches." His tone was harsh and he wasn't particularly gentle when he wiped at the cut with an alcohol pad.

"Just stick a Band-Aid on it," Joe said.

Archer spent a minute cleaning off the blood before speaking. "It wouldn't have been the end of the world to go to a hospital."

Yeah, it would have. Joe had spent far too many hours in hospitals. His job was dangerous so there'd been his own visits here and there, but that wasn't what had gotten him. It'd actually been all the time he'd been in waiting rooms. In his earlier years it'd been watching his mom waste away, then later hoping his dad would come out of his various surgeries okay. Then more recently waiting on Molly and *her* surgeries. If he never set foot in another hospital again it would be too soon. "Just stitch me up like you did last time."

Archer swore beneath his breath. "Lucas would be better. His hands are steadier."

"Or Reyes," Lucas said from his perch on the couch. He had a few scrapes and bruises, but nothing major because he was indestructible and maybe also a superhero. "Reyes has smaller hands."

Reyes was standing at the window playing a game on his phone, his thumbs racing at the speed of light, though he slowed down enough to show Lucas his "smaller" middle finger. Reyes was also covered in blood. Not his—their bad guy's. Setting the game aside, he came to Joe and looked him over. "I could do it. I'd give you a badass scar too."

"No," Joe said to Archer. "He'll do something stupid like make the stitches in the shape of a heart just to fuck with me."

Lucas just grinned but got up when Archer gestured for him. He too bent over Joe critically, making him feel like a bug on a slide. "Yeah," Lucas said. "You definitely need stitches."

"No shit," Joe said and sighed with acceptance. "Just do it already."

Lucas exhaled a short breath, which for him was the equivalent of an exasperated sigh. He retrieved the necessary items from Hunt's medical kit—more extensive than most urgent care's medical kits—and set about closing the gash in Joe's side.

Molly walked in during this and stilled. "What happened?"

"I'm fine," Joe said though he was sweating bullets because goddamn, getting stitched hurt like a son of a bitch.

"You're not fine!" Molly said and glared at Lucas. "What are you doing to my brother?"

"Archer," Lucas said. "Get her out of here."

"Don't you dare," Molly said.

But Archer stepped in front of her.

She dodged him and came up next to Lucas to look Joe over. "Oh my God." She gripped Lucas by the front of the guy's shirt. She was five-foot-two. If you asked her, she'd tell you she was five-foot-four, but she was full of shit. Lucas was over six feet and yet he let her yank him down so that they were nose-to-nose.

"Be careful with him," she said.

Jesus. "I'm fine!" Joe said.

Neither Lucas nor Molly looked at him. Still nose-to-nose, they just stared at each other, some sort of weird, angsty chemistry going on that Joe couldn't read.

"Did you hear me?" Molly asked Lucas.

"Woman, the people in China heard you."

"Does he need a hospital?" she asked.

"No," Joe said.

Archer slid an arm around her. "He's going to be fine, I promise. Just a little scratch. I want you to wait outside—"

"I need to stay here."

"Archer," Lucas said again.

Archer nodded and spoke directly to Molly. "What you need, what we all need, is that bottle of Scotch you keep in your bottom drawer. Can you get that for me?"

Molly looked at Joe and he managed to give her a smile and a nod. She then looked at Lucas.

No words were exchanged, just another odd, inexplicable beat. Finally, Molly let out a breath and vanished.

Lucas stopped stitching to watch her go.

"Hey," Joe said. "Are you staring at my sister's ass?"

Lucas blinked. "What? No."

"Yes, you were."

"Then why did you ask?"

"There's no way in hell that Lucas is dumb enough

to stare at my office manager and your sister's ass," Archer said. "Right, Lucas?"

Since this wasn't really a question and Lucas clearly knew it, he nodded and got back to stitching.

It took twelve stitches, and when Lucas was done he cracked the cold pack from the box and handed it over. Joe held it to his throbbing side and hoped it would keep the swelling down. He had plans for the night.

"You want to tell me what the fuck happened back there?" Archer asked.

Joe shrugged. Or started to but then stilled because shrugging hurt like a son of a bitch. "What happened was that we got the job done."

Archer shook his head. "I haven't seen anyone get the drop on you like that in years."

Joe could deny it, but Archer was right. He'd been distracted and had lost his focus long enough that the guy was not only able to pull a weapon on him but actually do some damage with it. He couldn't even remember the last time that had gone down.

Archer just looked at him for a long moment. "Remember when someone got the drop on me and I was shot?"

"Last year, yeah," Joe said. "I remember distinctly because Elle nearly killed us all for letting you get hurt."

"My mind wasn't on the job. How many times has that happened?"

"Never," Joe said.

Archer nodded and waited for Joe to catch up.

"Shit," Joe said. "You think I screwed up because my mind was on Kylie?"

"There he is," Lucas said. "I was starting to worry he had a concussion."

Joe blew out a breath. "Shit," he said again.

Archer snorted. "Man, Elle so called this. I should never have bet her. You just cost me a hundred bucks."

Reyes started to sing "Another One Bites the Dust" beneath his breath.

Lucas was looking horrified at the thought of Joe letting his concentration down over a woman. "Aw, man. You should've just let the guy stab you in the gut. It would've been less painful."

Joe ignored this and looked at Archer. "It won't happen again."

"I'm counting on that being true," Archer said. "I assume you're aware that you broke at least two of his ribs after he got his knife in you."

And Joe would've broken the rest if Lucas hadn't pulled him away from the guy. "He pissed me off."

Archer gave a rare full smile. "Go to bed, Lover Boy. To *sleep*."

Smart idea. But as already proven when it came to Kylie, Joe wasn't all that smart. Which is why he slid into his truck and didn't drive home.

He drove to Kylie's.

He parked and lifted his shirt to get a look at his side. The swelling was actually minimal and Lucas's small, neat row of stitches wasn't readily visible—if he kept his shirt on, that is. He leaned his head back and drew in a long breath, then slowly, purposely let it out again.

It was one in the morning and he was exhausted. And for once, he didn't have a plan A. Or B. Or any plan at all. Maybe he'd just stay right here and stare at her place like a lovelorn teenager for the rest of the night.

But passive wasn't on his list of character traits so he got out of his truck and told himself it was okay to show up this late because her lights were on.

Kylie opened the front door to his knock. She was a little sweaty and breathless, wearing a sports bra and capri leggings, one in Day-Glo yellow, the other in Day-Glo pink, blinding him. "Hey. Whatcha doing?"

"That's my question to you," he said.

"Couldn't sleep." She leaned on the door, clearly out of breath.

"So you were . . . handling your own business?" he asked hopefully. "Maybe with your lightsaber?"

She rolled her eyes. "Why do guys always immediately go there?"

"Because we're all just hopeful sex addicts looking for our next fix." He nudged her aside and let himself in. That was when he saw the yoga mat on the floor in front of the TV, which was paused midshow, giving him his first laugh all day. "*Golden Girls*?"

"It's the only thing I haven't marathoned yet." She turned off the TV and looked him over, her smile fading a little bit. "You okay? You look a little singed around the edges."

"Work," he said and scrubbed a hand down his face. "It was a long night."

"Everyone else okay?"

"Yeah. Well, maybe not the bad guy. He wasn't feeling like going to jail."

She was wide-eyed. "So he . . . ?"

"Tried to blow me and Lucas up with a hand grenade. But all he got was a Dumpster. Oh, and himself."

"Oh my God," she said, looking horrified.

"Like I said, it was an interesting night."

Her eyes narrowed and she stepped closer, putting her hands on him, looking at his shirt. "Is that . . . blood?"

He looked down at his front. His black T-shirt had stuck to him where he'd bled like a stuck pig. Shit. "It's nothing, just a scratch."

Going pale, she began pushing up his shirt.

"Really," he said. "All I needed was a Band-Aid, but—"

"*Off,*" she demanded, and who was he to argue with a bossy woman who wanted his clothes off?

He carefully slid his arm through and pulled the shirt over his head. In the next minute, he found himself being pushed to sit in a kitchen chair with a warm, sexy woman bent over him. "Oh my God, how many stitches?"

"Not too many," he said.

"You went to the ER and they left you all covered in blood like this?"

Before he could answer, she was cleaning the blood off and fussing over him.

"Sloppy nursing," she said.

"Yeah, well, Lucas isn't exactly gentle and nurturing."

Her head snapped up. "Lucas? Your coworker Lucas? *He* stitched you up?"

"Good as new."

She was looking at him like he'd grown a second head. "What's wrong with you? What's wrong with a hospital?"

"Don't like them," he said. "But hey, Lucas was a medic. He's always stitching one of us up. He's good."

She shook her head, muttering something to herself about stubborn alphas. Their gazes met, and as if she could read his mind about why exactly he didn't like hospitals, her eyes suddenly softened as she continued cleaning him up.

The kitchen was warm, and so were her hands, and he was tired. So tired. Leaning back in the chair, he closed his eyes, enjoying the feel of her standing so close, her warm breath on his neck, the scent of her, which his body now responded to like Pavlov's dogs.

When she was finished, she bent low and kissed his skin just above the white gauze holding him together. He opened his eyes and met hers.

"Better?" she asked.

He put his hand over hers. "Much."

"So now what?" she asked quietly. "What do you need right now?"

That was easy. "You."

Her breath caught. "Okay. Come on then." She held out a hand and led him to her bed. And maybe, a part of him hoped, into her heart, as well.

Chapter 23

#HoustonWeHaveAProblem

The next night was Molly's birthday party at O'Riley's. Kylie was happy to take a night off from thinking about her life to celebrate. Finn and Sean decorated the pub, something they did for everyone's birthday, which meant they all did a lot of celebrating.

Tonight's Wild West theme was Kylie's favorite. It wasn't much of a stretch for the pub, which had whiskey barrel tables and a bar crafted from repurposed longhouse-style doors. Adding to the effect were the hanging brass lantern lights and the horse-chewed fence baseboards.

Everyone dressed the part. The girls had met up at lunch and hit their favorite costume shop around the corner. Kylie hadn't had the time so she'd just added a hat and boots to her jeans and plaid button-down, and called it good.

The birthday girl was dressed to the hilt as a lady of the night and was the center of attention, which she seemed to enjoy.

"You beat me to that one," Tina said about Molly's costume. Tina was wearing something that was probably supposed to be a lady of the night but instead more resembled Little Bo Peep—if Little Bo Peep had been six feet tall, mahogany-skinned, and gorgeous. "I'm trying not to hate you."

"Hey, I'm not getting any, okay?" Molly said, adjusting her corset. "I thought I'd up my game tonight."

"I'll up your game, baby," said a guy on the other end of the bar.

The guy's buddy shook his head. "Man, are you nuts? That's Joe's baby sister."

The first guy went pale, stammered an apology, and nearly ran out of the pub.

"Dammit, Joe!" Molly yelled.

Joe, across the room and involved in a mean game of darts with Caleb, Spence, and Lucas, looked over. "What?" he yelled back.

"Stop ruining my sex life!" his sister yelled.

With a grimace, Joe put his fingers in his ears and turned away.

Molly rolled her eyes. "He's not going to stop. He's giving me anxiety. I need some action. My lady bits need some action, people!" she said. "Someone needs to man up!"

"Thought you were going to try online dating," Elle said.

"I did. But it turns out there are a lot of frogs out there." Molly looked around the pub a little wistfully. "I mean, it's not like I'm asking for too much. All I want is a six-foot-plus guy who's funny, smart, respectful, outgoing, well dressed, loyal, honest, hardworking, and obsessed with me. Oh, and he should have great stubble too. Or a beard."

Elle snorted. "Well, if that's all."

"Hey," Molly said, pointing at Elle without taking her eyes off the crowd. "You don't get to judge. You're wearing a diamond ring that could blind the whole city."

They all looked at the ring Archer had put on Elle's finger. It could indeed light up all of San Francisco. Maybe the entire state of California.

"I know diamonds are supposed to be a girl's best friend," Willa said, "but then leggings happened. Leggings are the new diamonds." She looked at Tina with her perfect hair and makeup and sighed. "The fact that you wear extensions and false eyelashes astounds me because I can't even be bothered to put on real pants."

"Girls, that's just sad," Tina said. "You gotta use it or lose it."

"I'm going to really hope that's not true," Molly said.

"Well, no matter what happens, pizza will always be there for you," Tina said. "Through thick and thin, in crust we trust."

They all drank to that and then the chitchat turned to Haley, who'd had a blind date the night before. "How did it go?" Willa wanted to know. She had a vested interest since she'd set Haley up with a girl-friend of hers.

"Well," Haley said, playing with the condensation on her glass of wine. "Sober-me and drunk-me are no longer on speaking terms."

"Dammit," Willa said. "It didn't work out?"

"I didn't say that." Haley looked at Tina. "Use it or lose it, right?"

They high-fived.

Kylie's gaze crept back to Joe, still across the room in a game of darts with Spence and Lucas. Given their intensity, it had to be a pretty serious game, which was in complete opposition to the fact that they'd all dressed for the Western theme.

Spence was in jeans and a cowboy hat. So was Lucas, both looking extremely hot.

And then there was Joe. He too was in a hat, but his was a backward baseball cap topped with dark sunglasses he'd shoved up there and clearly forgotten about. He wore an open flannel plaid shirt in dark blues over a white T-shirt and a pair of old, clearly beloved jeans well-worn in the stress points, and even from across the room it was obvious that he had some pretty excellent stress points.

She couldn't tear her gaze off him.

As if he felt her looking at him, he lifted his head and locked gazes with her. They hadn't spoken since he'd left her that morning still wet from their shower, naked and panting and practically purring.

His mouth curved in a barely-there smile and she felt her face heat.

Next to her, Archer and Elle were arguing over his

order, which had just arrived. "Look," he was saying, "I love you but I asked you what you wanted and you said nothing, so I ordered wings. The exact amount of wings I wanted to eat."

Elle narrowed her eyes. "But I only want a few—"

"*Exactly* the right amount, Elle."

She paused. "Okay, but I want you to remember this because later when you want to get lucky, I'm going to tell you that you're S-O-L because I've already had all the lucky I want today."

Archer opened his mouth, but she held up a finger. "*Exactly* the right amount," she said.

He stared at her and then laughed and hauled her onto his lap. Elle smiled and grabbed a wing, making *yummy* sounds as she ate it. Archer watched her, then leaned in and licked the sauce off the corner of her mouth, making his own *yummy* noise.

"Is that what love is?" Molly asked the room. "Sharing food when you don't want to?"

"Yeah," Kylie said softly. And it was also letting someone in when maybe you hadn't meant to. Again her gaze sought out Joe and again he looked at her right back, not bothering to hide it. He clearly spent zero time worrying about what anyone around them thought. It wasn't a problem for him.

Nope, his problem was that he didn't want to let love in.

Which of course had somehow, when she hadn't been looking, become *her* problem.

Later, after they'd all finished eating, Molly opened her presents. When she got to Joe's and unwrapped the gorgeous mirror Kylie had made, she went stock-still before lifting suspiciously sheeny eyes to Joe.

"It's the right one, yes?" he asked in the universal voice of male panic when a woman appeared to be on the verge of tears.

"Yes, you idiot," she said and then limped her way closer and threw herself at him.

"Okay." Joe patted her on the back. "Okay, then."

"Such an idiot," Molly muttered and held on.

He grimaced. "Are you crying or drooling?" he asked, trying to break free.

"An asshole idiot." Molly only held him all the tighter. "I love you, you big jerk." She pulled back and gave him a shove.

And *that,* clearly, Joe knew how to deal with. He didn't budge, of course, but he did laugh and looked greatly relieved that his sister was over her moment.

Anyone could see that they had a close, strong relationship. But sometimes, like now, Kylie also caught glimpses of an odd, nameless tension between the two of them that she didn't quite understand.

After the last present had been unwrapped, everyone scattered, to dance or play pool or get another drink. Molly plopped next to Kylie.

"You can take the boy off the street," she said, "but you can't take the street out of the boy. He really hates it when I get all emotional over him."

"You like to bait him," Kylie said.

Molly shrugged. "It's my civic duty as his sister, right? You have any siblings?"

"No," Kylie said. She'd often wished for a sister or a brother, someone to share the load with, someone with the same blood so she'd always have them at her back. Friends like Molly, Elle, Pru and all the others had filled the gap for her, but deep down there was a hole where family should be.

Molly was watching Joe. "He pretends he's so tough, but I'm his kryptonite. Thanks for making that gorgeous mirror for him to give to me."

"He paid for it."

"Of course he did," Molly said. "Joe knows better than most that nothing comes free. Not even friendship—or whatever it is that you two are really up to. My point is that he'd never expect anything from you."

Kylie knew this. She wasn't sure how she felt about it. "Friends do stuff for friends."

"Not where we come from," Molly said. "My dad told me he met you. He also told me you're going to be the one to bring Joe to his knees."

Something deep inside Kylie reacted to that. She wanted to say it was denial. And maybe a week ago it would've been. Deep, dark, head-in-the-sand denial. But today, right now, after all the things she and Joe shared, all the intimacy . . . it wasn't denial at all.

It was hope, which was infinitely more dangerous.

Chapter 24

#IllBeBack

Molly glanced at Kylie. "You look like you either just swallowed a bee or had an epiphany."

Kylie managed a laugh, but yeah. She'd just had a hell of an epiphany.

She was falling for Joe.

So not good and so not smart, but before she could freak out about it too badly there were some cheering and a few groans across the bar.

Joe had won at pool.

"Yeah," Molly said, laughing wryly as her brother collected cash for his victory. "Definitely the street rat in him still comes out here and there. He can't change *everything*."

Kylie tore her gaze off Joe and looked at Molly. "Change? What has he changed?"

She shrugged. "Growing up, he was always . . . well, untamed."

"Don't see how that's changed at all," Kylie said dryly.

Molly laughed. "Trust me, he's definitely mellowed, a lot. Oddly enough, the military did that for him. Or to him. Same with working at Hunt. He's more focused now. Driven. And . . . caring."

"You guys are close. He cares about you very much."

"Yes," Molly said. "But a good part of that is guilt."

"Guilt?"

Molly hesitated and then pushed her beer away. "Okay, clearly I've hit my quota."

"Guilt?"

Molly grimaced and looked away. "It's an old, long story from before we both changed—for the better, I should add." She shifted her bad leg and grimaced again.

"I'm sorry," Kylie said. "It's clearly a painful story and none of my business—"

"He blames himself," Molly said.

"For what?"

Molly was quiet a moment and then she sighed. "I see how he looks at you, you know. And you're my friend, but . . ." She hesitated. "Don't hurt him, okay? Only I get to do that."

"I'm not going to hurt him," Kylie said. "To be honest, I'm not sure I even could. And in any case, it's not like that between us."

"Come on."

"It's not," Kylie said, knowing she sounded defensive but, well, she *felt* defensive since even she didn't believe herself. Because they *were* like that, at least somewhat. But she'd meant what she'd said. She didn't think she had the ability to hurt Joe. He held too much of himself back for that.

"We all watched him drag you out of here the other night," Molly said. "After you tried to say you weren't anything to each other. I know you're sleeping together."

"Well, not *sleeping* exactly." Kylie bit her lower lip. "Except maybe once or twice, but those times don't count because he didn't come over until really late. And it's not like he keeps stuff at my place. The few things he's got there are a toothbrush and a T-shirt, and the T-shirt's only because I stole it and—"

"Wait," Molly said in shocked disbelief. "Are you telling me that my brother Joe-the-lone-wolf slept at your house? As in eyes closed, mouth open, snoring, lost in *z*-land?"

"Actually, I don't think he snores—"

"But he left a toothbrush at your place," Molly said.

"Well, yeah, cuz that's just good manners, brushing your teeth in the morning, right?"

Molly was just staring at her, mouth agape. "Okay, let me get this straight. You're saying that Joe actually spent the night with you. Like you woke up and he was still there."

Kylie nodded, an odd feeling beginning to tighten in her chest. "Why? What's so weird about his staying with me? Is it because you don't think I'm good enough—"

"No. *No*," Molly rushed to say firmly, taking

Kylie's hand. "I promise, it's not anything to do with you and *everything* to do with Joe and who he's been for so long that I didn't think he had it in him to adjust. And actually . . ." She smiled. "Okay, so it is about you a little bit, but in the very best way." She paused and cocked her head. "Do you guys talk a lot?"

"Not exactly."

"Yeah. He's not much for words, is he?"

Kylie managed a laugh. "No, he's much more of a show-don't-tell guy."

"But see, that's the thing," Molly said earnestly. "He's usually not all that good at showing either. Or he hasn't been. Not with anyone. He doesn't do emotions or feelings easily."

"I'm getting that," Kylie said. "What I'm not getting is why."

Molly looked around them. The pub was crowded and yet no one was paying them any attention. Seemingly relieved, she turned back to Kylie. "He won't ever tell you," she said quietly, "but it's not his fault he's this way. It's . . . mine."

Confused, Kylie shook her head. "Is this about the guilt thing?"

"Yes. Our dad, he's better now than he used to be, but when we were growing up, his PTSD was really bad. He'd act . . . oddly. Paranoid. If we weren't home by dark, he locked us out. Literally. As in he'd bolt the place up and nothing and no one could get in, whether we were inside or not."

Kylie tried to imagine what that had been like for

the siblings, especially in the neighborhood they'd grown up in, but couldn't. "That must have been terrifying for you. And dangerous."

Molly nodded. "Very, but it wasn't Dad's fault, really. He just wasn't . . . present. And he had a hard time keeping jobs because of it. So Joe was motivated at a young age to provide. He learned some interesting skills, such as how to break us into the house so we didn't have to sleep outside, among other things." She paused. "Like shoplifting to keep us fed."

Kylie's heart squeezed. "I'm so sorry. No kid should have to go through that."

"At least we had each other." Molly looked across the crowded bar and out the windows into the night. "But obviously, we lacked supervision. That's how it happened."

"How what happened?" Kylie asked.

"When Joe was young—and stupid—he got in with the wrong crowd. They wanted him to do bad stuff." She paused and met Kylie's gaze, her own hooded with bad memories. "Like I said, Joe's got skills. The kind of skills that are really great for felons. But that isn't Joe. He's one of those rare guys who's just all the way to the bone good, you know?"

Kylie nodded because she *did* know. "So he refused to do anything wrong."

Molly nodded, expression still troubled. "Yeah, but it didn't go over so well. They tried to force his hand."

"How?" Kylie asked. "Joe isn't the sort of guy to do anything he doesn't want to."

"Ha. So you *have* met my brother, aka Mr. Obstinate." Molly hesitated and then, when she spoke again, her voice was soft. "They tried to make him."

A chill went down Kylie's spine. "Made him how?" Her stomach sank. "Did they hurt him?"

"No." Molly reached for her drink again and downed it. "They hurt someone close to him."

Kylie met her gaze, her heart pounding. "You?"

Molly nodded and Kylie's heart sank hard. "Oh, Molly, I'm so sorry."

Molly shook her head. "It really wasn't his fault but I don't think he believes that. No one blames him, certainly not me." She shrugged, like she was mentally shucking off the memories, and though Kylie wished she knew the whole story, she didn't want to ask Molly to relive anything more than she already had.

"Look at them," Molly said, nudging her chin toward the dance floor where Archer and Elle were now dancing, swaying in a loose embrace.

Even from the distance of half the bar, Kylie could see how much Archer loved Elle. They kissed, his hands sliding up Elle's slim body, his usually very serious, intense face still very serious and very intense, but totally into Elle.

"If they can find love," Molly said, "it means anyone can find love."

"To be honest," Kylie said, "I don't think it's for me."

"Well, since I'm pretty sure it isn't for me either, I'm not the one to talk you into feeling otherwise. But I can admit, I'd hoped you and Joe might work out."

Kylie knew deep down she'd been hoping the same thing. But when she looked up again, Joe was at the pool table, being waylaid by a dark, gorgeous brunette. She had her hand on his forearm and was telling him something that was making him laugh.

Molly twisted to see what she was looking at. "Oh, that. Don't worry about Dee. She and Joe have been knocking boots together on and off since high school, but I'm pretty sure it's been a while."

Joe laughed again and something deep in Kylie's chest reacted. She stood up. "I think I'm calling it a night."

As if he could hear her, which wasn't possible over the noise of the bar, Joe looked up and their eyes met.

And then Kylie did something she'd told herself she wouldn't do anymore. She turned tail and ran. She got all the way to the street, where she was fumbling with her phone, trying to access her Uber app, when a hand reached out and turned her around to face a tall, deceptively stoic shadow with an achingly familiar face.

"Joe," she said, breathless from nerves. "Hey. Didn't see you."

"No? Not even when you were looking right at me in the pub?"

Okay, fine. He'd caught her. Whatever. She didn't want to get in a fight with him. She actually wanted to do the opposite after what Molly had told her. But sometimes her emotions were like a pack of wild horses.

Uncontrollable.

Joe ignored the storm she was sure he could see in her expression and silently directed her to his truck. He drove her home, got out, and walked her to her door. There, he took her keys and let them both in, after which he did a thorough check of her place before coming back to the living room. "The woman you saw," he said, "she's an old friend. We don't see each other anymore."

Sweet that he would offer the information without her asking, and even sweeter that he seemed to want to make sure she wasn't feeling jealous. "It's okay," she said. "The problem is me. But forget that. We don't need to talk about that."

"Okay, good." He stepped in to her and took her bag off her shoulder, which he then tossed onto the couch. "Talking isn't our strong suit anyway."

She snorted and he smiled, stroking a finger over her temple, tucking a strand of hair behind her ear. "Last chance, Kylie. Speak up or forever hold your peace."

Her heart skipped a beat. She wanted to get to their strong suit . . . oh how she wanted that. But she also wanted to ask about Molly before she lost her chance. Only she wasn't sure she had a right to his past. "I spent a few minutes with your sister tonight," she said quietly.

"Yeah," he said, nudging her back a step so he could shut the shades, closing them in against the rest of the world. Then he helped her out of her jacket, tossing that to the couch as well before stepping in to her, pressing his body to hers. "She loved the mirror," he said. "You're a genius."

Already breathless, she said, "It was your idea."

"Yeah, but it was your work. You do beautiful work," he murmured, kissing his way down her throat. "You've got great hands."

She snorted a laugh but her humor drained when she remembered the rest of her conversation with Molly.

Joe lifted his head and searched her expression, his own smile fading as well. "What is it? Something's on your mind."

"Now's probably not a good time to talk about it."

"Just say it, Kylie."

She drew in a ragged breath. "Molly told me what happened. When you guys were younger."

"Told you what?"

"How she was hurt so that you could be manipulated into doing something you didn't want to do."

He remained frozen in place for a single second before letting out a long exhalation and dropping his hands from her.

"I'm sorry," she said. "I shouldn't have brought it up."

Moving away, he turned to stare out her front window. "It was a long time ago."

"She said you blame yourself."

He made a rough sound in the back of his throat and she came up beside him, put a hand on his rigid arm, waited until he turned to meet her gaze. "She said you shouldn't, Joe. Blame yourself."

He closed his eyes and when he opened them, unlike his usual calm, his gaze was turbulent and filled with bad memories. "It *was* my fault," he said. "All of it. And I should go."

She didn't want to push him to talk about something that gave him pain. She didn't feel like she had any right to those bad memories, but if she could lessen his pain in any way, she wanted to. "Stay," she said softly. "Please?"

"I won't be good company," he warned.

"It's okay. I've got ice cream, a comfy spot in my bed just for you, and *Pretty Little Liars* on my DVR. We can watch a season ahead of your dad and then tell him spoilers." Then she held her breath for his answer, knowing without understanding exactly why that this was a turning point and if he left right now, there'd be no going back. She'd lose him.

Chapter 25

#YouHadMeAtHello

At Kylie's offer, Joe heard himself let out a rough laugh. She was looking up at him with those warm, loving eyes, the ones he was starting to realize he couldn't resist. "What kind of ice cream?"

With a smile, she turned to go into the kitchen, but he caught her hand and reeled her in. "Never mind the ice cream. All I need is you."

She gave him another soft smile and they sat on her couch together. "It's a long story," he warned. "And it's ugly. I messed things up. Badly. You sure you want to hear it?"

"I want to hear whatever you can tell me," she said, voice low and very serious, eyes matching the tone. "Always."

He rested his forehead against hers. "Molly's leg and back. That's all on me. All of it and worse."

He did his best not to think about that time in his life and he was good at it. He'd never told anyone about any of it. But this wasn't just anyone—this was Kylie—and he drew in a ragged breath. "I was stupid."

She opened her mouth but he shook his head at her and put a finger over her lips. "Shh," he said. "I'm going to tell you, but I don't need you to defend my dumb ass." He paused, remembering. "We lived in that shit neighborhood, and Molly . . ." He shook his head. "She'd drawn the attention of one of the asshole thugs hanging around. She was fourteen and I'd just turned seventeen. I'd gone along with the gang's stupidity up until then because they promised if I did, they'd leave Molly alone. I believed them. I shouldn't have. When they wanted me to steal a car and I refused, they took her. To persuade me."

"Oh, Joe," she whispered. "What did you do?"

"I hunted them down and got her back. It took three days." He *hated* thinking of those long minutes and hours and days, the utter heart-stopping panic over what might have been happening to Molly. "I finally found out where they were holding her. Just as I arrived, she somehow escaped out a third-floor window. She was perched on a ledge, desperately trying to reach a tree branch that wasn't quite close enough."

Kylie stared at him. "I'm hoping that's where the story ends, but somehow I know that it isn't."

"She jumped for it and missed, and then fell to the ground," he said. "She broke her back in two places.

She's had three surgeries but the nerves in her right leg are permanently damaged."

"Oh my God."

"She used to run track," he said. "She wanted to be an Olympian. That was her dream. It was going to be her way out."

Kylie slid closer to him, pressing her body to his as if she knew he needed warmth, her warmth. Not that he deserved it, but he wasn't strong enough to push her away, so instead he pulled her in close.

"She told me it wasn't your fault, Joe," she murmured. "She believes it." She tipped her head up to his. "And so do I."

She was giving him way more credit than he deserved.

"So is what happened to Molly the reason why you tend to be so . . ." She trailed off.

"Crazy?" he asked.

"Well, I was going to say overprotective," she told him with a small smile. "Is this why you won't let me all the way in, because you're afraid your lifestyle will get me hurt?"

He stilled at her incredible—and accurate—assessment.

"Joe . . ." She paused as if searching for the right words. "I get that you're out there saving the world, trying to help people and maybe clean up your karma at the same time, but no one seems to think it needs cleaning except you. You're too hard on yourself."

He knew that later he'd be going ten rounds with himself in his own head about this, about telling her the whole story. It was bringing it all back to the surface and it wasn't a good time for that, not with the countdown on and only days left to figure her shit out.

But Kylie wouldn't understand that. She didn't bother hiding her emotions like he did. She had no interest in keeping herself in control. And actually, her willingness to let go was one of the things he loved about her. There was just something incredibly appealing about how she put herself out there, not worrying about outcome or the possibility of getting hurt.

Which made her the brave one, not him. Honestly, he had no idea why he even bothered to try to resist her. Resistance was futile with this woman who'd gotten under his thick skin when he hadn't been looking. She thought he held back with her, but he'd been fooling himself because he wasn't holding back at all.

Just thinking about it made his chest tight. So did imagining her not being in his life. He'd learned first-hand what it was like to have her all to himself. He was getting used to sharing his free time with her, and his personal space. He even loved sleeping with her after they made love, holding her all night, allowing himself to give in to his selfish need to keep her close.

All of which was forcing him to face a fact he hadn't seen coming—his solitary life was starting to feel just a little too solitary.

He knew he should walk away right now, before

he got in any more over his head. But who the hell was he kidding? It was too late. He was already going down for the count.

Kylie slid her hands beneath the hem of his shirt and paused with her fingers splayed wide over his bare skin.

He went hard and sucked in a breath. "You know I can't think worth a damn when you have your hands on me."

"Huh," she said, *not* taking her hands off of him. "Didn't know that." She gave him an innocent look and bit her lower lip.

With a groan, he hauled her in flush against him. He knew he'd given away how badly he wanted— actually, make that *needed*—her, because when their gazes met, the look in her eyes was enough to make his heart stop and his lungs run out of air.

She needed him too.

He stared into her face, searching for what, exactly, he had no fucking clue, before he closed his arms around her. Kissing her hard, he lifted her up, and when she wrapped her legs around him, he carried her to the bed.

He tossed her down on it, leaving her free to gasp for air as he stripped and then crawled up her body, tugging off her clothes as he went. His emotions were a chaotic mix of things he couldn't get a grasp on, though lust and passion were high on the list. When he'd condomed up and was poised between her legs, she tipped her head back, her eyes closing in anticipation of what was to come.

"Kylie," he said softly. "Look at me."

Her head came up and her eyes opened slowly. They were glazed with passion and he had to use all of his self-control not to dive into her right then. "Can you feel what you do to me?" He pressed into her lightly.

She sucked in a sharp breath and nodded as her nails dug into his shoulders. "Yes."

"I'll never get tired of this." He pushed in another inch and bent to kiss her. "I'll never get tired of how you make me feel." He rolled his hips and slid all the way home.

With a low moan, she wrapped her arms around his neck and tightened her legs on him. As he began to move, her hips rushed to meet his every thrust and when she came, she took him right over the edge with her.

They were still gasping for air when his phone— from his pants somewhere on the floor—alerted him to an incoming text. He dropped his forehead to hers and concentrated on the only thing he could— breathing.

"Maybe it's nothing," she said, her hands in his hair, her body still quivering beneath his.

"Maybe." But they both knew it wasn't. He took the time to give her a soft kiss and then another. And another . . .

She pulled free with clear regret. "You have to go," she said.

His laugh was short. "Story of our relationship." He was halfway out the door when he heard her ask the room a question.

"So we have a relationship now?"

He glanced back, really hoping that was a rhetorical question. But she was looking to him for an answer.

At whatever she saw on his face, a rough laugh escaped her. "Okay, so maybe not," she murmured.

Every woman he'd ever known including his own sister fought like this, with battles he never saw coming. And he'd never received a copy of the rule book. He wanted to keep walking out the door. He wanted that a whole lot more than he wanted to have this conversation, but this was Kylie. He couldn't just walk away from her. Wouldn't. He blew out a breath. "Kylie—"

"No, wait," she said. "Me first. I know I let you think I was okay with this, with just this physical thing between us. And I was. I really was."

His heart kicked hard. "But . . . ?"

"But now . . ." She let out a long breath and shook her head. "Suddenly, I'm not." She met his gaze, her own steely but also hurt. "I'm worth more, Joe. I'm realizing I want to be with a man who's capable of giving me that more. Maybe even capable of giving me everything."

He stilled. "Are you dumping me, Kylie?"

"I guess I'm asking if you're ever going to want to be that man."

Hell. If she wasn't dumping him, she would be soon, because he was going to be honest, the only way he knew how to be. "Being with you on the job, or as friends, or in bed . . . it *all* works for me, Kylie. Every second of it. But if you're asking me what we have or need me to promise more right now, I can't."

"I get that," she said. "I can't make you want to be with me just because I discovered that's what I want."

His heart pinched. He wanted to put words to the feelings bouncing around in his chest, making him miserable, but if he did, she'd realize just how emotionally challenged he really was. He wasn't talking mild-to-moderately emotionally challenged either. He was talking *severely* emotionally challenged here.

But he'd discovered things too. Such as when he was with her, he felt . . . alive. And when he wasn't with her, all he thought about was being with her, about the things he wanted to do with her. And to her . . .

He was a solitary man by nature who as a rule didn't do serious relationships. They were messy and required things he couldn't give. But thinking about Kylie and how comfortably she fit into his life didn't make him feel threatened at all. It actually made him feel . . . mellow. At peace.

In truth, she felt like the best thing to have happened to him in a long time—which didn't mean he'd relax his stance. He couldn't. And knowing that, he fought to control his emotions.

It was shockingly hard, which was proof that she could turn him upside down without even trying. And that simply couldn't happen. "I want to be with you too," he said. "And yeah," he added when she looked at him in surprise, "I didn't see that coming either. But we both know why I can't. I honestly don't know if I even *should* open myself up for more, if I'm capable of it."

"Are you sure it's that?" she asked. "Because maybe you just don't want to be so emotionally invested that you're left vulnerable again."

Look at her calling him on all his bullshit. He was both proud and horrified that she knew him so well, that he'd let her know him so well. "It's not about me," he said. "It's about you. You're the one I'd be putting at risk and I won't do it."

She sat up on the bed. "You're talking like you're still Special Ops. But, Joe, you're home now. You're no longer in that line of work."

"No, but what I do now can be even worse," he said, "because my guard's down. Something can still happen—"

"I'm not a helpless fourteen-year-old girl," she said quietly. "I'm not going to get drawn into something bad because of your lifestyle."

"You don't know that."

"Joe, you can't keep the people in your life safe from everything," she said.

"Maybe not, but I can sure as hell try."

She stared at him for a long minute and he knew a whole new level of terror when her eyes got suspiciously shiny, before she wrapped herself up in the sheet and went into her bathroom and shut the door.

The click of the lock sent a message loud and clear.

He told himself he was glad. It'd had to be done. He should be relieved that she finally fully understood him and where he was coming from.

But relief was just about the opposite of how he felt as he headed into whatever tonight's work emergency was.

Chapter 26

#ElementaryMyDearWatson

Half an hour later Joe found himself hanging off a roof with his team, posing as window washers fifteen flights off the ground.

Apparently window washing at night was a real thing. They'd needed the cover because they were in stealth surveillance mode for a criminal investigation involving a million-dollar embezzlement suit. And as was the case about 90 percent of the time on a stakeout, things were annoyingly quiet.

So quiet that he was thinking too hard about, what else . . . Kylie. He just kept seeing the look on her face when he'd spelled out how he wasn't going there with her. And where was all the work action to take his mind off the things he'd said? Because right about now he'd have preferred being flung twenty-five feet in the air through drywall again over thinking this hard. When his phone vibrated with an incoming text, he jumped on the distraction.

> **Dad:** I'm going to watch another episode of Buffy The Vampire Slayer.

> **Joe:** It's the middle of the night. And wtf, you keep watching without me.

> **Dad:** Do you want to watch Buffy The Vampire Slayer or not?

> **Joe:** Well yeah, but wait for me. I'm still working.

> **Dad:** Buffy The Vampire Slayer doesn't wait for nobody.

> **Joe:** Say Buffy The Vampire Slayer one more time.

> **Dad:** Buffy The Vampire Slayer one more time.

Joe gave up and slid his phone away. A gust of wind came along and knocked their platform into the side of the building.

Lucas closed his eyes and moaned like he was dying. Heights didn't bother Joe any but they drove Superman insane. Joe had once seen him jump into a raging river to catch a bad guy without blinking an eye, so he was amused. The guy was so invincible it was fun to see any weakness from him.

"Hey, Lucas," Reyes said, also amused. "Look."

Lucas opened his eyes and Reyes jumped up and down a few times. The platform swayed.

And Lucas gripped the railing with white knuckles and swore the air blue.

"You kiss your mama with that mouth?" Max asked.

"Shut it," Archer said.

And everyone shut it.

But Lucas remained green.

"Hey," Max stage-whispered to Joe. "Heard you're with the woodworker chick."

Reyes snorted and when everyone looked at him he shrugged. "He said 'woodworker.'"

Joe rolled his eyes. "How old are you, twelve?"

"What?" he asked innocently. "She works on wood. That's all I meant. You're the one who took it there, man. She working on your wood, Joe?"

"Reyes is about to go flying without a parachute," Joe said to Archer. "You good with that?"

"Yes," Archer said.

"Hey," Reyes said but backed very carefully out of Joe's reach, putting his hands up in surrender. "Just saying. You two are looking pretty cozy."

"Your point?" Joe asked coolly.

Reyes laughed. "You should lock her down as soon as possible, man. Any woman who can put up with your bad attitude is worth keeping. Plus, she's smoking hot."

"It's supposed to be about more than just her body," Max said. "Rory says it's about *personality*."

"True," Reyes said. "They have like ten of those, so you can always just choose one."

"Our perp's entering the building so look alive," Archer said. "If you boys are ready to shut the fuck up and work, that is."

Five minutes later, their guy walked into his office talking on the phone, where he implicated himself all over the place. He never even gave the "window washers" a second look and they got the whole conversation recorded.

"That's all we need," Archer said. "We've got enough for the DA to take the case forward. You're all off for the night."

Joe knew he couldn't go back to Kylie's, not after pushing her away, so instead he went and watched *Buffy* with his dad before checking out the last apprentice on their list. Phillip Wilde out of San Jose worked as a master carpenter, making furniture on the side. But as Joe suspected, it was yet another dead end. Phillip had quit a year ago and, according to a neighbor who came out in his bathrobe and was willing to chat, now lived in the Florida Keys, making beach chairs for tourists.

He waited until the next day after work to tell Kylie. He was standing outside Reclaimed Woods in the courtyard when she exited. She looked surprised to see him and regret slashed through him.

"What are you doing here?" she asked.

"Wanted to talk to you."

"Thought that wasn't our thing, talking."

Yeah, he deserved that.

She sighed. "Never mind me. What's wrong?"

That she could read him so easily was no longer

a surprise. Although he had no idea how she could when no one else ever seemed able to, but he was getting tired of worrying about that. "The list of apprentices is a dead end," he said. "We need to talk about a new angle."

"But we still have one more to check on," she said. "Phillip, out in San Jose."

"I checked into it. Phillip moved to Florida last year."

She crossed her arms. "So now you've cut me out of the investigation as neatly as you cut me out of your life? We had a deal, Joe."

"I didn't cut you out of anything. I was trying to save us some time."

"Okay," she said, smile gone and maybe steam coming out of her ears. "Well, let me save you some more of your precious time. I'm going in another direction on this investigation. You're fired."

He caught her before she could walk away. "Oh no," he said. "It's not going to be that easy. You're stuck with me."

"I gave you the mirror for Molly. We're square." Yanking free, she started walking across the courtyard, her eyes on her phone.

"Hell no we're not square," he said, following her. "We're not done here until you're safe."

She snorted.

"What does that mean?" he asked.

Instead of answering, she slid into a waiting Uber.

He barely got in with her before she could slam the door on his nose. Since she was doing the whole not speaking to him thing, and since he wasn't interested in fighting with her with an audience, the ride was silent until they were dropped off in Soma.

"What are we doing here?" he asked as she took off walking. "Kylie," he said warningly when they ended up on a narrow backstreet that was really more of an alleyway.

"Shh." She slipped into a gated yard and vanished.

Shit. He followed to find her climbing a rickety old fire escape. He had a few choices. He could argue with her. He could pull her off the fire escape. Or he could do the crazy thing and join her.

He joined her.

Since his climbing skills were far superior to hers, he caught up with her and helped her up onto the next level. The small apartment building was three floors. Looked like four units on each floor. Kylie stopped when they were closest to the third-floor far-right unit, which revealed a kitchen.

"My mom's place," she whispered and looked at her watch. "She'll be home from work right about . . ."

A woman walked into the kitchen.

"Now," Kylie whispered.

"Why didn't you just wait for her out front?"

"Because the last few times she and I talked, I couldn't shake the feeling that she's keeping something from me. At first I thought she just needed more money, but now I'm not sure. I'm worried about her but I can't just come right out and ask her anything. She's cagey."

"You give her money?"

"*Shh.*"

Fine. She didn't want to talk about it. He got that. He concentrated on the scene at hand. The woman in the kitchen had Kylie's long hair, but unlike Kylie, who mostly pulled hers up, her mom's hair was styled to within an inch of its life. She wore artful makeup that Tina from the coffee shop would admire and that, combined with a very tight dress and knee-high boots, had Joe confused. She didn't look old enough to be Kylie's mom. But a more careful look told him the makeup and clothing had fooled him.

She tossed her purse onto the kitchen counter and whirled to face the younger man who'd come in behind her. Smiling, she hopped up on the kitchen table and beckoned the guy with a crook of her finger. Then she had the man standing between her legs and they were apparently trying to eat each other's face off.

Kylie grimaced. "That's a new one."

"What, her having a man in her kitchen?"

"No," she said. "*That's* common. But the actual man is new. He's not her boyfriend. Which is clearly what she didn't want me to know."

"Why not?"

"Because she goes through men like other women go through shoes. And she knows it irritates me because she throws the good ones away."

Kylie's mom pulled back from the kiss and turned to the window.

Both Kylie and Joe shrank out of view as she opened the glass all the way, inadvertently helping Joe's and Kylie's cause, because now they could hear the kitchen conversation.

"Whew," Kylie's mom said as she fanned her face. "That's better. You've got me all hot and bothered."

The guy looked smug. "Then why did you stop me?"

"I spoke to Kylie yesterday."

Next to Joe, Kylie froze.

"And?" the guy asked. "Did you tell her your good news?"

"No. Not yet. She's not ready to hear it yet. You have to work that girl into things slowly or she freaks out."

Joe looked at Kylie, who still wasn't moving.

"When she was little," her mom said, "she'd lose it at the first sign of any drama or change. If I stopped dating someone. If I started dating someone. She's a creature of habit and can't handle any changes. It's why her grandpa took her in."

"Your dad?" the boyfriend asked. "The rich artist dude?"

Interesting way to phrase it, Joe thought. Interesting, and more than a little suspect.

"Yeah," said Kylie's mom distractedly. "He said he knew how to handle her, and he did. He was way better at it than me, too, and she was happy there. But he raised her to be like him—an old man. So if I had tried to tell her all in one call that I'd dumped Charlie and then started seeing you and now we want to elope, she'd have lost it."

"You're a grown woman, baby. And she's your daughter."

"Yeah, well, Kylie's and my relationship is a bit . . .

backward. She's always thought of herself as the mom, and in truth, she's often had to be."

"You know what you need? A distraction," he said huskily. "Let's go to the bedroom, where I do my best work."

Joe rolled his eyes at the line and when the two lovebirds had left the kitchen, he looked over at Kylie. He wasn't even sure if she was breathing. He reached out to touch her, but she shook her head.

"I'm fine."

No, she wasn't, but she would be, he vowed. "How many boyfriends have there been?" he asked and knew by the look on her face that it'd been too many. "Did you get what you needed to hear?" he asked. "We done here?"

Looking a little lost, she nodded and started to climb down. Fast. "Kylie—"

Too late. She'd made it to the second-floor landing when her foot caught on a rung. Somehow that loosened the ladder, sending it cascading to the ground, Kylie in free fall along with it. The crash landing had him reliving the Molly nightmare all over again, helplessly watching her fall out of that tree. He rushed to climb down to the ledge and then dropped the rest of the way to the ground next to Kylie's prone body. "Don't move—"

"No, I'm okay," she said, bouncing right up to quickly start walking back to the street.

"Kylie, stop. You're not okay. You just blew out both knees on your jeans. Let me see your palms."

"I'm fine," she said, not stopping, not letting him

touch her. Again she was on her phone, probably getting another Uber.

Her voice was shaking and her hands were too, but in some ways, her mom was right. Kylie needed to do things in her own way and in her own time, and Joe got that. He could give her the time she needed to get herself together. She had until they got back to her place, and then her time shutting him out was over. And yeah, he got the irony here. He'd shut her out first. But he was having a hell of a time *keeping* her shut out.

Chapter 27

#HastaLaVistaBaby

Kylie was still mad as she and Joe waited for an Uber. Mad at her mom, mad at her mom's new boy toy, mad at the fire escape, and last but certainly not least, mad at Joe. To sum it up, she was mad at everyone and everything in her life.

Including herself.

Because dammit. *Dammit,* she could've really fallen for the smart, resourceful, resilient, stoically silent man behind her. But he'd cut off that possibility before he could feel the same. It infuriated her. No, wait, that wasn't quite true.

It hurt her feelings.

But she wasn't going to ask for more from him. She was going to move on. No more Gibs or Joes in her life.

Refusing to cry, which she had a tendency to do

when she was really angry, she continued to ignore Joe as he insisted the Uber driver take them to his truck. Once there, he made a quick run up to his office for something—she didn't care what—returning with a backpack slung over his shoulder, after which he drove her home. She unlocked her front door and limped into her apartment, throwing her things onto the couch before moving straight to the kitchen.

She still had ice cream in the freezer. She'd thought she'd needed Joe in her life. She'd thought she needed to talk to her mom. She'd thought she needed a lot of things, but it turned out that all she really needed in that moment was comfort food. Comfort food never failed her. Hauling out the ice cream, she slapped it into the microwave for fifteen seconds to soften it and then grabbed a spoon. Leaning against the counter, she dug in, eyes closed, concentrating only on the taste of the little chocolate chips melting on her tongue.

Thank God for chocolate.

Joe hadn't followed her into the kitchen at first. Probably checking out the apartment, but she sensed when he showed up because her nipples got hard. Which was really annoying. She opened her eyes and yep, sure enough, he stood close, assessing her.

Normally when she was feeling way too many feelings, no one and nothing could get through to her. But the sight of him pulling Twinkies along with a first-aid kit from his backpack was enough for her to feel her eyes fill with tears. So *that's* what he'd gone up to his office for. "I'm fine," she said, sounding totally not fine, dammit.

He picked her up and set her on the kitchen counter and then handed her the Twinkies. "My emergency stash."

"You keep Twinkies as an emergency stash?" she asked.

"Oh yeah. Don't tell Archer."

"Cute," she said and felt a little chunk of her anger fall away. But only a little. "Thanks."

He took a good look at her hands. Her right palm was scraped up pretty good. He cleaned it out and bandaged it. Then he pulled her knees apart and stepped between them. "Tilt your head back a little," he instructed quietly, his hands resting on her thighs, warming her from the inside out.

She bared her neck, feeling a little bit like Little Red Riding Hood making herself available to the Big Bad Wolf. Joe pushed her hair away from her face and took her head in his big, warm hands, his gaze taking in the spot on her temple where she'd smacked it on her less than perfect fire escape landing. "Tender?" he asked, probing gently.

"No." Not that she'd admit to it anyway.

He brushed a small kiss to the spot, which she felt all the way through her body. *Hold firm,* she told herself. *You're hurt and angry with him, remember?* Sexy times, no matter how good he made them, couldn't take that hurt and anger away. Yes, she'd been mentally sidetracked by the sweet offering of the Twinkies but she was past that now.

He unzipped her sweatshirt and tugged it off, leaving her in just a thin camisole top, making her glad her nipples had gotten ahold of themselves and calmed down.

"How about here?" he asked, touching her shoulder where she'd also scraped herself and taken off a few layers of skin.

Since she couldn't find her voice, she shrugged.

Ignoring her bad 'tude, he kissed that spot too, his lips lingering a bit longer, and all bets were off as far as her happy nipples were concerned. Every move he made spiked her heart rate as he continued his inspection, which was really playing havoc with her ability to hold on to her anger.

In fact, it was slipping right through her fingers in spite of her determination.

"And here?" he murmured, stroking the juncture between her neck and shoulder.

"I don't know." But she sighed as his mouth touched her there, brushing whisper-soft kisses across the tender skin. Then he gently set her down on her feet and met her gaze.

"Strip," he said.

She gave a rough laugh at this because one, *hell no*. And two, even if she was willing to go there with him, she wasn't nearly as comfortable in her skin as he was in his. He had no body issues at all and could walk around naked without even giving it another thought—nor should he—but she gave it lots of thoughts.

Joe stood there, taking up more than his fair share

of the kitchen, waiting patiently with some humor in his gaze. "I want to see your knees. You're bleeding through your jeans."

Oh. Right. Her hands went to the waistband of her jeans and hesitated.

"What?" he asked.

She grimaced. "It feels weird to take off my pants in front of you when it's not for sex. Like we're playing dirty doctor or something."

"How about after I get a look, you can order me to strip too," he said and smiled. "You can be the sexy nurse."

"What if I want to be the doctor?" she asked.

"Honey, once you've got me naked, you can be whatever you want to be."

Rolling her eyes, she unbuttoned and unzipped and then had to execute a little shimmy to get the slightly too tight jeans down. She blamed Tina's delicious and fattening muffins, but couldn't get too worked up about that because if she was being honest, there was something almost unbearably erotic about stripping while Joe remained fully dressed. As her pants hit the floor, she felt her breathing change.

Joe took one look at her baby blue lacy thong and his breathing changed too. But he lifted her back up to the counter without comment. She squeaked because without her jeans, the tile was *cold*. He laughed softly, evilly, and then got down to doctoring.

When he had her knees patched up, he slid his hands to her butt and scooted her snug up against him, her thighs on either side of his hips. She squeezed him with her legs and felt him lean into her, his arms gently closing around her. He kissed her jaw, his lips nibbling oh so softly at her skin, and she had one cohesive thought.

I'm in such trouble . . .

"Joe?"

"Yeah?"

"I get to be the doctor now."

"Doctor away," he said, voice low and husky.

"What hurts?"

"Everything."

Oh boy. She kissed him and then her brain shorted out and she closed her eyes because he was sliding one hand up to the back of her neck while his mouth did something pretty amazing as it worked its way across her collarbone. Flashes and bolts of heat slashed through her and whatever pain she'd been in was forgotten. She shifted to once again give him better access and he intercepted her mouth with his, making her moan as their tongues touched and another fresh bolt of lust ripped through her.

Joe kissed like he did everything else in his life— with an easy confidence and a skill that defied the odds. Being kissed by him took her out of herself and made her forget everything else. She could feel him hard through his jeans, and memories of what he felt like inside her tore another moan from her that he drank in greedily.

He used that hand he had low on her back to press her close as they moved against each other until she tore free, still breathing hard. It was crazy to her that he could get her halfway to orgasm with just a kiss, but without his mouth on her right now, thinking about it was more than a little embarrassing.

"Bed," he said firmly and then carried her there. He was losing his clothes with quick efficiency when her brain kicked in.

Could she do this, just have sex and keep her heart out of it? She got off the bed and hesitated, unsure. Where was her red wig when she needed it?

The room was dark, only a small pool of light at the base of the window where the moon slanted in. She had no trouble seeing the outline of the dark, muscled shadow as he sat up and studied her. "I can go to the couch," he said quietly. "Whatever you want. Just don't ask me to leave you alone tonight."

She chewed on her lower lip.

"Kylie."

"I'm trying to decide what I want to do with you."

"What are the options?" he asked.

"Kill you or kiss you."

He laughed. "Here, let me help you decide." Reaching out, he tugged her into him so that she stood between his spread thighs.

She sighed. "I find it really irritating that you smell so good. I want to bite you."

He gave her a small smile. "Bite away."

"I'm really mad at you, Joe."

"I know. Let me make it all better."

For now, he meant. But maybe not. Even in the dark she could see the need and yearning and hunger on his face. He wanted her every bit as much as she wanted him. Staring at him, she gave a slow nod and in one dizzying move, he snagged her around the waist and tugged her back onto the bed.

And then turned on the light.

"Hey," she complained and lifted a hand to block her eyes. "Turn that off."

"I want to see you."

"You know what I look like!"

"Not when we're naked," he said.

"I'm not naked—" She broke off when he slid off her panties. Okay, now she was naked.

"We've never done this before," he said.

She gaped up at him. "What are you talking about? We've done nothing *but* this."

He smiled but shook his head. "Not as *you*. You've always been in a wig as a disguise. But now you're you."

She was finding it very hard to talk with his big, delicious bod holding her down. "I wasn't in disguise that other morning in the shower," she said.

"Semantics. Your sweet curves were all warm and wet and covered in soap. I lost my mind."

"How about the other night when you showed up late—"

"That's just it," he said. "It was late. And dark." He pushed her hair from her face and made himself very at home between her legs. "Where were we?"

With her about to walk. But now she had him this close and she couldn't hold on to her resolve. Not ready to have the conversation with him in this position, hell, not wanting to have it at all, she rolled so that *she* was on top. Better. Now he was sprawled out beneath her, all sinew and heat, and she couldn't think. *One last time,* she told herself. *You can have him this one last time before you walk away.* "I think we were just about to rock each other's world."

"I like the sound of that." Then *he* rolled, and before she could blink, she was pinned beneath him again.

And not, apparently, because he was in any sort of hurry to get to it. No, it was as if it was the complete opposite. A switch had been thrown and suddenly he seemed to have all the time in the world as he worked his way down her body, kissing, licking, nibbling, and then kissing again, every single inch of her. She was writhing, begging him for more, but he couldn't be rushed as he made his way back to her mouth for a kiss that was hot, deep, and slow, and she absolutely melted. He kissed her like that for long minutes, seemingly content to just drink her in as they rolled over the bed, taking turns on top. She reveled in the dominant position for long, rare moments, reacquainting herself with every inch of him, wondering if she'd ever get enough of feeling his heat, his hard muscles quivering beneath her tongue. And when she took him just a little too far, when he groaned her name and pulled her up to straddle him, she took his hands in hers and pushed them over his head as she brought him deep inside her.

The ambient glow from her bathroom night-light lit his warrior's body in bold relief, highlighting the sheen of his skin and the flex of his muscles moving beneath it, all the way down past his abs to where their bodies were joined. She watched, helplessly fascinated, as his body surged into hers, again and again and again. Her eyes drank in the details of him, the faint line of hair down his belly, a long, thin scar across his ribs, the line of stitches from the other night, another scar in the hollow of his shoulder.

The muscles in his neck were corded, his head thrown back in pleasure, and his eyes, locked on hers, sent her right over. She felt him go too, his mouth at her throat as he shuddered along with her . . .

They were still gasping for air, still lying tangled together where they'd collapsed. From somewhere in the dark room, Joe's phone buzzed. The nature of his job and the story of their lives. He ignored it but Kylie was barely able to recognize this fact. She was that far gone in what they'd just done. It felt as though he'd peeled back all her layers and broken into her heart. There were feelings, oh so many feelings, and she knew, dammit, she *knew,* she wasn't alone in this.

Not that she was going to wait around for him to realize that. As she worked at putting air into her lungs and waited for the feeling to return to her extremities, she realized the pillows were gone. Her lamp leaned drunkenly against one wall. The blankets and sheets had disappeared and the fitted sheet had been pulled loose, lying twisted and damp beneath them.

The only thing moving was Joe's hand, slowly stroking up and down her damp back as she continued to struggle to regain her breath and some semblance of control. Only when she was clearly relaxed, bone-less, and very near a pleasure coma in fact, did he go for his phone.

When he did, she pulled the blanket off the floor to cover herself. Joe glanced over at her, clearly amused by her sudden modesty. But as he listened to a message, his smile faded.

"What?" she asked when he'd disconnected.

He didn't answer, just began pulling on his clothes.

She sat up. "Joe."

He paused with only his jeans on, low-slung and sexy even now. "Remember the cowboy apprentice, Eric?" he asked.

"Of course. What did he want?"

Joe looked pained.

She stared at him. "Joe."

"He found the imposter's card. He's got a number for the guy."

Chapter 28

#CarpeDiem

Kylie's heart took a good hard fast leap at the first real progress toward getting back her penguin. Finally, they were getting somewhere. Except . . . She met Joe's gaze. "Tell me something."

"What?"

"Were you going to fill me in on Eric's call if I hadn't asked?"

He hesitated and she felt the shock roll through his system. "Seriously?" she asked.

"Okay, hold on a second," he said, shoving his fingers through his hair in a rare tell of frustration. "Yes, I did briefly consider not telling you . . . *yet* . . . but I knew you'd get all up in arms over that. I was going to tell you, Kylie."

"But maybe not until you'd checked it over."

That one he didn't answer, but he didn't have to. The truth was in his eyes.

Stunned, she shook her head and stared at him, unsure how to feel. She'd never thought about trust being a premeditated, calculated thing before, but apparently it was. She didn't like it, not one little bit. Jumping up, she pulled on some clothes before grabbing her phone. "What's the guy's name and number?"

"Kylie—"

"*Joe.*"

He didn't sigh but he looked like he wanted to. "We don't have a name," he said. "Just the business—Wood Specialties—and a number."

"Fine. Just the number then." She made the call on speaker. The voice mail was a brusque male voice saying one word. "Beep."

"I'm interested in your work," Kylie said. "Call me back." She left her number and disconnected.

Joe was finishing getting dressed. He grabbed his keys. "I'm going to the office to do a search on that number and get an address."

"Great idea." She slid her purse over her shoulder. "I'm going with you."

"It's the middle of the night."

She just looked at him and he blew out a breath and lifted his hands. "Fine," he said.

"Fine."

Half an hour later they were in his office and had the address of Wood Specialties, located on a houseboat in the marina. They also had a name for the guy who owned it.

Kevin Baker.

Kylie sat down hard in Joe's office chair.

Joe was watching her carefully. "You know him?"

"I used to," she said. "He's one of my mom's old boyfriends. One of the few I actually liked. He was nice to me. And he liked my grandpa. He did a little work for him now and then, although he left right around the time of the fire."

Joe took his eyes off his computer screen and looked at her. "And you didn't think he should be on the list of suspects?"

"No, I didn't," she said a little testily, hugging herself. "I never would've considered Kevin for taking the penguin. He wasn't an apprentice. And out of all of my mom's boyfriends, he was my favorite. He's a nice guy and the only one who bothered to be even halfway nice to the daughter of his crazy girlfriend."

Joe blew out a breath, which spoke volumes. They both knew she hadn't had a lot of nice guys in her life who'd put her first. And she had the feeling that Joe believed they were about to ruin the memory of one of the few. "It's not him," she said. "No way."

"Maybe not," Joe said. "But it's time for a whole new list called THE BOYFRIENDS, and Kevin goes right to the top. He's a woodworker?"

"Kind of, but he preferred painting. He wasn't great at either."

Joe was quiet for a second. "That first night after I agreed to help you, I got ahold of the official notes on the fire. I talked to the arson detective who'd worked the case."

She stared at him. "Why?"

"You'd asked for my help," he said. "I never go into anything unprepared."

"No, I mean why didn't you tell me?" she asked. "Or share the notes?"

"Because there wasn't anything in there that you didn't already know." He paused. "And I thought reading about it all over again would upset you."

She took that in for a moment and nodded.

"Kylie."

She met his gaze.

"You weren't in any way blamed for the fire."

"Only because there wasn't enough evidence."

He shook his head. "You're not at fault."

"You don't know that. It could've been my fault."

"It wasn't," he said firmly, calmly.

Something about his unwavering belief in her while still holding back his heart made her mad. "How do you know?"

"Because I know *you*," he said. "Maybe even better than anyone else."

Seeing as this was very likely true, she didn't respond. And also because she wanted to say, *If you know me so well, why won't you let yourself love me?* But that was *way* too desperate and needy and she was done with that. "What do you think you know about me?"

He gave a small smile. "That you're crazy stubborn, crazy smart, and crazy careful." His smile widened. "You're also crazy OCD when it comes to your work. No way did you leave the soldering iron on. Someone else must've come along after you and done it. You had nothing to do with that fire and I'm betting that when we get to the bottom of this, I'll be able to prove it to you once and for all. Now tell me everything else you know about Kevin."

"He never really got anywhere with his art," she said. "He ended up working for an art dealer and learning the ropes. Haven't heard about him for a while, but last I did, he was working independently for several galleries across the country. I need to talk to him." She stood up and headed to the door.

He caught her by her purse strap.

"You're not leaving me behind," she said tightly, knowing that's exactly what he wanted to do. "I'm going to see him."

"I get it," he said. "And I'm with you. But not at two in the morning. It doesn't feel safe. We need a plan and backup."

She crossed her arms, both believing him and also doubting him. "We never needed backup before."

"We were never close before. And this feels close. And dangerous." He put his hands on her arms, bending a little to look into her eyes. "Putting you in danger is unacceptable to me. We're going to wait until morning, when we've made a plan and thought it all through."

All of that made sense but he'd shown his hand earlier. He intended to cut her out of this. Back when she'd been little and her mom had dug her heels in about something or another, being totally unreasonable—as Joe was being now—she'd learned there was only one way to handle the situation. Play dead. So she nodded and bit back her argument. "Okay," she said. "Fine."

Joe, not nearly as easy a mark as her mom, went brows up at her way-too-easy acquiescence. "Okay, fine?" he repeated.

She didn't respond, just freed herself and headed to the door. On the way, she slid a look at Joe's desk and couch, and sensual erotic memories of being on them with Joe flashed bright in her mind. And in her heart. She hardened that heart and walked out the door.

Joe followed, and if he was plagued by those same memories, he kept it to himself pretty well. Did he even remember? She glanced back at him and found his eyes dilated to almost black.

Yeah, he remembered. He drove her home and she was out of his truck and heading to her front door almost before he parked.

When he caught up with her, clearly planning on going inside with her, she sent him a long *oh hell no* look.

"I'm going to make sure you get inside safely," he said.

"I always do."

Joe didn't bend on this. "You've been rattling cages and looking under rocks. I'm going to walk you inside your damn apartment, Kylie."

She lifted her hands, giving the unspoken message of *fine, but you're still an asshole.*

And given his sigh, he got that message loud and clear.

"So, what time?" she asked.

"What time what?"

She narrowed her eyes suspiciously. "What time are we going to talk to Kevin?"

"I'll check with the guys and let you know." He walked her in and checked her place. And then turned to her, most likely to state his case on staying, but before he could, she opened the front door in silent invitation.

He ran a hand over his jaw. He hadn't shaved that morning and she was viscerally reminded of the night before, his lips touching her in intimate places, the brush of his stubble against her skin. In fact, she still had the slightest whisper of burn on her inner thighs and she wrapped her arms around herself to control the tremor.

And to keep herself from stopping him from leaving at all.

"Kylie—"

"No," she said and let out a rough laugh because damn if just the sound of her name on his lips didn't make her want to cave. With another mirthless laugh aimed directly at herself, she nudged the door open wide.

After holding her gaze, he nodded, ran a finger along her jaw, and did as she wanted. He left.

Chapter 29

*#FirstRuleOfFightClubIs
YouDontTalkAboutFightClub*

Joe went straight back to the office, doing his damnedest to set aside his personal emotions. There was a job to do, and the job always came first. But his chest ached like a son of a bitch with something he wasn't used to feeling—fear.

Fear of losing her.

But he'd made his bed so he texted Archer because it was time for reinforcements. Archer agreed and luckily the team didn't blink about coming in at three a.m.

As they did for every job, they gathered intel and went through it with a fine-tooth comb. Joe had already done most of the legwork, with the exception of looking into Kylie's mom's boyfriends.

And that's where they hit pay dirt.

Or more correctly, Lucas did. He pushed his iPad

to the center of the table in the conference room so everyone could see it.

Joe stared at the intel in disbelief. Kevin was indeed an art buyer now, but there were some ugly things deep in his past. The guy had been arrested on suspicion of arson.

Twice.

And both times had gotten off.

"Coincidence?" Lucas asked.

"I don't believe in coincidences," Archer said.

Neither did Joe. He wanted to go into the marina hot and drag that ass-munch right to jail, and he wanted that like yesterday. But he no longer ran on sheer emotion, balls, and lack of common sense. Patience had been drilled into him, along with the ability to make and execute a plan under any circumstances.

"Best to go in at dawn," Archer suggested. "In that area, if we go in now, any lights we use will be reflected off the water and too easily seen." He looked at Joe. "What time will Kylie be here?"

Joe hesitated and Archer went brows up. "You're leaving her out of this?"

"Yes."

"Your funeral," Archer said with a shrug. "Let's catch that asshole with enough evidence so she can be done with this."

By that time it was four a.m. Everyone agreed to meet back in one hour and they all scattered, either to find food or catch a catnap.

Except Lucas. He stayed in the conference room, waiting until he and Joe were alone.

"What else is going on?" he asked quietly. "You're off."

"I'm fine."

"You get in a fight with Kylie?"

Joe gave him a *back the fuck off* look, which Lucas ignored. "How did you screw it up?"

"Why would you assume I screwed it up?"

"Because you're a moron when it comes to keeping a good woman," Lucas said.

Hard to be insulted at the truth. "It'll be fine."

"Yeah?" Lucas asked skeptically. "What's the last thing she said to you?"

"Why?"

"Did she smile at you? Touch you? Kiss you goodbye?"

"Actually," Joe said, "she laughed at me."

"Hell, dude. When a female laughs at you during an argument, she's turned the corner from pissed to psycho and she's about to murder your ass. You need your six covered?"

"I think I'm good," Joe said wryly. Kylie wasn't going to kill him. She was going to do worse—she was going to dump his sorry ass.

Knowing it, he drove home to shower and recharge. But when he pulled up to his place, there was the glow of an interior light that he knew he hadn't left on. Pulling his gun, he let himself inside.

Molly was curled up on his couch with a bottle of tequila and his hidden stash of Girl Scout Thin Mints.

"It's early to be drinking," he said. "What's wrong?"

"I'm not drinking—though I thought about it. I'm just eating." She shrugged. "And nothing's wrong."

"Then why are you robbing me blind?"

"I was hungry. Why did you have the cookies in the freezer behind the booze?"

"To keep them safe from you." He snatched the box from her and helped himself to a rack. Breakfast of champions. "How did you know to search for them in there?"

She gave him a long look. "I know *all* your secrets."

"No, you don't."

"I do," she said.

"Shit." He blew out a breath and sank to the couch next to her. "You want to talk about something? Just say what you need to say. We both know you're not going to give me any peace until you do."

She nudged her elbow into his side. "Look at you, understanding the female psyche. So you *can* do it."

Leaning back, he closed his eyes. "I don't have the time or patience to play guessing games, Molly. Spit it out."

"Okay," she said. "Whatever's going on with you and Kylie—"

"Nothing. *Nothing's* going on."

She raised a brow.

"It's not," he said.

"You blew it?" She looked him over. "You did. Dammit, Joe."

He decided to plead the Fifth on that one. It was the only play he had.

"Fine, whatever, it's your love life. But she's got the

right to confront this dickwad who's been terrorizing her. You can't cut her out. She'll never forgive you."

When he just narrowed his eyes, she gave him the look right back. No one, and he meant *no one*, could give him shit or call him on *his* shit like his sister. No one else was allowed. And actually, she wasn't allowed either. She just didn't care that she wasn't allowed. "I'm not cutting her out of anything," he said.

"Oh please. Don't forget, I work where you work. I run the office, for God's sake. I get the same texts and e-mails all the guys get. You're going in at dawn and you're doing it without her. My question is this— are you insane or just stupid?"

Honestly, there was a strong chance that he was both. His phone buzzed an incoming text. "Hold that thought," he muttered and pulled out the phone to look at the text in order to make sure it wasn't one of the guys or Kylie.

Dad: Did you talk to the asshole yet?

Joe: Dad, I think you texted the wrong person.

Dad: Yep, meant that for your sister.

Joe: Wait. What asshole? Did you mean me?

Dad: . . .

Joe shook his head and put his phone away. "What does Dad want you to talk to me about?"

"He wants you to fall for Kylie. We have meetings about it. I'm to report back."

Joe just stared at her, trying to absorb this. "And you're going to report back what, exactly?"

"That it's too late. You've blown it to smithereens."

Joe's eyes began to twitch. "I didn't—"

"Look," she said, mercifully cutting him off. "I'm going to tell you something."

He grimaced. "Do you have to?"

She shook her head. "You can't joke this away, Joe. You need to hear it. If you handle this without her and it all goes down and it turns out that this Kevin guy really is the one, you take away her chance of getting closure."

He opened his mouth, but she held up a finger and then pointed it at him. "Just like you took away my closure," she said.

He stilled in shock. "Fuck that, Molly. I didn't—"

"But you did." She nudged her shoulder to his. "I mean, yes, you came for me when I was in trouble. After they took me, you never gave up searching for me, 24–7, even when the cops told Dad that I'd just run away. *You* knew that I hadn't taken off on some teenage whim. You knew I was in trouble, and thankfully you were like a bloodhound on the scent." Her voice went soft and emotional. "And I'm so, *so* very grateful for that." She inhaled a deep, shaky breath. "You have no idea how grateful."

He closed his eyes, sick to his gut because she was *grateful?* He'd nearly gotten her killed. *He* was the fucking grateful one, grateful that she'd ever spoken to him again, that she'd kept him in her life. That she still loved him was his own little miracle. "Molly—"

"But you didn't give me closure, Joe. After you got me to the hospital, you went back and handled the situation on your own, and by 'handled' I mean you went all vigilante on their asses and put your life in jeopardy in a very large way."

At the memory of her battered body lying still on the sidewalk after her fall, he jerked to his feet, unable to sit. "*I'd* put you in that situation," he said tightly. "You were innocent—"

"And so were you," she said, standing too, going toe-to-toe with him, her voice rising.

But his voice didn't. *She* was the passionate one in the family, the only one who let her emotions fly high and proud and loud. Very loud. He buried his, always. "I was *never* innocent," he said.

"You were! Joe, you never did what they wanted you to! It wasn't your fault that they were asshole punk-ass thugs. You got to me as soon as you could."

"Not soon enough."

They stared at each other. Finally, Molly broke the eye contact. She blew out a breath and they both looked down at the leg she still had so much trouble with.

"I got *myself* into trouble," she said quietly. "You know this. They told me if I just sat there and kept my mouth shut, they weren't going to hurt me. They just wanted to scare you. But I got impatient."

"This is a shock."

A small smile curved her lips at his quip and, relieved, he reached for her hand. It was the one thing he knew how to do for her, defuse her temper.

She held on and squeezed. "I got impatient," she said again. "And I got hurt because my fourteen-year-old self came up with the brilliant idea to try and escape. Please let that sink into your thick skull, Joe. When you went after them and nearly killed them, and then got in all that trouble because of it—"

"I couldn't just let them get away with what they'd done."

"Of course you could have!" she said. Actually, she was back to yelling. "The system would've taken care of them. You saw to it that they were caught, Joe, and that was amazing. You were just a kid and yet you still managed to do what no one else could. But then you took it upon yourself to mete out the justice." She dropped his hand and gave him a hard push to the chest. "And because of that, you were taken away from us. From Dad. From me. And I know you feel guilty, Joe. I get that. But don't *you* get it yet? *I* feel guilty too."

He was dumbfounded. "What the hell for?"

"Because every day that you had to be in the military and become even tougher and harder than you already were, that was my fault. Now you're so far removed from us that I can't even reach you half the time. I thought you weren't ever going to find your way back to feeling human, and then Kylie came along. She changed you. She brought you back to me. And now you're going to blow it all over again by taking away *her* closure too."

"How?" he asked, baffled. "How am I taking away her closure?"

"Because you're going to finish this for her, without her. I never got to look those asshole thugs in the eyes and say, 'You did your worst and I'm still breathing'! And I *needed* to do that, Joe! And so does Kylie. She needs to be in on the play for Kevin. You have to see that, right? Tell me you see that."

Just bringing all this up had him feeling . . . raw. Hollow. And something else he hadn't felt in a long time. Emotional. "I wasn't trying to take away your closure," he said. "But God, Molly, you almost died. I had to—"

"Be at my side," she said. "That was all you had to do and all I ever needed." She took a deep breath and lowered her voice. "Listen, you can't protect me all the time, and no one expects you to. It's the same with anyone in your life, okay? Kylie's a big girl. She'd rather have you at her side while she fights her battles than have you fight them for her."

Shit. That actually made sense. Which meant she was right.

She stepped closer and put her hand on his chest. "I need you to really hear this, Joe, and believe me. And then let it go. And *then* I need you to understand you're doing the same thing all over again to Kylie and she's not going to be as forgiving as your sister. See, I *have* to forgive you. We're blood. I'm going to always love you whether I like it or not. But Kylie doesn't have to forgive you at all. And if she doesn't, and she dumps your sorry ass for real, I'm afraid you're going to go back to . . ." She clamped her lips tight together, her eyes going suspiciously damp.

"To what?" he asked softly.

"To the man who doesn't smile or laugh or let himself feel."

He closed his eyes. "Molly," he breathed, and pulled her in for a hug. She held on tight, so damn tight that it was almost impossible to swallow the lump in his throat.

She was right. He couldn't protect her all the time and he had to accept that. Same with Kylie. And if he loved her—and damn, but he really did—he had to let her do this.

I love her?

Holy shit. He actually had to drop his ass to his couch because his legs got wobbly. Pulling out his phone, he texted the guys that there was going to be a change of plans. Kylie would go in first and talk to Kevin and get her damn closure if it killed him.

And it might.

They'd have her back, they'd make sure she was safe, and when she was satisfied by whatever answers she could get, they'd be there to finish it if needed and to drag Kevin's ass to jail. "I've got to go," he said.

Molly smiled. "Tell her hi for me."

Joe drove through the early morning wondering why the hell it'd taken him so long to realize that this was the only way it could go down.

And then there was the bigger epiphany of the night, the one he was trying damn hard not to dwell on.

He loved Kylie, a fact far more terrifying than any job he'd ever taken on.

He parked in front of Kylie's place. The lights were no longer on. It was four thirty in the morning. She was undoubtedly asleep. He hated to wake her, but this couldn't wait. There wasn't much time before they'd meet up with the team.

But she didn't answer the door. Or her phone. And when he helped himself and broke in, he just about stopped breathing.

She wasn't home.

He knew exactly where she'd gone. And why. He'd cut her out and now she was doing the same to him. He tried calling her again. Still no answer.

Joe was trained to handle himself in any situation, but nothing had prepared him for this moment. For knowing she'd gone off on her own—because of him.

He should never have tried to shield her. He should've just gone with her and trusted she could handle whatever they'd found, together.

Worse, he realized something else—that as much as he couldn't stand the thought of losing her, he'd lost her anyway by not trusting her. In his life, he tried really hard not to do anything stupid, but he'd definitely failed there. People tended to make assumptions based on words, but in Joe's experience, people rarely said what they really meant. So he didn't go by words. He went by steady, consistent actions.

And all of Kylie's actions told him she loved him too.

Unfortunately, *his* actions hadn't told her the same

thing in return. Which really did make him an ass. His chest hurt, no doubt from understanding that this was how his life was going to feel without Kylie in it.

Empty.

He ran to his truck, calling Archer and the guys to move everything up to right this minute. He called the police. He called *everyone* and hoped he wasn't too late.

Chapter 30

#SnapOutOfIt

Kylie sat at her mom's small kitchen table, drinking hot chocolate with little tiny marshmallows. When she'd been young, she'd had to drag a chair over from the table to climb up onto her grandpa's cabinets to reach the box of prepackaged powder. He'd kept it hidden from her because she'd had no self-control, loving how she always felt like Wonder Woman when all the sugar hit her system.

But her mom didn't hide the stuff and Kylie was on her third cup.

Wonder Woman still hadn't shown up.

But an entire volume of doubts had. When push had come to shove and Joe believed he'd had a viable suspect, he'd planned to handle it without her. He would've left her behind, when only days ago he'd promised to *never* leave her behind. "Men suck," she said.

"Yeah, they do." Her mom came to sit at the table with her, carrying her own cup of hot chocolate. Or more accurately, rum with a dab of hot chocolate. "Men *always* suck. You sure you don't need a kick?" She held up a flask.

"I'm sure," Kylie said. Her mom had a lifelong history with men sucking. Not that the woman had ever refrained from men, of course. In the old days, she'd visit Kylie at her grandpa's, dote on her for a while, or at least until another man came along, and then poof, she'd be gone.

Logically, Kylie knew she was angry at Joe because he was giving her bad flashbacks to her past. To when her mom hadn't ever put any weight into who Kylie was, wanting so much more from her life than to be a mom in the first place.

It'd been excusable when her mom had been a very young teen mom, but the pattern had been set and kept. She'd always chosen men over her daughter.

And in turn, she'd chosen men who chose work over her.

Maybe Kylie was overreacting. Okay, so she was *definitely* overreacting. All Joe was trying to do was keep her safe. She got that. She really did. But emotions like hurt and frustration didn't respond to common sense. The bottom line was that this wasn't a simple misunderstanding between them. They saw the world differently. A man like Joe would *always* be able to set her aside for something else. And she'd had enough of that for a lifetime. She deserved better. She needed to move on and get it for herself.

The funny—and sad—thing was, out of all the ways she'd thought their relationship would come to an end, this hadn't even been in the realm of possibilities, her realizing that she loved him and also that he wasn't the One for her. With her chest far too tight, she downed the rest of her hot chocolate, beginning to rethink her no-rum stance.

"So are you ever going to tell me what brings you here at . . ." Her mom glanced at the clock on the range. "Four thirty-eight in the morning? I'm not buying that it's because you got hurt by some guy. You've never been all that invested in the opposite sex, certainly not enough to let one get to you."

Ha. That was a good one. But she shoved that deep because that had nothing to do with why she was here. The thing was, she wasn't stupid. No matter that Joe didn't trust her to use her brain, she knew better than to go after Kevin on her own. She'd never do that.

But she wanted answers and her mom might be the one who could give them to her. "It's complicated," she started.

Her mom smiled. "Kylie, honey, everything with you is."

Kylie sighed and told herself not to get mad. She was here for answers, not a fight. And anyway, she supposed she could be a little complicated.

"It's just that you seem . . . sad." Her mom's eyes were surprisingly free of cynicism. "Are you?" she asked. "Sad?"

Well, that was one word for what Kylie felt. *Devastated* was another. "Do you remember Kevin Baker?" she asked.

Her mom scrunched up her forehead. "Kevin . . . yeah, sure. He was the one who was a good cook, right? Always making pancakes in the morning. You loved his pancakes."

Kylie had indeed loved Kevin's pancakes. He'd let her sit on the counter and stir the batter. "It's possible he might have my penguin," she said.

"What penguin?"

"Remember Grandpa's carvings?"

"Oh, yeah." Her mom went brows up. "You still have one of them?"

"Had," Kylie said. "Someone stole it and then started sending me pictures of it, saying I couldn't have it back unless I authenticated two pieces as Grandpa's."

Her mom frowned. "But I thought everything went up in flames in the fire."

"I thought so too, but one of the pieces looks legit. The other looks like a forgery."

"Then why would someone want you to authenticate it—" She broke off. "Oh," she breathed. "Someone's got a scam cooking. Wow. It's kind of brilliant." She caught Kylie's expression. "And wrong," she added. "Very wrong. You think it might be Kevin?"

"I don't want to think it, but there's some evidence that puts him on the radar, so I want to talk to him."

"What kind of evidence?" her mom asked.

"He took a piece to Eric Hansen, one of Grandpa's apprentices, and tried to sell it as his own. Later, he moved on to claiming the work *was* Grandpa's."

"Are you kidding me? That little piece of shit." Her mom stood up and grabbed her purse and keys.

"Wait," Kylie said, following her to the door. "Mom, what are you doing?"

"Going to pay Kevin a visit. If anyone's going to make money off my dad's talents, it's going to be us."

"No. Mom, you can't just—"

But her mom was out the door.

Kylie ran after her and caught up just as she was getting into her car. Kylie jumped into the passenger seat. "Mom, seriously. You can't—"

"I'm going to straighten this out. No one rips off a Masters."

Kylie held on as they catapulted out into the street. "Do you even know where Kevin lives?"

"Yes."

"But you broke up years ago."

"He lives on his uncle's boat. The old man died before I ever even met Kevin. Trust me, he's not moving from that boat until he's dead and buried."

"Okay, stop," Kylie said. "Turn around. We need to go home. There are other people handling this. The authorities can—"

"The authorities have never helped me out a day in my life. Don't fool yourself, Kylie. We're on our own." She pulled into the marina parking lot, which was dark. Very dark. It was getting close to dawn, but the day wasn't going to come with much light. The sky was heavy with an incoming storm.

This wasn't good. In fact, this was bad. Very, *very* bad. Kylie pulled out her phone to call Joe, but she had no service. "Mom, check your phone. Do you have any reception?"

Her mom pulled hers from her purse. "One bar. Not enough for shit."

"Which means you've *got* to stop because we can't call for backup. We're not going to be the stupid chicks in the horror flicks, okay? So just pull back out onto the street and keep driving until we get cell service, and then we'll—"

"This first," her mom said. "I just want to ask him some questions, no big deal. Wait in the car if that makes you feel better. I'll be right back." She pulled the car up to the shadows at the edge of the parking lot and hopped out of her still running car.

"Mom—"

But she was gone, heading for the docks.

Dammit. Kylie crawled over the console, into the driver's seat, and drove through the lot, one eye on her phone. She didn't want to leave her mom but she had to call Joe. When one bar finally appeared, she nearly collapsed in relief. It wasn't enough for a call, but she thought maybe she could get a text out. "Siri," she said, eyes on the spot where her mom had vanished. "Text Joe. I'm at the marina with my mom, who's gone in to talk to Kevin. Send." She tossed her phone down, drove closer to the maze of docks, parked, and went after her mom. Maybe the woman hadn't been all that great a maternal figure, but she was still the only one Kylie had. There was no way she could just sit in the car and wait for help.

She tried to stay in the shadows as she headed to

the dock. Once there, she was out in the open, but the sky was still dark and there were no lights. Stymied by the huge maze of docks, Kylie slowed to listen but couldn't hear a thing except for the water slapping up against the pylons. *"Mom?"*

No answer, but she thought she could hear the clicking of her mom's sandals to the right, so she turned that way and nearly groaned at the amount of boats.

An entire row of them, as far as the eye could see.

But only one had an interior light on. Kylie headed that way, her stomach filled with dread. She so did not feel good about this. After creeping closer to the lone boat with the light, she hid behind a pylon and peered into one of the windows.

The interior of the boat was tight quarters, jam-packed with . . . wood furniture. She crept closer to get a better look and froze. Most of the pieces were cookie-cutter pieces, a stack of the same headboards, another of identical nightstands, but mixed in were a few other things, such as a table that looked an awful lot like the one in the picture she'd received. Another was a unique grandfather clock that she recognized from her grandpa's shop. The shop where everything had supposedly burned.

Chapter 31

#SayHelloToMyLittleFriend

Panicked, Kylie once again called out for her mom. When she didn't get a response, she moved to the ladder and boarded the ship, jumping to the deck. *"Mom!"*

Still no answer, but she could hear voices now, her mom's and a man's, both raised. She rushed to the hatch door, not sure how to feel when she found it unlocked. A few steep steps and she found herself below deck in the area she'd seen through the window from the dock.

Just beyond that, her mom and Kevin stood in a tiny galley, toe-to-toe, nose-to-nose. In unison the two of them turned and looked at Kylie, her mom not surprised, Kevin *very* surprised.

"Kylie?" He sounded shocked. "What are you doing here?"

Feeling oddly emotional at the sight of him, she pointed to the grandfather clock. "Where did you get that?"

He looked confused. "What's going on?"

"Kylie's question first," her mom said.

"Okay." Kevin looked at the grandfather clock. "Your grandpa gave it to me."

Kylie shook her head. "He couldn't have. It was in his shop on the night of the fire, still unfinished."

"He hadn't finished a lot of things," Kevin said. "Kylie . . ." Expression warm, he stepped closer. "It's really good to see you. I—"

"Hold on." She held up her hand, staring at the clock. "How is it here if it burned?"

He hesitated and she let out a rough breath. "You were at his shop that night. And you, or someone, took it and finished it." She waited for him to say otherwise, hoping against hope there was a good explanation that didn't involve him betraying her grandpa *and* one of the few good childhood memories she had.

But he said nothing.

"Explain," her mom said to him. "Explain right now."

"Listen," Kevin said directly to Kylie, ignoring her mom. "Clearly, there's some confusion. Your grandpa gave me this piece *before* the fire, and it *was* finished. But great news, you've just confirmed it's his work. Can I get you to authenticate that in writing?"

"I'm not confused." She'd offered to help her grandpa finish the piece and he'd been delighted with her interest. Only they hadn't had the time before it was too late. She looked around and saw a Polaroid camera on the galley table, which made her heart start a heavy drumming in her chest. "Is that your camera?"

Kevin followed her gaze and sighed, scrubbing a hand over his face. When he looked at her again, his bafflement was gone, replaced by resignation. "All you had to do," he said, sounding very tired, "was agree to authenticate my work so I could make enough money to fund my own gallery instead of working for a bunch of big corporate idiots who know nothing about the art of furniture making."

"I couldn't do that," she said. "I couldn't authenticate what wasn't his. Surely you knew that."

He shrugged. "You made your choice, I suppose. But now I have to make mine."

Kylie's heart sank to her toes and she slowly slid her hands into her pockets. Her right hand encountered her phone. She swiped the screen and thumbed what she was pretty sure would be her phone app. Then she tapped the screen near the top, hoping like hell that first, she had service now that she was away from all the buildings and on the water, and second, that she was calling the last person she'd attempted to call—Joe.

"I can't believe this," her mom said. "I knew right from the start that you were a bad apple."

"Right," Kevin said dryly. "Or why else would you have dated me?"

Her mom's eyes narrowed. "And what's that supposed to mean?"

Kevin snorted. "It means you only date assholes. And you're a mom! What kind of idea was that supposed to give Kylie? It's amazing that she's not all kinds of screwed up."

Ha. Little did he know, Kylie thought. "Okay," she said quickly when her mom started looking around, probably for a bat to hit Kevin over the head with. "This is about Grandpa's work, not you two's past—"

"Shut up," they both said in unison, glaring at each other.

"You said you were the exception!" her mom yelled at Kevin.

"And you said you'd changed!" Kevin yelled back.

Kylie sighed and, keeping one eye on the children, she looked around for something to help the situation and caught sight of a couple of pieces of furniture against the far wall. An armoire and a matching mirror. "Oh my God," she said. "Those are my grandpa's too." She looked at Kevin. "They were also in his shop on the day of the fire, where supposedly everything burned."

"Most," he said. "But not everything."

Her mom's eyes were wide. And pissed. "How did you get this stuff?" she asked. "His stuff?"

Kevin shrugged. "You know how the guy was. Brilliant artist, shitty businessman."

"So you took advantage of him through me?" Kylie's mom asked.

"Hey, he'd offered to pay me to finish some things for him," Kevin said. "And I did exactly that, only he didn't pay me. He couldn't."

"He'd never do that," her mom said. "He was the most honest man I ever met."

Kylie had gone still. "The horses," she whispered.

"What?" Her mom looked at her. "What horses?"

But Kevin was nodding, confirming Kylie's fear. "He did love the races," he said. "And the betting."

The truth was, her grandpa had been a gambling addict—though Kylie had believed him to be a *recovered* addict. Her mom was looking stunned. Kylie's grandpa had been so good at so many things and it seemed one of those things was keeping secrets.

"He kept promising me he'd get me the money," Kevin said. "Only it never happened."

"Why didn't you just tell me?" her mom asked.

"Because he begged me not to. He didn't want anyone to know." Kevin sent Kylie an apologetic glance. "But I needed money too. So I helped myself to one of his pieces now and then and sold them."

"That's stealing," her mom said.

"I called it getting paid. He owed me."

Kylie's gaze fell on something right past the Polaroid camera. A high-grade food processor. Her penguin was perched on it, inches from certain destruction by rotating whipping blades if the processor got flipped on. Her stomach fell and in shock, she shook her head. "How is it that he never caught you taking stuff from his shop?"

She saw the flash of guilt and her gut tightened. "He did catch you," she said.

"Once," he admitted. "He walked in on me late at

night loading up a few things into my truck. He said something like, 'I knew someone was stealing from me. I just didn't think it would be you.'"

That was exactly like her grandpa, seeing only the good in people. "He cared about you. I'm sure he was devastated."

"Devastated? Not exactly," Kevin said. "He pulled a gun on me and I dove to the ground when he actually squeezed off a round."

"Wait—*he shot at you?*" Kylie gasped in shock.

"No, he shot at the ceiling. A warning, I guess. The bullet ricocheted off something and hit the electrical socket where the soldering iron was plugged in. The place went up in flames in seconds. It was a fluke. He just meant to scare me off. Like this." Reaching behind him, Kevin produced a gun.

With twin gasps, Kylie's mom and Kylie both dove to the floor.

"I'm not going to shoot you," he said, sounding horrified at the thought. "I'm trying to show you what happened that night and how it couldn't happen again in a million years. It was truly a one in a million shot." He squeezed the trigger and *bam,* a bullet hit the ceiling. And ricocheted off somewhere else.

And then . . . nothing.

"See?" he said, shrugging. "Accident."

Kylie shot to her feet, such fury flowing through her that her entire body was shaking with it. "You can't just fire a gun into a closed area. You'll hurt someone!"

"I wasn't aiming at either of you."

"Oh my God!" Kylie managed. "There's a reason they don't like dumbasses to have guns, you know!"

"You're overreacting."

"I'm overreacting?" she asked. "Are you kidding me? All these years I blamed *myself* for that fire!"

"Well, that was stupid," Kevin said. "You weren't even there."

"I was earlier in the day! And you *knew* I blamed myself!" she cried. "You could have told me all this right after it happened!"

"Oh, right. And I'm sure the police would've understood about me just taking what I was owed." He let out a mirthless laugh. "I might've gone to jail. And I'd have hurt your grandpa's reputation while I was at it. Did you think of that? He was good to me—I mean, other than the whole not paying me thing. I didn't want to jeopardize his career."

"You lying, two-faced, thieving bastard," Kylie's mom said, getting back to her feet.

"Seriously?" Kevin asked, taking a step back from her. "*You* want to go there? How many times did you *borrow* money from him?"

"I'm his blood! If you don't admit to occasionally stealing money from your parents then you're not being honest."

"I never stole money from my parents," Kevin said.

Nor had Kylie, but she couldn't think. She was shaking with anger and her head was spinning. "Why didn't anyone find the gun or the bullet that night?"

"Your grandpa freaked that he'd lost his temper. He said the gun wasn't registered. He made me take it and I don't know why they didn't find the bullet or casing. I took the gun and left, not knowing the fire was already smoldering, gaining steam. I'd never have left him there if I'd known what would happen."

"I can't believe this," she said. "I thought for sure you'd have a good explanation and be just another dead end. I didn't want it to be you. You were nice to me. I thought you liked me. But then you bailed on us, and now . . . now you're a deserter *and* a thief."

Kevin's eyes softened. "I liked you too, Kylie, and I never bailed on you guys."

"Yes, you did," her mom said. "You told me that we were good together, that you saw a future. Then one day you said you had to go to New York for a job but you'd call when you got back."

"And I meant all of that, and I *did* call," Kevin said. "Your latest conquest answered."

Her mom rolled her eyes. "Well, if you're going to let that stop you."

Smoke was beginning to curl down from the ceiling, seeping in through the cracks and the vent. Kylie stared at it in growing horror. "Uh, guys?" she said, but neither was paying her any attention.

"I think you're full of shit," her mom said to Kevin.

"No, I really did see a life with the three of us." He turned to Kylie. "Your mom said she'd wait for me. I was only gone three weeks, but I bet she didn't even wait a day."

"Hey," her mom said defensively, but when Kevin

raised a brow, she tossed up her hands. "Okay, fine. So I was a shithead back then."

"Hello!" Kylie said, jabbing a finger at the smoking ceiling. "Forget the past! We've got a problem—"

"And to be fair to me," her mom went on, "I was young and stupid. I didn't know a good guy from a bad one. I always picked them based on what they could do for me. And worse, I always picked them over my own offspring." She sent Kylie a watery smile. "But I was lucky enough to have a daughter willing to be patient with me. And I'm going to learn to put her first, starting now. Come over here, baby." She held out a hand to Kylie and wriggled her fingers.

"Mom," Kylie said through a tight throat and, reaching out, took hold of her hand. "We all need to get off the boat. *Now*."

"Holy shit," Kevin said, finally noticing the crazy amount of smoke tunneling through the cracks. "We're actually on fire. Did I do that?"

"Yes, Urkel, you really did that!" Kylie's mom tugged Kylie toward the door, but before they could get there, the ceiling suddenly collapsed, crashing down on top of them. Some of it was on fire, but thankfully not the pieces that hit Kylie. It took her a minute to dig out but she finally sat up, coughing, looking around for her mom. *"Mom!"*

"Here." Her mom appeared as she sat up, covered in dust. In front of them, flames were flickering now, gaining strength.

Kylie dragged herself to her feet and then pulled her mom up too. "Where's Kevin?"

"I don't know!"

"Kevin!" Kylie yelled as her mom yanked her toward their exit. Together they stumbled and staggered up the stairs and off the boat, onto the dock, whipping back around to look for any sign of him. "Kevin!" Kylie yelled again and again, chest tight, panic gripping her. "Did he get above deck?" she asked her mom.

"I don't know, baby."

Suddenly the night lit up with a symphony of sounds and lights. First responders arriving en masse, appearing through the hazy smoke like avengers. Kylie felt herself sway a little bit and she sank to the dock as she stared at the craziness in fascination.

An outline of a man broke from the pack, running down the docks. "Found her," Joe said into his comm, heading right for her, his team materializing behind him. "Kylie," he said, voice rough, dropping to his knees in front of her.

Aw, look at that. He was worried about her, his eyes reflecting that and a lot more. In spite of himself, he cared about her. She knew that much. It wasn't entirely his fault that he was so emotionally challenged, she thought, putting a hand on his jaw. "You're so pretty, Joe. It's really a shame that you're such a dumbass."

Lucas choked out a laugh but, at Joe's glare, quickly turned to Kylie's mom. "You okay, ma'am?"

"I will be if you never 'ma'am' me again," her mom said, looking singed around the edges but thankfully unhurt.

Joe turned Kylie's face to his, running his finger

over a bump on her forehead that made her wince and slap his hand away. "Kevin's still on the boat," she said and gripped the front of his shirt in her fist. "We've got to save him."

Joe pointed to a figure of a man sitting on the other end of the dock with an oxygen mask over his face.

Kevin.

She sagged in relief, sort of falling into Joe. He still knelt in front of her, looking her over, face grim, jaw tight—whether in reaction to her "dumbass" comment, or just the fact that she was here where she shouldn't have been, she didn't know.

"I didn't mean to be here," she said. "I—"

He put a finger over her lips. "We'll circle back to that later, when your hair's not still smoking."

"I texted you."

"Yes, and it said 'Siri, text Joe.'"

"What?" She shook her head. "No, she was supposed to tell you where I was. That bitch. I also called. Did she tell you that?"

"I got the call. We were connected the whole time, which is how I got here in time to see you save yourself. Proud of you, Kylie."

She tried to meet his gaze at that, but suddenly the ground was shaking so violently she was having trouble speaking. "Wh-wh-what's happening?"

"Shh," Joe said, pulling her in close. "You're in shock."

"Am not— Hey," she said as Joe ran his hands over her, looking for injuries. "I'm okay." But then she ruined that statement by nearly coughing up a lung. "Really. Totally fine," she finally managed with a very hoarse voice.

This didn't appear to ease his tension one little bit as he continued to hold on to her. "You're bleeding."

"What? No, I'm not. I'm—" She looked down and saw a long rip in her jeans from hip to knee, revealing a huge gash in her leg with lots of blood and gore. "Huh," she said, her heartbeat pounding like a drum in her ears as her vision started to fade. "Look at that . . . I *am* bleeding." Her vision went all cobwebby.

"Kylie." Joe sounded more intense than she'd ever heard him and that was saying something. "Kylie, stay with me."

Ha. If only he really meant that.

Chapter 32

#YouAintHeardNothingYet

Joe's heart was still on overdrive from the crazy race to the marina while listening to Kylie handle the situation via her cell phone. The connection had been spotty so he'd missed a bunch of what was said, but the gunshot had come through loud and clear and he'd gone into heart failure until he'd heard her voice again. "Kylie, the paramedics are going to take a look at you now."

She weaved and clutched at him. "I'm sorry you're upset."

"Let's worry about you."

"Five-by-five rule," she said, cupping his jaw with both hands to stare into his eyes. "If it's not going to matter in five years, don't let it upset you."

He shook his head and hugged her close, pressing his face into her hair, trying not to embarrass himself, but he was going to need a moment. "You're going to matter in five years, Kylie."

She didn't respond to that. Instead she pulled back to look earnestly into his eyes. "You get why I went without you, right? I didn't mean to, but I had to go with my mom. I couldn't let her go after Kevin by herself."

"And you were amazing, baby," her mom said, dropping to her knees on Kylie's other side now. "But let's allow the hot guys to do their job and take care of you, okay?"

"I can take care of myself." Kylie looked around with a frown. "Why is the ground *still* shaking?"

"Still you," Joe said gently. He took an emergency blanket from Lucas and wrapped it around her shoulders. He was worried about the gash along her thigh, as it was bone-deep. There was another cut at her temple and along one cheek. Her pupils were dilated. And she was breathing like she'd just run a few miles. None of it added up to anything good. "You did great, Kylie. You took care of your mom. Now you're going to let us take care of you."

She closed her eyes. "But I'm fine."

"And don't I know it. But I've got you now. I love you, and I've got you."

No answer.

He stroked the hair from her face. "Kylie."

Nothing. She'd gone limp in his arms and for the second time in an hour, his heart about stopped. The next few minutes were a blur of action as he handed her over to the paramedics, not leaving her side until they'd loaded her up in the ambulance.

Her mom climbed in beside her, and then the double doors shut in his face and they were gone.

"Hospital," he said to Lucas and headed straight for his truck.

Lucas beat him to it—quite the feat. "I'm driving," he said.

Since Joe didn't want to waste time fighting, he took shotgun and then proceeded to backseat-drive Lucas all the way there. "Turn here, it's faster. Take the next left. Run the yellow."

"Joe?"

"Yeah?"

Lucas glanced at him. "You want to get there in how many minutes?"

"I'd do it in ten," Joe said.

Lucas nodded. "If you shut the fuck up, I'll get you there in eight."

So Joe shut the fuck up. And Lucas got them to the hospital in the promised eight minutes.

But it was several hours before Joe got to see Kylie. She'd needed to be sedated to remove the drywall that was still embedded in her leg. Several other cuts, including the one on her temple, had needed stitches.

In the meantime, it was the dreaded waiting room for him, which had filled up. Kylie's entire gang from the Pacific Pier Building was there, including his own sister, who gave him a big, hard hug and then smacked him upside the head.

"That's for Kylie," Molly said.

"Hey." He rubbed his head. "It's not my fault she's in here."

A lie. He'd let her down. He'd let them both down and he didn't know how he could forgive himself.

"That's not what I meant," Molly said and then sighed and hugged him again. "Joseph Michael Malone, Kylie being in here *isn't* your fault."

She hadn't middle-named him since they'd been young so she clearly meant business.

"And I smacked you," she went on, "because the rumor mill says you waited until she was passed out to tell her you love her."

He gaped at her and then whipped around to look at his guys.

Lucas. Archer. Max. Reyes.

Lucas waved.

Joe flipped him off.

"Oh please," Molly said. "Don't even try to blame any of them for your idiocy. We talked about this too. You're still too slow on the trigger."

"Wow," he said.

His sister went hands on hips. "Did you know that no one says 'wow' better than a guy who's been accused of something he actually did?"

Joe pulled out his phone and looked at the dark screen. Where the hell was a call when you needed one?

"Sorry," Molly said. "But the person you're hoping is going to call you has been sedated, and even if she wasn't, she'd be ignoring your sorry ass."

Joe turned and walked out of the room. Because

once again his sister was right—not that he could tell her so or she'd gloat. But he had indeed been *way* too slow, on several counts. He was supposed to protect Kylie. Instead he'd kept her out of the loop and she'd gotten hurt—on his watch. That was going to eat at him for a good long time.

He paced around and finally bribed a nurse he'd dated the year before to direct him to Kylie's room. He waited there until her mom left before slipping inside himself.

Her eyes were closed and she appeared to be sleeping peacefully enough, so he dragged a chair as close to her bed as he could get and sat.

He didn't realize he'd dozed off until he heard her low, raspy voice murmur, "Go home, Joe."

She was sitting up carefully, hair wild, moving slow enough to tell him she hurt from head to toe. Her body was a tightly coiled spring, whether from the pain or stress, he had no idea. Both, no doubt. "How do you feel?" he asked.

"Better than you. You look like hell."

Yeah, well, the past twelve hours had nearly killed him.

She stared up at him and then closed her eyes. "We're not doing this," she whispered.

"Not doing what?"

"You think it's your fault I got hurt," she said. "So now you're going to change your stance on wanting a relationship with me out of guilt. But I won't do it, Joe. I don't want you under those circumstances. I want you to have wanted me all along."

Heart heavy, he shook his head. "It's not that, Kylie. I—"

"Oh my God, you're awake!" Her mom came back into the room with a relieved smile. "I brought Jell-O. Red, green, yellow . . . *all* the Jell-O!" She set a tray on Kylie's lap. "And I just talked to your doctor. He says I can bust you free in a few hours. And then I'm taking you out of town to recoup for a few days. I've got a friend in Aptos who's letting us use his beach house!"

Kylie grimaced. "Mom—"

"Please, Kylie." She sat at Kylie's hip and took her hand in hers, gripping it tight, pressing it to her chest. "Please let me do this for you."

Kylie stared at her mom and then nodded. Then she leaned back and closed her eyes—without looking at Joe again.

"Kylie," he said.

"My head hurts," she whispered, and just like that both he and her mom were ushered out of her room so she could rest some more. And later, when she was discharged, she left town with her mom and what was left of the tatters of Joe's heart.

Chapter 33

#OfAllTheGinJointsInAllTheTownsInAllTheWorld

One week later

Kylie carefully navigated her way out of the Uber in front of her place. It wasn't easy with her bag and her crutches—she wasn't supposed to put weight on her leg yet—but she managed because she needed to be alone.

Or more accurately, away from her mom.

They'd had a surprisingly and shockingly good time at the beach house. Her mom had been sweet and attentive and helpful, all new traits. She'd even cooked for Kylie. And they'd had to call the fire department only one time and that had been mostly because her mom wanted to see if Aptos had any cute new firefighter recruits, so she'd burned some cookies and set off the fire alarm.

But it was time for Kylie to get back to her life. Her friends missed her. Gib missed her. Work missed her. Vinnie missed her.

She wanted to get back to normal. Or as normal as her life could be. To say she still felt off balance about how everything had gone down would be an understatement. The boat was still off-limits due to the ongoing investigation, so she had no idea what, if anything, had been recovered. But as far as she knew, the penguin hadn't been found in the fire and that was devastating. Still, now she knew she didn't need it to remember her grandpa by.

Kevin, who'd not been injured beyond minor smoke inhalation, was cooperating fully, and for that she was grateful. But it was far more than the fire that had her spinning. It was her broken heart. She'd done her best not to go there all week with her mom, but just walking up to the front of her place was like ripping off the Band-Aid.

Memories flooded her as she walked inside. Joe, and all those times he'd stood on this very porch right at her back, watching out for her. Joe, gently nudging her inside and then up against the wall, where he not so gently kissed the daylights out of her. Joe, tipping his head back and laughing at something she said. God, she loved his laugh. Joe, buried deep inside her, his hands on her face, eyes locked on hers, revealing emotion that he never seemed to have the words for.

With a shuddery exhalation, she made her way through the living room. When she heard something behind her, she turned to find Joe standing in the doorway as if she'd conjured him up.

He was in his usual work gear, loaded for bear, clearly straight from the job and appearing as if maybe he'd just walked off the cover of *Guns & Ammo*.

He looked like the best thing she'd seen all week—not that she wanted him to know it, so she steeled both herself and her heart. Clearly he'd set some sort of security or alarm to alert himself to her arrival and that should've infuriated her. But be still her beating heart . . . he seemed to be holding something. "Is that a bag of Tina's muffins?" she asked, trying to remain unmoved.

"Your mom said you hadn't been eating very much."

"You've been talking to my mom?"

He shrugged. "You weren't answering my calls or texts."

She let out a deep sigh. "What are you doing here, Joe?"

"I needed to see you." He hadn't moved from where he stood against the opposite doorway. "I needed to see for myself that you were alright."

She spread her arms. "Almost good as new."

He gave a small smile. "It's really good to see you. I missed you, Kylie."

"I know."

He seemed surprised and she smiled. "I guess you don't know that you actually aren't that hard to read once you let someone in, although your expression

when you look at me is usually mostly either be-
mused or amused." She shook her head. "I was never
sure what to make of that, but the girls told me it's a
look of love." She kept her gaze level on his, daring
him to disagree with her, but he didn't.

This gave her a surge of hope that her poor body
didn't know what to do with. So she mixed it in with
her lingering anger and it was like a chemistry ex-
periment. It exploded inside her. "I'd take heart over
that except then you go and do stupid things like that
night at my place when everything came to a head.
You made me so angry when you lied to me, telling
me you'd let me be involved— No," she said when
he opened his mouth. "You *lied,* Joe, by omission or
whatever. Don't even try to deny it. And that's not
even the worst part. You sleep with me, and it's not
just sex. You touch me and kiss me and look at me in
a way that tells me it's so much more, but you deny
it. You want me to think it's just a toss in the hay that
you could walk away from at any point. But it's not."
She had to stop there and swallow a ball of emotion
stuck in her throat. "And that's not something you
do to a friend," she managed to say, although she
was no longer speaking all calm and quiet. "That's
something you do to a one-night stand. And I won't
be someone that you don't have the decency to tell
the truth to, or someone you just sleep with when it's
convenient. I won't be a toy, Joe. Not even for you."

He finally pushed off from the doorway and
stalked toward her, eyes glittering dangerously.
"You're not a toy, Kylie," he said in a very serious

voice. Maybe the most serious voice she'd heard from him yet. "Not even close." He came to a stop right in front of her. He set the bag of muffins aside and drew a deep breath. "With the exception of my dad and my sister, I've always been alone—" He set a finger over her lips when she started to speak. "I've never done relationships," he said. "I've never lived with a woman. I've never gotten attached to anyone because it's easier to keep them all distant than to let them in and be vulnerable because of how I feel about them. It's not right, but it's been my MO for a long time, and it's what makes me do things like let you think I don't love you."

She sucked in a breath to speak, but he applied a gentle pressure to her lips. "It's what made me screw up that night we were going after Kevin," he went on. "I realized it and came back for you, but you were already gone." He paused and shook his head. "Okay, that's not entirely true either. *Molly* made me realize it and she was right. You're a part of me, Kylie, the very best part. You're not just my friend or my lover. You're . . . everything."

This shocking admission had all the air in her lungs escaping out in one big, shocked rush, and she pulled his finger from her lips. "I have a question," she whispered.

He gave a single, wary nod.

"Why did you ever agree to help me that first day, when I got the first picture?"

At first he didn't respond, but she forced herself to wait him out. She might not be well versed in interrogation techniques, but she knew the only way to get a stubborn male to answer a question when he didn't want to was to ask it and then remain silent. But it was the hardest thing she'd ever done and she had to literally bite her tongue to press her minuscule advantage.

"I don't think I should say," Joe finally told her.

She gaped at him. "What? Why not?"

"Because I don't make a habit of giving my adversary information that can be used against me."

"Adversary?" she asked. "Is that how you see me?"

"Kylie," he said on a rough laugh. "We've been in a chess game since day one and you're winning. When I'm not looking, you sneak pieces on your side of the board. You don't need any help from me."

She stared at him and then found her first genuine smile in *days*. "You missed me," she whispered, the knowledge giving her way too much smug pleasure. "I think I want to hear you say it."

He was silent as he carefully scooped her up and gently deposited her on the couch. She was grateful as her muscles were quivering with fatigue. She watched from her perch as he locked her front door and checked the house.

When he came back to her, he sat on the coffee table facing her, mood still serious. "Yes."

"Yes?" she inquired.

"Yes, I missed you. I missed the hell out of you. I missed us. This," he said, gesturing between them.

"So there's really a this?" she asked softly, almost afraid to talk, scared that if she did, he'd stop.

He leaned forward and once again scooped her into his warm, strong, *wonderful* arms. He took the spot where she'd just been, settling her in his lap. "Long before our first kiss that first crazy night, I knew there was a this." He nuzzled at her ear. "It terrified me. I was in some pretty good denial there for a while, but I couldn't hold on to it." He pulled back and met her gaze. "You trusted me. You looked at me like I was something of worth to you. You believed in me, and there haven't been a lot of people in my life to do that." Leaning in, he covered her mouth with his.

It was a really amazing kiss and she was trying to climb him like a tree when he broke free. Her heart stopped at the look on his face. "What?" she whispered.

He sank his fingers into her hair. "I need you to tell me now, Kylie."

"Tell you what?"

"That you love me."

All the stress and tension drained from her as she slid her arms around his neck and relaxed into him. "I love you back, Joseph Michael Malone."

He didn't smile. "I wasn't sure you heard me at the marina."

"I did. I'll never forget it. I also heard that Molly yelled at you at the hospital, middle-naming you. There's a group text."

"I'm really going to have to beat the shit out of my team," he said mildly. He cupped her face and brought it close to his, and their next kiss was far more serious than the one before it. This time when they broke for air, clothes were missing.

"Be sure," Joe said.

"I'm sure that if you stop, I'll find your gun and shoot you."

He smiled, probably at the thought of her trying to overpower him. "I meant be sure about *me*. You know a relationship with me won't be easy. There will probably be days when we'll want to kill each other."

"There are days like that now."

"Funny," he said and kissed her again, stopping just as it got really good. "I almost forgot," he said. "I have something for you." He reached into one of his pants pockets and pulled out a small wooden carving.

She blinked. She could tell he'd carved it himself, but beyond that she had no guesses. "Did you make a . . ." She turned it around in her palm but it looked like only one thing. "A penis?"

He paused to stare at the carving and then laughed. "Okay, yeah. Let's go with that." He waggled a brow. "For when I can't be with you. Beware of splinters."

She grinned and pulled him down for another heart-stopping kiss. "Stay with me, Joe," she said against his mouth. "Always be with me so I don't need the wooden penis."

He laughed again and the easy sound of it made her smile up at him. "This feels like a dream," she murmured.

He tossed the wooden carving aside and nudged

himself into the vee of her thighs. "How about this? Does *this* feel like a dream?"

Heat pooled low in her body and she had the sudden urge to divest him of the rest of his clothing. "Definitely not."

"Good. Now eat your muffins. You're going to need the energy for what I have planned."

Liking the sound of that, she nearly swallowed a blueberry muffin whole when he brought it to her. When she was done, he carried her to her bed, where he carefully set her down before slowly crawling up her body until he could look straight into her eyes. "We should discuss terms."

"Of course," she said, rocking up into him. "But I think I need a preview of the perks on offer before I can negotiate properly."

"My pleasure." He brushed his lips gently against hers before getting serious and deepening the kiss.

It was a long time before she could think again, and her first thought was she had no idea what was going to happen, but she had no doubt they were going to make this work.

Joe laced his fingers in hers and brought them to his lips. It was a small, sweet gesture, but as she'd already learned with him, actions always spoke louder than words and *his* actions told her everything she needed to know. "You're mine now," she whispered.

He smiled, apparently not at all concerned. "I'm okay with that."

"And I'm yours."

"My wildest dream come true," he said.

Epilogue

Two weeks later

On Kylie's first day back to work, Joe walked into Reclaimed Woods to find Gib at the front counter. The guy looked up from his computer, expression carefully blank.

"Problem?" Joe asked.

"I like the guys you work with," Gib said. "Archer. Lucas. Reyes and the others. I like your good friend Spence too, and Caleb, because he just spent a fortune on some of my stuff. I'm also fond of your sister. Molly's good people. Really good."

Joe wasn't sure where this was going, but he nodded. He liked all of those people too.

"But I've never liked you," Gib said.

Joe felt a rough laugh leave him. "Yeah, well, that's not exactly new information."

Gib didn't smile. "I'm going to trust that everyone knows something about you I don't, that you're a good guy."

What was he supposed to say to that?

"You going to take good care of her?" Gib said.

Joe nodded. "I am."

Gib went back to his computer screen.

And thus, apparently temporarily vetted, Joe headed through to the back. He found Kylie in a huge apron, covered in sawdust, large protective goggles on her face. She was bent over a saw, milling something that was sending sparks and more sawdust into the air that circled her like a puffy cloud as she worked with great concentration.

Afraid to startle her, he stood there and watched a moment, marveling at how just laying eyes on her warmed his heart and eased his soul. He'd grown soft, he realized, by allowing her in. But there was no going back for him. He'd rather suffer the weakness of loving her and having her in his life than reverting to his empty life before her.

He was just damn lucky—and grateful—that she seemed to feel the same way, that she'd been willing to fight him, fight for him. He waited until she stopped, turned off the saw, and eyed whatever she was working on before moving closer.

She whipped around and, at the sight of him, sent a brilliant smile in his direction, at once making his day, his week, his month, his entire life.

"Hey," she said. She tossed off the goggles and threw herself at him.

He caught her up and lowered his head, finding her lips with his, trying to promise everything he didn't have words for.

"Mmm," she said when the kiss ended, leaving her eyes closed, her mouth curving. "Missed that."

He'd left her bed six hours earlier and he was quite certain he'd kissed her thoroughly then too. Every inch of her. "I've got something for you," he said.

Her eyes flew open as he carefully lowered her back to the ground. Her leg was healing up just fine, but it still bothered her some and he could tell by the slight tremor in her body that she'd pushed herself too far today. "Sit."

"Gimme," she said. "One of Tina's muffins?" she asked hopefully.

"Something even better. Sit first."

She rolled her eyes but sat on a stool.

He pulled her beloved penguin from his pocket.

Her mouth curved in a little *oh!* of surprise as she held out her hands for it. "It didn't burn," she breathed, hugging it to her chest.

"There wasn't a lot that made it out," he said, "but several of your grandpa's pieces actually did. It was all being held as evidence until today."

She looked up, her eyes meeting his. "There's more," she guessed.

He reached into another pocket and pulled out a second small wooden carving. Another penguin, the mirror image of the one she held.

She gasped. "Ohmigod, there *are* two? This one was on the boat too?"

"No."

She looked up. "Then where?"

"A while back you told me you thought maybe there might be more carvings, so I did some digging and tracked it down."

She looked boggled. "What? *How?*"

"Your mom had your grandpa's files, or what was left of them, and I went through them. I found a bill of sale from years ago and contacted the buyer, who was actually an ex of your grandpa's. He'd sold her the penguin and she still had it. She said it was a memory keeper. When I told her your story, she changed her mind. She wanted you to have it more than she wanted to keep it." He shrugged. "So she sold it to me."

Kylie was staring at him, very still. "It had to be insanely expensive."

He shrugged again.

"Joe."

He stroked a finger over the curve of her ear, tucking an errant strand of hair behind it. Because he didn't want to stop touching her, he let his fingers slip into her wild waves of hair. "I wanted you to have it."

Her eyes went a little shimmery with unshed tears. "But—"

He put a finger over her lips. "I wanted to."

She was silent a moment, like she was so moved she couldn't speak. "No one's done anything like that for me," she finally whispered and blinked the tears away. "Thank you."

He took the two penguins and showed her how they went together like two pieces of a jigsaw puzzle. They'd been made as two halves of a whole.

"They fit," she said, marveling.

"They do," he agreed and met her gaze. "And so do we, Kylie."

She shook her head, reaching for him. "You're amazing, you know that?"

"I don't," he said, lifting her up against him again, closing his eyes, loving the feel of her in his arms. "Maybe you should tell me, slowly and in great detail."

She took him home and did just that.

Keep reading for a sneak peek
at Jill Shalvis' next women's fiction novel,

RAINY DAY FRIENDS

Coming Summer 2018!

Chapter 1

*Anxiety Girl, able to jump to the worst
conclusion in a single bound!*

Most of the time Karma was a bitch, but every once
in a while she could be surprisingly nice, even kind.
Lanie Jacobs, way past overdue for both of those
things, told herself this was her time. Seize the day
and all that and, drawing a deep breath, she exited
the highway at Wildstone.

The old Wild West California town was nestled in
the rolling hills between the Pacific Coast and wine/
ranching country. She'd actually grown up not too
far from here, though it felt like a lifetime ago. The
road was narrow and curvy, and since it'd rained earlier, she added tricky and slick to her growing list of
issues. She was already white-knuckling a sharp turn
when a kamikaze squirrel darted into her lane, causing her to nearly swerve into oncoming traffic before
remembering the rules of country driving.

Never leave your lane; not for weather, animals, or even God himself.

Luckily the squirrel reversed its direction, but before she could relax a trio of deer bounded across the road. "Run, Bambi," she cried, hitting her brakes, and by the skin of their collective teeth, they all missed each other.

Sweating, nerves sizzling like live wires, she finally turned onto Capriotti Lane and parked as she'd been instructed.

It took a moment for her pulse to come down from stroke level. She'd been taught anti-anxiety techniques, but she'd never quite figured out how to make any of them work while in the actual throes of an anxiety attack.

It's all good, she told herself, but because she wasn't buying what she was selling, she had to force herself out of the car like she was a five-year-old starting kindergarten instead of being thirty and simply facing a brand new job. Given all she'd been through, this should be easy, even fun. But sometimes adulthood felt like the vet's office and she was the dog excited for the car ride—only to find out the real destination.

Shaking her head, she strode across the parking lot. It was April, which meant the rolling hills to the east were green and lush and the Pacific Ocean to the west looked like a surfer's dream, all of it so gorgeous it could've been a postcard. A beautiful smoke screen over her not-so-beautiful past. The air was scented like a really expensive sea-and-earth candle, though all Lanie could smell was her forgotten hopes and dreams. With wood chips crunching under her shoes, she headed through the entrance beneath which was a huge wooden sign that read:

CAPRIOTTI WINERY, FROM OUR FIELDS
TO YOUR TABLE . . .

Her heart sped up. Nerves, of course, the bane of her existence. But after a very crappy few years, she was changing her path. For once in her godforsaken life, something was going to work out for her. *This* was going to work out for her.

She was grimly determined.

The land was lined with split rail wooden fencing, protecting grapevines as far as the eye could see. The large open area in front of her was home to several barns and other structures, all meticulously maintained and landscaped with stacks of barrels, colorful flower beds, and clever glass bottle displays.

Lanie walked into the first "barn," which was the reception and offices for the winery. She was greeted by an empty reception counter, beyond which was a huge, open-beamed room containing a bar on the far side, comfy couches and low tables scattered through the main area, and walls of windows that showed off the gorgeous countryside.

It was warm and inviting and . . . empty. Well, except for the huge mountain of white-and-gray fur sleeping on a dog bed in a corner. It was either a

Wookie or a massive English sheep dog, complete with scraggly fur hanging in its eyes. If it was a dog, it was the hugest one she'd ever seen and she froze as the thing snorted, lifted its head, and opened a bleary eye.

At the sight of her, it leapt to its four paws and gave a happy "*wuff!*" At least she was hoping it was a happy *wuff* because it came running at her. Never having owned a dog in her life, she froze. "Uh, hi," she said and did her best to hold her ground. But the closer the thing got, the more she lost her nerve and she whirled to run.

And then she heard a crash.

She turned back in time to see that the dog's forward momentum had been too much. Its hind end had come out from beneath it and it'd flipped onto its back, skidding to a stop in front of Lanie.

She—because she was definitely a she, Lanie could now see—flopped around like a fish for a few seconds as she tried to right herself, to no success. With a loud woof, the dog gave up and stayed on her back, tail wagging like crazy, tongue lolling out of the side of her mouth.

"You're vicious, I see," Lanie said and, unable to resist, squatted down to rub the dog's belly.

She snorted her pleasure, licked her hand, and then lumbered back to her bed.

Lanie looked around. Still alone. Eleven forty-five. She was fifteen minutes early, which was a statement on her entire life.

You'll be the only human to ever be early for her

own funeral, her mom liked to say, along with her favorite—*You expect way too much out of people.*

This from the woman who'd regularly forgotten to pick up her own daughter after school.

Lanie eyed the sign on the reception desk and realized the problem. The winery was closed on Mondays and Tuesdays, and today was Monday. "Hello?" she called out, feeling a little panicky. Had she somehow screwed up the dates? She'd interviewed for a two-month graphic artist job here twice, both via Skype from her Santa Barbara apartment. Her new boss, Cora Capriotti, the winery office manager, wanted her to create new labels, menus, website . . . everything, and they wanted her to do so on-site. Cora had explained that they prided themselves on being old fashioned. It was part of their charm, she'd said.

Lanie didn't mind the temporary relocation from Santa Barbara, two hours south of here. She'd actually accepted the job *because* of it, secretly hoping that if she was in Wildstone again maybe she and her mom might reconcile. In any case, two months away from her life was exactly what the doctor had ordered.

Literally.

Pulling out her cell phone, she scrolled for her new boss's number and called.

"We're out back!" Cora answered. "Let yourself in and join us for lunch!"

"Oh, but I don't want to interrupt—" Lanie blinked and stared at her phone.

Cora had disconnected.

With another deep breath that was long on nerves and short on actual air, she walked through the great, open room and out the back double French doors. She stepped onto a patio beautifully decorated with strings of white lights and green foliage lining the picnic-style tables. But that wasn't what had her frozen like a deer in the headlights facing down a speeding Mack truck.

No, that honor went to the people crowded around two of the large tables, which had been pushed close together. Everyone turned to look at her in unison, all ages and sizes, and then started talking at once.

Lanie recognized that they were smiling and waving, which meant they were probably a friendly crowd, but parties weren't her friend. Her favorite party trick was *not* going.

A woman in her early fifties cleared the pack. She had dark brunette hair liberally streaked with gray, striking dark brown eyes, and a kind smile. She was holding a glass of red wine in one hand and a delicious-looking hunk of bread in the other, and she waved both in Lanie's direction.

"Lanie, right? I'm Cora, come on in."

Lanie didn't move. "I've caught you in the middle of something. A wedding or a party. I can come back—"

"Oh, no, it's nothing like that." Cora looked back at the wild pack of people still watching. "It's just lunch. We do this every day." She gestured at all of them. "Meet your fellow employees. I'm related to everyone one way or another, so they'll behave. Or else." She smiled, taking away the heat of the threat. "In any case, welcome. Come join us. Let me get you a plate—"

"Oh, that's okay, I brought a salad." Lanie patted her bag. "I can just go sit in my car until you're finished—"

"No need for that, honey. I have lunch catered every day."

"Every day?" She didn't realize she'd spoken out loud until Cora laughed.

"It's our social time," Cora said.

At Lanie's last job, people had raced out of the building at lunch to escape each other. "That's . . . very generous of you."

"Nothing generous about it," Cora said with a laugh. "It keeps everyone on-site, ensures no one's late back at the job, and I get to keep my nosy nose in everyone's business." She set aside her bread, freeing up a hand to grab Lanie's, clearly recognizing a flight risk when she saw one. "Everyone," she called out. "This is Lanie Jacobs, our new graphic artist." She smiled reassuringly at Lanie and gestured to the group of people. "Lanie, this is everyone, from the winemaker to the front desk receptionist, we're all here. We're a rather informal bunch."

They all burst into applause and Lanie wished for a big, black hole to sink into and vanish. "Hi," she managed and gave a little wave. She must have pulled off the correct level of civility because they all went back to eating and drinking wine, talking amongst themselves.

"Are you really related to all of them?" she asked Cora, watching two little girls, twins given their matching toothless smiles, happily eating chocolate cupcakes, half of which were all over their faces.

Cora laughed. "Just about. I've got a big family. You?"

"No."

"Single?"

"Yes." Lanie's current relationship status: *sleeping diagonally across her bed.*

Cora smiled. "Well, I'll be happy to share my people, there's certainly enough of us to go around. Hey," she yelled, cupping a hand around her mouth. "Someone take the girls in to wash up, and no more cupcakes or they'll be bouncing off the walls."

So the cupcakes were a problem, but wine at lunch wasn't. Good to know.

Cora smiled at Lanie's expression, clearly reading her thoughts. "We're Californians," she said. "We're serious about our wine, but laid-back about everything else. In fact, maybe that should be our tagline. Now come, have a seat." She drew Lanie over to the tables. "We'll get to work soon enough."

There was an impressive amount of food, all of it Italian, all of it fragrant and delicious looking. Lanie's heart said *definitely* to both the wine and the lasagna, but her pants said *holy shit, woman, find a salad instead.*

Cora gave a nudge to the woman at the end of the table who looked to be around Lanie's age with silky dark hair and matching eyes. "Scoot," Cora said.

The woman scooted. So did everyone else, allowing a space on the end for Lanie.

"Sit," Cora told Lanie. "Eat. Make merry."

"But—"

"Oh, and be careful of that one," Cora said, pointing to the woman directly across from Lanie, this one in her early twenties with the same gorgeous dark hair and eyes as the other. "Her bad attitude can be contagious."

"Gee, thanks, Mom," she said with an impressive eyeroll.

Cora blew her daughter a kiss and fluttered away, grabbing a bottle of wine from the middle of one of the tables and refilling glasses as she went.

"One of these days I'm gonna roll my eyes so hard I'm going to go blind," her daughter muttered.

The twins ran through, still giggling, still looking like they'd bathed in chocolate, which caused a bit of a commotion. Trying to remain inconspicuous, Lanie pulled her lunch out of her bag, a homemade salad in a container, sans dressing.

"Are you kidding me?" Cora's daughter asked. "Do you *want* her to come back here and yell at us for not feeding you properly? Put that away." She stood up, reached for a stack of plates in the middle of the table, and handed Lanie one. "Here. Now fill it up and eat, and for God's sake, look happy while you're at it or she'll have my ass."

Lanie eyeballed the casserole dishes lining the center of the tables. Spaghetti, lasagna . . .

"Don't worry, it all tastes as good as it looks," an

old man said from the middle of the table. There was
no hair on his head, but he did have a large patch
of steel-gray fuzz on his chest sticking out from
the top of his polo shirt. His olive complexion had
seen at least seven decades of sun, but his smile was
pure little-boy mischief. "And don't worry about
your cholesterol either," he added. "I'm seventy-
five and I've eaten like this every single day of my
life." He leaned across the table and shook her hand.
"Leonardo Antony Capriotti. And this is my sweet-
heart of fifty-four years, Adelina Capriotti. I'd use
her middle name, but she refuses to sleep with me
when I do that."

The older woman next to him was teeny tiny, her
white hair in a tight bun on her head, her spectacles
low on her nose, her smile mischievous. "Gotta keep
him in line, you know. Nice to meet you."

Lanie knew from her research on the company
that it'd been Leonardo and Adelina to start this
winery back in the seventies, though they'd since
handed over the day-to-day reins to their daughter,
who Lanie now realized was her boss Cora. "Nice to
meet you both," she said.

"Likewise. You're going to give us a new updated
look and make me look good," he said. "Right?"

"Right," she said and hoped that was actually true.
No pressure or anything . . .

He smiled. "I like you. Now eat."

If she ate any of this stuff, she'd need a nap by
mid-afternoon. But not wanting to insult anyone, she
scooped as little as she felt she could get away with

onto her plate and pushed it around with her fork, trying to resist temptation.

"Uh-oh," Cora's daughter said. "We have a dieter."

"Stop it," the woman next to Lanie said. "You'll scare her away and end up right back on Mom's shit list."

Cora's daughter, whose shirt read: *Live, Laugh, and Leave Me the Hell Alone*, snorted. "We both know that I never get *off* the shit list. I just move up and down on it. Mom's impossible to please."

"Don't listen to her," the other woman said to Lanie. "I'm Alyssa, by the way. And Grumpy-Ass over there is my baby sister Mia."

Mia waved and reached for the bread basket. "I'm giving up on getting a bikini body so pass the butter, please. Grandma says the good lord put alcohol and carbs on this planet for a reason and I'll be damned if I'm going to let him down."

Her grandma toasted her.

"Mia and I work here at the winery," Alyssa said and gently patted the cloth-wrapped little bundle swaddled to her chest. "This is Elsa, my youngest."

"Elsa, like the princess?" Lanie asked.

"More like the queen," Alyssa said with a smile, rubbing her infant's tush. "She's going to rule this roost someday."

"Who are you kidding?" Mia asked. "Mom's going to hold the reins until she's three hundred years old. That's how long witches live, you know."

Lanie wasn't sure how to react. After all, that witch was now her boss.

"You're scaring her off again," Alyssa said and looked at Lanie. "We love Mom madly, I promise. Mia's just bitchy because she got dumped last night, was late for work this morning, and got read the riot act. She thinks life sucks."

"Yeah, well, life *does* suck," Mia said. "It sucks donkey balls. And this whole waking up every morning thing is getting a bit excessive. But Alyssa's right. Don't listen to me. Sarcasm. It's how I hug."

Alyssa reached across the table and squeezed her sister's hand in her own, her eyes soft. "Are you going to tell me what happened? I thought you liked this one."

Mia shrugged. "I was texting him and he was only responding occasionally with a 'K.' I mean, I have no idea what 'K' even means. Am I to assume he intended to type 'OK' but was stabbed and couldn't expend the energy to type an extra whole letter?"

Alyssa sucked her lips into her mouth in a clear attempt not to laugh. "Tell me you didn't ask him that and then get broken up with by text."

"Well, dear know-it-all sister, that's exactly what happened. And now I've got a new motto: *Don't waste your good boob years on a guy that doesn't deserve them.* Oh, and side note: no man does. Men suck."

Lanie let out a completely inadvertent snort of agreement and both women looked over at her.

"Well, they do," she said. "Suck."

"See, I *knew* I was going to like you." Mia reached for a bottle of red and gestured with it in Lanie's direction.

She shook her head. "Water's good, thanks."

Mia nodded. "I like water too. It solves a lot of problems. Wanna lose weight? Drink water. Tired of your man? Drown him." She paused and cocked her head in thought. "In hindsight, I should've gone *that* route . . ."

A man came out onto the patio, searched the tables, and focused in on Alyssa. He came up behind her, cupped her face, and tilted it up for his kiss. And he wasn't shy about it either, smiling intimately into her eyes first. Running his hands down her arms to cup around the baby, he pulled back an inch. "How are my girls?" he murmured.

"Jeez, careful or she'll suffocate," Mia said.

"Hmm." The man kissed Alyssa again, longer this time before finally lifting his head. "What a way to go." He turned to Lanie and smiled. "Welcome. I'm Owen Booker, the winemaker."

Alyssa, looking a little dazed, licked her lips. "And husband," she added to his resume. "He's my husband." She beamed. "I somehow managed to land the best winemaker in the country."

Owen laughed softly and borrowed her fork to take a bite of her pasta. "I'll see you at the afternoon meeting," he said, bent and brushed a kiss on Elsa's little head, and walked off.

Alyssa watched him go. Specifically watched his ass, letting out a theatrical sigh.

"Good God, give it a rest," Mia griped. "And you're drooling. Get yourself together, woman. Yesterday you wanted to kill him, remember?"

"Well, he *is* still a man," Alyssa said. "If I don't want to kill him at least once a day, he's not doing his job right."

"Please, God, tell me you're almost done with the baby hormonal mood swings," Mia said.

"Hey, I'm hardly having any baby hormone-related mood swings anymore."

Mia snorted and looked at Lanie. "FYI, whenever we're in a situation where I happen to be the voice of reason, it's probably an apocalypse sort of thing and you should save yourself."

"Whatever," Alyssa said. "He's hot and he's mine, all mine."

"Yes," Mia said. "We know. And he's been yours since the second grade and you get to sleep with him later so . . ."

Alyssa laughed. "I know. Isn't it great? All you need is love."

"I'm pretty sure we also need water, food, shelter, vodka, and Netflix."

"Well excuse me for being happy." Alyssa looked at Lanie. "Are you married, Lanie?"

"Not anymore." She took a bite of the most amazing fettuccini alfredo she'd ever had and decided that maybe calories on Mondays didn't count.

"Was he an asshole?" Mia asked, her eyes curious but warmly so.

"Actually, he's dead."

Alyssa gasped. "I'm so sorry. I shouldn't have asked—"

"No," Lanie said, kicking herself for spilling the beans like that. "It's okay. It's been six months." Six months, one week, and two days, but hey, who was counting? She bypassed her water and reached for the wine after all. When in Rome . . .

"That's really not very long," Alyssa said.

"I'm really okay." There was a reason for the quick recovery. Several, actually, not the least of which was the fact that after Kyle had passed away, some things had come to light. Things such as the husband she thought she'd known and loved had hidden an addiction from her.

A wife addiction.

So far two other women had come out of the woodwork claiming to also be married to Kyle. Not that she intended to share that humiliation. Not now or ever.

You're my moon and my stars, he'd always told her.

Just one lie in a string of many . . .

Cora came back around and Lanie nearly leapt up in relief. Work! Work was going to save her.

"I see you've met some of my big, nosy, interfering, boisterous, loving family and survived to tell the tale," Cora said, slipping an arm around Mia and gently squeezing.

"Yes, and I'm all ready to get to it," Lanie said.

"Oh, not yet." Cora gestured for her to stay seated. "No rush, there's still fifteen minutes left of lunch." And then she once again made her way around the tables, chatting with everyone she passed. "Girls," she called out to the cupcake twins who were now chasing one another around the other table, "slow down, please!"

At Lanie's table, everyone had gotten deeply involved in a discussion on barrels. She was listening with half an ear to the differences in using American oak versus French oak when a man in a deputy sheriff's uniform came unnoticed through the double French doors. He was tall, built, and fully armed. His eyes were covered by dark aviator sunglasses, leaving his expression unreadable. And intimidating as hell.

He strode directly toward her.

"Scoot," he said to the table, and since no one else scooted, in fact no one else even looked over at him, Lanie scooted.

"Thanks." He sat, reaching past her to accept the plate that Mia wordlessly handed to him without pausing from her conversation with Alyssa. The plate was filled up to shockingly towering heights that surely no one human could consume.

He caught Lanie staring and went brows up.

"That's a lot of food," she said inanely.

"Hungry." He grabbed a fork. "You're the new hire."

"Lanie," she said and watched in awe as he began to shovel in food like he hadn't eaten in a week.

"Mark," he said after swallowing a bite, something she appreciated because Kyle used to talk with his mouth full and it had driven her to want to kill him. Which, as it turned out, hadn't been necessary. A heart attack had done that for her.

Apparently cheating on a bunch of wives had been high stress. Go figure.

"You must be a very brave woman," Mark said.

And for a horrifying minute, she was afraid she'd spoken of Kyle out loud and she stared at him.

"Taking on this job, this family," he said. "They're insane, you know. Every last one of them."

Because he had a disarming smile and was speaking with absolutely no malice, she knew he had to be kidding. But she still thought it rude considering they'd served him food. "They can't be all that bad," she said. "They're feeding you, which you seem to be enjoying."

"Who wouldn't enjoy it? It's the best food in the land."

This was actually true. She watched him go at everything on his plate like it was a food-eating contest and he was in danger of coming in second place for the world championship. She shook her head in awe. "You're going to get heartburn eating that fast."

"Better than not eating at all," he said, glancing at his watch. "I've got ten minutes to be back on the road chasing the bad guys, and a lot of long, hungry hours ahead of me."

"One of those days, huh?"

"One of those years," he said. "But at least I'm not stuck here at the winery day in and day out."

It was her turn to go brows up. "Are you making fun of my job at all?"

"Making fun? No," he said. "Offering sympathy, yes. You clearly have no idea what you've gotten yourself into. You could still make a break for it, you know."

That she herself had been thinking the very same

thing only five minutes ago didn't help. Suddenly feeling defensive for this job she hadn't even yet started, she looked around her. The winery itself was clearly lovingly and beautifully taken care of. The yard in which they sat was lush and colorful and welcoming. Sure, the sheer number of people employed here was intimidating, as was the fact that they gathered every day to eat lunch and socialize. But she'd get used to it.

Maybe.

"I love my job," she said.

Mark grinned. "You're on day one. And you haven't started yet or you'd have finished your wine. Trust me, it's going to be a rough ride, Lanie Jacobs."

Huh. So he definitely knew more about her than she knew about him. No big deal since she wasn't all that interested in knowing more about him. "Surely given what you do for a living, you realize there's nothing 'rough' about my job at all."

"I know I'd rather face down thugs and gang-bangers daily than work in this loony bin."

She knew he was kidding, that he was in fact actually pretty funny, but she refused to be charmed. Fact was, she couldn't have been charmed by any penis-carrying human being at the moment. "Right," she said, "because clearly you're here against your will, being held hostage and force-fed all this amazing food. How awful for you."

"Yeah, life's a bitch." He eyeballed the piece of cheese bread on her plate she hadn't touched. It was the last one.

She gestured for him to take it and then watched in amazement as he put that away too. "I have to ask," she said. "How in the world do you stay so . . ." She gestured with a hand toward his clearly well-taken-care-of body and struggled with a word to describe him. She supposed *hot* worked—if one was into big, annoying, perfectly fit alphas—not that she intended to say so since she was pretty sure he knew exactly how good he looked.

"How do I stay so . . . what?" he asked.

"Didn't anyone ever tell you that fishing for compliments is unattractive?"

He surprised her by laughing, clearly completely unconcerned with what she thought of him. "My days tend to burn up a lot of calories," he said.

"Uh-huh."

He pushed his dark sunglasses to the top of his head and she was leveled with dark eyes dancing with mischievousness. "Such cynicism in one so young."

A plate of cupcakes was passed down the table and Lanie eyed them, feeling her mouth water. She had only so much self-control and apparently she was at her limit because she took one, and then, with barely a pause, grabbed a second as well. Realizing the deputy sheriff was watching her and looking amused while he was at it, she shrugged. "Sometimes I reward myself before I accomplish something. It's called pre-award motivation."

"Does it work?"

"Absolutely one hundred percent not," she admitted and took a bite of one of the cupcakes, letting out a low moan before she could stop herself. "Oh. My. God."

His eyes darkened to black. "You sound like that cupcake is giving you quite the experience."

She held up a finger for silence, possibly having her first ever in-public orgasm.

He leaned in a little bit, and since their thighs were already plastered together, he didn't have to go far to speak directly into her ear. "Do you make those same sexy sounds when you—"

She pointed at him again because she still couldn't talk, and he just grinned. "Yeah," he said. "I bet you do. And now I know what I'm going to be thinking about for the rest of the day."

"You'll be too busy catching the bad guys, remember?"

"I'm real good at multitasking," he said.

She let out a laugh, though it was rusty as hell. It'd been a while since she'd found something funny. Not that this changed her idea of him. He was still too sure of himself, too cocky, and she'd had enough of that to last a lifetime. But she also was good at multitasking and could both not like him and appreciate his sense of humor at the same time.

What she couldn't appreciate was when his smile turned warm and inviting because, for a minute, something passed between them, something she couldn't— or didn't—intend to recognize.

"Maybe I could call you sometime," he said.

Before she could turn him down politely, the little

cupcake twins came running, leaping at him, one of them yelling, "Daddy, Daddy, Daddy! Look what we got!"

Catching them both with impressive ease, Mark stood, managing to somehow confiscate the cupcakes and set them aside before getting covered in chocolate. "Why is it," he asked Lanie over their twin, dark heads, "that when a child wants to show you something, they try to place it directly in your cornea?"

Still completely floored, Lanie could only shake her head.

Mark adjusted the girls so that they hung upside down off his back. This had them erupting in squeals of delight as he turned back to face Lanie again, two little ankles in each of his big hands. "I know what you're thinking," he said into her undoubtedly shocked face. "I think it every day."

Actually, even she had no idea what she was thinking except . . . he was a Capriotti? How had she not seen that coming?

"Yeah," he said. "I'm one of them, which is why I get to bitch about them. And let me guess . . . you just decided you're not going to answer my call?"

Most definitely not, but before she could say so out loud, Cora was back, going up on tiptoes to kiss Mark on the cheek. "Hey, baby. Heard you had a real tough night."

He shrugged.

"You get enough to eat?" she asked. "Yes?" She eyed his empty plate and then, with a nod of satisfaction, reached up and ruffled his hair. "Good. But don't for a single minute think, Marcus Antony Edward Capriotti, that I don't know who sneaked your grandpa the cigars he was caught smoking last night."

From his seat at the table, "Grandpa," aka Leonardo Antony Capriotti, lifted his hands like *who, me?*

Cora shook her head at the both of them, helped the girls down from Mark's broad shoulders, took them by the hand, and walked away.

No, Lanie would most definitely *not* be taking the man's call. And not for the reasons he'd assume either. She didn't mind that he had kids. What she minded was that here was a guy who appeared to have it all: close family, wonderful children, a killer smile, hot body . . . without a single clue about just how damn lucky he was. It made her mad, actually.

He took in her expression. "Okay, so you're most definitely not going to take my call."

"It's nothing personal," she said. "I just don't date . . ."

"Dads?"

Actually as a direct result of no longer trusting love, not even one little teeny, tiny bit, she didn't date *anyone* anymore, but that was none of his business.

He looked at her for another beat and whatever lingering amusement he'd retained left him and he simply nodded as he slid his sunglasses back over his eyes. "Good luck today," he said. "You really are going to need it."

And then he was gone.

He thought she'd judged him. She hated that he thought that but it was best to let him think it. Certainly better than the truth, which was that the problem was her, all her. She inhaled a deep, shaky breath and turned, surprised to find not just Cora watching, but his sisters, grandpa, and several others she could only guess were also related.

Note to self: Capriottis multiplied when left unattended.